Home Before Dark

Home
Before Dark

Michael Molloy

HEINEMANN : LONDON

First published in Great Britain 1994
by William Heinemann Ltd
an imprint of Reed Consumer Books Ltd
Michelin House, 81 Fulham Road, London SW3 6RB
and Auckland, Melbourne, Singapore and Toronto

A CIP catalogue record for this title
is available from the British Library

ISBN 0 434474665

Printed and bound in Great Britain
by Clays Ltd, St Ives plc

Prologue

4.30 p.m. Tuesday, 14 December

He could remember every detail of the little terraced house: the paved front garden, carefully arranged with terracotta pots; a bow window, recently added, that was out of character with the flat-fronted cottages on either side. The bright watercolours in the white-painted hallway – bought on holidays he guessed: Spain, North Africa, Italy, Malta. She must have enjoyed the breaks to want these garish reminders. Everything was immaculately clean; but there was a curious sour smell that he'd encountered before. They'd found a bottle of spilt milk in the kitchen but it wasn't that, the milk was fresh: delivered that morning.

'Life is so unfair,' Mrs Frederick Burford-Crofton said as she passed a cup of tea containing four lumps of sugar to her brother; then she sighed and stirred the sliver of lemon that floated in her own weak infusion.

Superintendent Colin Greaves brought his attention back to the palm court of the Ritz Hotel and smiled. 'To what injustice are you referring, Lizzie?'

'Well, just look at you,' she continued. 'You eat and drink whatever you like; and yet you stay disgustingly thin.' She spread a slim hand over her flat stomach and said: 'I only have to look at a slice of bread or one wretched potato and I need a week in a health farm to repair the damage.'

'You used to eat like a horse.'

'Not any more, darling. Fred says it's like living with a canary these days.'

A black and white cat watched him when he entered the living room. It was wary, ready for flight.
Everything was in place. Cushions plumped, magazines squared neatly on the coffee table before the television set. The housework had been done recently. There was hardly a speck of dust on any polished surface. Nothing to keep him there. He knew it was time to go into the bedroom.

Greaves forced himself to think of his brother-in-law. 'How is Fred keeping these days?' he asked.

Mrs Burford-Crofton sighed again. 'Impossible! He never stops working, I've had to go down on my knees to get him to agree to this holiday.'

Greaves sipped some of his tea and ate one of the tiny sandwiches on the table before them. 'But you always go to the West Indies at this time of year.'

'And it's always a struggle,' his sister replied sharply. She sat back in her chair and looked at him in an accusatory manner. 'When are you going to give him a hand? You have a duty to the family you know.'

She accompanied the last part of the sentence with a wave of her hand to someone behind Greaves. He did not turn around but questioned her with a slight inclination of his head.

'Elinore Trimmington,' she explained. 'With that

tiresome daughter. I did hope I wouldn't see anyone I knew today. I look like a scarecrow.'

Greaves smiled again and glanced at her elegant form. 'Where did you buy your outfit – the Belgravia Oxfam shop?'

'Don't try and change the subject. I asked you a question.'

Greaves drank some more of his tea. 'I'm forty-one years old, Lizzie. It's too late for me to begin a new job.'

'Nonsense,' she replied firmly. 'You're eight years younger than me, that makes you thirty-nine.' She looked steadfastly into her brother's steady gaze and then grinned. 'All right, you're forty; but not a day older – I won't have it.'

When he entered the tiny bedroom, the constable had to shuffle away to make room for him. The naked body lay on the bed, limbs sprawled awkwardly. She wasn't beautiful; a plain, middle-aged woman, thick-waisted, her pale hair thin and streaked with grey. The features were distorted, like the others: eyes bulged grotesquely and the mouth open, revealing a swollen tongue. There were dark bruises on her throat. He stood close enough to see where the skin had been pierced slightly; there was a thin smear of blood around the wound. The smell was stronger now, the old familiar scent that was the part of his work that he hated the most: the smell of death.

'Who found her?' he asked the constable who stood beside him. He was young, trying hard to keep his voice level when he replied to the question.

'Her daughter, sir, when she came home from school.'

3

'Did you bring the keys with you?' Greaves asked, forcing his mind to the present once again.

Elizabeth opened her handbag and rummaged short-sightedly for a few moments.

'Why don't you put your spectacles on?' Greaves asked.

'I don't need them,' she answered shortly. 'Especially when Elinore is about. I don't want her telling everyone: "I saw Lizzie Burford-Crofton in the Ritz and she's falling to pieces" – Ah, here they are.' She produced a bunch of keys and handed them to him. 'Fred says will you go gently with the cellar. It needs to be restocked.'

Greaves nodded. 'That's all taken care of. Sarah's father is going down a few days early with the children.'

'In Christmas week? I thought this was the busiest time for shopkeepers?'

It was Greaves's turn to sigh. 'I've told you before, Sarah's father is a retired doctor, her husband's family were shopkeepers.'

His sister nodded and Greaves realised, not for the first time, that Lizzie would always have a mind like the inside of her handbag – everything there, but hopelessly muddled.

'And how is Sarah?' she asked. 'What's the name of the newspaper she works for?'

'The *Gazette*.'

'That's right – one of the little ones. I always have trouble remembering.'

'She's been very busy recently – she needs a holiday as well.'

Lizzie surveyed the spread of sandwiches and cakes she had ordered. 'Just look at all this food. You haven't

4

eaten anything.' She paused for a moment and then said: 'Marion will be staying close to us, we're bound to run into her. Do you want me to give her any message?'

He shook his head. 'She's married again, Lizzie, we don't have any contact these days.'

She looked at him quickly, her long pretty features forming an expression of concern.

'You were such a good match . . . these people you know nowadays: shopkeepers, doctors, journalists . . .'

Greaves studied his sister again with a mixture of exasperation and affection. Dear kind, silly, snobbish Lizzie. He smiled. 'Some might think them the right company for a copper.'

'Don't say that,' she answered. 'It's such a vulgar American word – policeman, if you must.'

'Our family started out as traders,' he reminded her. 'And some of the trade was pretty gamy by all accounts. I should think a policeman would lend a certain amount of respectability to the genealogy.'

'We were merchants,' she said sitting up straighter. 'Empire builders – one of the families that put Hong Kong on the map.'

'Well the Chinese are going to take it off the map again.'

'Don't remind me,' she replied. 'Fred says it's another piece of history that's passing us by.'

Greaves resisted the impulse to explain that history could not pass one by, like a pedestrian being overtaken like a motor car. Instead he looked up and saw a tall figure studying the room until he glanced in his direction. Greaves caught his attention and gestured for him to join them.

'Sorry to intrude, sir,' the figure said when he stood beside the table.

'Not at all,' Greaves replied. 'Sit down and join us. I don't think you've met my sister. Lizzie, this is a colleague of mine, Detective-Sergeant Nicholas Holland.'

Sergeant Holland shook hands and sat down, but he stayed on the edge of his chair. Lizzie was now smiling at him with all her customary charm. Despite her devotion to her husband, she was still a fine-looking woman – and Holland was a handsome young man.

'Would you care for a cup of tea, Sergeant?' she asked. 'Have some of these sandwiches, they're quite delicious.'

Holland accepted the tea but Greaves could tell he was not relaxed.

'Something come up?' Greaves asked.

Holland nodded.

'Same as the others?' Greaves asked, frowning with sudden concern.

'Yes,' Holland replied. 'But this one is still alive.'

'What happened to the others?' Lizzie asked, leaning forward.

'They were strangled,' Greaves answered quietly.

Chapter One

From the far end of the garden, Sarah could hear the telephone ringing; it was a welcome distraction. For the past two hours she had been working under a sullen sky, heavy with the threat of rain, and her mood now matched the bleak winter landscape about her. Gardening was always a reminder of her childhood, the times when she had helped her father in the school holidays; and so she understood the reason for the sadness that engulfed her. It was almost Christmas and that had been the hardest time for them after her mother had died. Her father had done his best but he had not always been able to cope with his own grief; subsequently, the happiest time of the year for most families had been, for them, a reminder of the loss they endured.

When her own children were born she had tried hard to make it a joyful occasion, but secretly this time of year had always reminded her of the sadness she had known in her own childhood. This year, however, something curious had happened. For the past four weeks she had been working on a series for her newspaper about the lives of children who were living rough on the streets of the great cities and it had proved to be a cathartic experience.

Originally the intention had been for her to write two short pieces on the subject; but the *Gazette*'s political cartoonist had produced a powerful illustration to accompany the first article. It was based on the drawing that appeared in Dickens's *A Christmas Carol*, showing the starving waifs sheltered by the spirit of Christmas Yet To Come. This drawing – combined with Sarah's article – had caught the attention of the public and moved them in a manner that sometimes happens but can never be predicted. Sarah had been instructed to turn the minor series that had been planned into a campaign.

The reaction from the public had grown with each piece until wary government ministers had stopped making anodyne statements and started to promise legislation. But the work had taken its toll on Sarah; she had never been able to completely detach herself from the lives of the people she encountered in her job. It gave a powerful edge to her copy, but at times could be emotionally draining. Talking to the children had been heart-breaking – there had been so many of them. A fragile army of lost souls: inarticulate, frightened and hopeless. Their wasted bodies and blank features had eventually merged into one pinched, grey face that stayed in her mind's eye and had come to dominate her memory.

The last article in the series had appeared that morning, filed from Liverpool. Sarah had returned to London the night before, weary to the bone, and called the news desk to inform them that she would be in the office the following afternoon. That morning she had risen later than usual and decided to spend some time tidying the neglected garden.

Since she had started the work she had been trying to remember her mother's face, but somehow the features refused to form. They remained as faded and wispy as the smoke that rose from the smouldering fire which she had heaped with the last of the autumn leaves. All that would come to her was the image of the same sad child. It was a disturbing phenomenon, and it caused her to feel both guilty and somehow callous.

Pushing the thought from her mind, she turned and walked briskly back to the house, entering by the french windows. The strident telephone sounded so irritable she wondered if she was going to enjoy the conversation.

'It's me,' George Conway said when she answered. 'Why the hell did you take so long?'

'Dead leaves,' Sarah replied.

'That sounds like one of those Russian novels that are too depressing to read,' he said genially.

'No, real dead leaves: I'm burning them in the garden.'

'Don't they go on the compost heap?'

Sarah smiled. Good old George. Like all effective news editors, he was even interested in things that didn't interest him at all. 'Some do,' she said, indulging his insatiable curiosity. 'We've got lots so we burn the last of them. What do you want, George? I'm not due on until three o'clock.'

'I thought you might like to come in early and have lunch with me at the Godfather's.'

She hesitated and looked at her watch; it was nearly midday and her clothes and hair smelt of woodsmoke. Sarah had been anticipating a leisurely bath before going on duty. She was about to turn down the invitation when George added: 'I thought you might like to discuss the new editor who was appointed this morning.'

'Who is it?' she asked quickly.

George chuckled. 'Sorry, can't tell you on the phone.'

'Are you going to make me ring somebody else in the office?'

'They won't know,' George said smugly. 'The announcement goes out at one o'clock. Top secret until then.'

'I'll see you in the restaurant.'

'Meet me at the bar. I want to have a drink before we eat.'

'To celebrate – or dull the pain?'

'More to still a giddy feeling,' he said enigmatically, adding, 'Great work from the North, by the way, you've earned your salt this month.' Then he rang off.

Sarah looked down at the half-grown golden Labrador that had emerged from the kitchen and now sat at her feet. 'I've got to go out early, Sam,' she said to him as if she were talking to a child, 'but Mrs Lomax will be here soon so she'll look after you until the others get home.'

The dog's tail thumped on the carpet while she spoke, then he followed closely after her when she made for the bathroom.

Sarah gazed regretfully at the empty tub for a moment, before turning on the shower. Although no one could have been more devoted to their children, she enjoyed the quiet times alone she'd spent in the house. It was a rare occurrence these days. As she stood

10

beneath the stinging water she thought about the years before her husband had been killed. Then, all she'd had to do was care for her children and tend the house and garden. Now that fairly recent period of her life seemed as distant to her as childhood – blurred and unfixed in her memory like half-remembered photographs. The reason she had been alone so often then was that Jack had spent much of his time abroad as a television reporter.

'What on earth did I *do* in those days?' she asked the dog, who now sat watching as she towelled herself. But she knew the answer. Throughout her marriage to Jack, Sarah had been the very model of contented domesticity. She had felt no guilt or sense of unful-filment; no angst that her total preoccupation with homemaking was stifling her development or capa-bilities as a woman.

Sarah loved her family and the house in Hampstead where they had always lived. So much so that for a longish time after Jack's death she had lived in a fog-like daze, unable to accept reality. Then, with the need to preserve their home and feed her children, the prac-tical part of her nature had re-emerged. It had given her the drive to regain the job as a reporter she had held before her marriage.

Through her work, she had met Colin Greaves, a man quite different to her husband; yet she had come to love him with the same degree of commitment. Where Jack had been carefree and outgoing, Greaves's emotions were private and his manner reserved. Her husband's good looks had made women turn to look at him. Colin, when he wanted to, could pass un-noticed in a crowd.

11

And so, in a few months, her life had changed completely and the old slow, safe pace had quickened into something far more challenging and unpredictable.

The bedroom she now entered had been the one that she'd shared with Jack during their married life, but when Greaves had come to live with her they had decided to sleep elsewhere in the house. Sarah's dressing table was still there and most of her clothes in the wardrobe, but the bed was not made up and the abandoned room had gradually been encroached upon by her twin boys, who had been moving in more of their possessions in recent months. There were signs of their stealthy occupation all around her now: books, sports gear and odd cardboard boxes full of boyhood detritus. A half-built model of a Roman town stood on a card table in the centre of the room and her dressing table was cluttered with scalpels, pieces of balsa wood and odd scraps of paper. Among her jars of make-up was a large container they had discarded. She picked it up now and glanced at the label. It was called Spray Mount and the words 'safety advice' caught her attention.

'Contains: petroleum distillates, pentane, propane, butane,' she read aloud. 'Vapour may be harmful. Vapours may ignite explosively. Keep away from heat.' She shook the can gently and could hear liquid swill inside. 'Just what I need on my face,' she muttered, then placed the can and the rest of the junk in one of the cardboard boxes next to the bed.

She finished dressing and was about to apply her make-up when the telephone rang again. This time it was her father.

12

'Is Colin there?' he asked briskly. 'I rang him at work but they wouldn't tell me where he was.'

'He's on a big job, Dad,' Sarah replied.

'Can't he even take a telephone call?'

'It's pretty important. I've hardly spoken to him for days.'

'What's it about?'

Sarah realised with sudden surprise that she didn't know. Her preoccupation with the recent series had taken up a lot of her time.

'I don't actually know, but he's awfully tied up.'

'Damn,' she heard her father mutter. 'I wanted to ask him what kind of whisky he preferred.'

'Single malt,' she said with as much authority as she could muster.

'Are you sure?' Henry Linton said suspiciously. Sarah was a poor liar and her father a shrewd judge of his daughter.

'Positive. Look I've got to go, Dad. I'm late for work. I'll telephone you later.'

'I shall be out later,' he said stiffly. 'Don't worry, I'll ring when you're less busy.'

Sarah thought about the call while she swiftly applied her make-up. As in the aftermath of most of her conversations with her father, she felt a vague sense of guilt. Even as a child, he had always managed to make her feel that she fell short of his highest expectations. She did not doubt his love; but sometimes she doubted his admiration for the career she had chosen.

Colin knew all this; and it was partly why he had suggested that they should all spend Christmas together at his sister's weekend house in Oxfordshire.

Sarah's father, a country doctor, had insisted that he contribute to the cost and Colin had finally bowed to his determination and asked him to buy the drink. Since then, he had fretted over the selection of wines and made frequent calls to consult her over the food she would be preparing.

Sarah had just replaced her lipstick in her handbag when she saw the dog sit up and listen intently.

She could hear nothing, but she knew that someone he liked was approaching the house. If it had been a stranger, he would already have been barking in the hallway. By the time she had reached the top of the stairs, Sarah heard a key scrabbling in the lock and then Mrs Lomax, Sarah's housekeeper, called out: 'Hello, it's only me.' The dog ran ahead and was already finishing the biscuit he had been given when Sarah entered the kitchen.

'Welcome home,' Mrs Lomax began. 'Did you have any trouble getting into the house? Don't those new keys take some getting used to? Like something on a jail door. When I was a girl nobody bothered to lock their houses round our way – mind you, nobody had anything worth nicking in those days.' Pat Lomax was a cheerful soul who believed that any thought entering her head deserved to be uttered immediately.

'Colin insisted on having them installed,' Sarah answered. 'He said you could have broken into the house with a bent hairpin.'

'Well it's all for the best then – considering the people you get going about these days.'

'I've got to go in early, Pat,' Sarah said. 'I was going to make shepherd's pie for the children's supper.'

'I'll manage, love,' Mrs Lomax answered, switching

on the electric kettle in preparation for one of the many cups of tea that sustained her throughout the day. Then she turned back to Sarah. 'Did you hear about that poor woman in Branshaw Gardens last week?'

Sarah shook her head and waited in anticipation. Pat was a woman in late middle age who came from a large family in the building trade. They had lived in Hampstead for several generations and their network of information never missed an item of gossip about the area, no matter how trivial – or significant.

'It was the same as what happened on the other side of the Heath,' she continued. 'Poor woman murdered in her own house. Her little boy found her when he came home from school. They were both connected with your kiddies' school, you know?'

'No, I didn't,' Sarah answered.

'Yes,' Pat nodded. 'The first one was a teacher for a bit. The one in Branshaw Gardens went to school there – our Doreen knew her.'

Sarah felt a sudden moment of compassion for the victim and her family that was physical, like a hand pressing against her chest. 'Dear God, what is the world coming to?' she replied.

Pat reached down and stroked the dog. 'It's getting as bad as it was in wartime,' she said.

'Wartime?'

Pat straightened up again. 'That's right,' she said. 'My brother Bill was a special copper in those days. He says there was a lot of murders then. People moving about, marriages breaking up. He says it was the restlessness that got into them, like the devil. Things got better after a few years of peacetime. Now he reckons it's started all over again.'

She turned to a pile of unironed washing that lay close to the sink. 'Them boys have gone through those shirts you bought at the beginning of term,' she said.

'What about Emily's?' Sarah asked.

'Good as new,' Pat answered. 'She's never any trouble.'

'I'll buy some more on Saturday,' Sarah said. She noticed the time. 'Oh, I must go. See you tonight.'

'Don't worry about being late,' Pat answered. 'I've brought a video with me, so I won't be in a rush to get home.'

'What is it?' Sarah asked as she walked towards the door.

'*The Sound of Music*,' Pat answered in a satisfied voice. 'That'll get the boys upstairs early.'

Sarah hurried from the house still smiling and headed her little Renault south towards Farringdon Road where the offices of the *Gazette* were located. Recently Pat had discovered a new technique for hounding her twin sons into bed, a selection of film videos that sent them complaining to the refuge of their own quarters. Emily did not pose the same problem; she spent most of her evenings with her boyfriend, listening to records in her bedroom, which occasionally raised worries of a different sort.

The traffic was heavy around King's Cross so it was just after one o'clock when she found a parking space and hurried to the Italian restaurant that was near the Holborn end of Gray's Inn Road. As soon as she entered she saw George Conway sitting on a high stool at the little bar; he was holding a large tumbler of Scotch in his left hand and had almost

16

finished the bowl of peanuts on the copper-covered counter.

The proprietor of the restaurant stood close to the cash register and surveyed the crowded room with pleasure. Luigi Bartellini – known to the staff of the *Gazette* as the Godfather, despite the fact that he had never been nearer Sicily than his home city of Milan – smiled with more than professional pleasure when Sarah entered.

'Mrs Keane,' he said with a slight bow, 'as always, you bring a touch of the summer to a cold winter's day.'

Sarah thanked him and took the stool next to George, who had watched Luigi's elaborate display of courtesy in the mirror behind the bar and made a noise somewhere between a snort and a grunt to signify his disapproval.

As usual, George Conway resembled a badly made bed. It wasn't that his clothes were cheap, they were just defeated by the extra layers of fat that covered his powerful frame. Even his short-cut hair grew in unruly tufts and his face was the colour and texture of a house brick. He pulled at his broken nose and said in a voice that was loud enough to carry as far as Luigi: 'Why do you let that wop look at you as though you'd just handed him your knickers for a tip?'

Luigi turned his back on the other customers in the room and gave George a V sign to demonstrate there were no hard feelings between them.

'A woman of my age is glad of any little attention she can get, George,' Sarah replied easily. The barman, knowing her preference, held up a bottle of Frascati, then poured a glass in response to her nod of agreement.

17

'Forty seems younger than springtime to me these days,' George said wistfully.

'Thirty-nine,' Sarah corrected him.

'I wasn't talking about you,' he answered with a lopsided grin. 'My latest paramour is forty-seven, and a grandmother. Did you know the world is suddenly full of divorced grandmothers, Sarah? Mature, sexually active women with bodies honed to perfection by Jane Fonda exercise videos.'

'I thought you'd gone back to your second wife?'

'I'm talking about my second wife,' he said, taking more of the peanuts. 'She wanted me to live with her again, and raise her child as though she were my own.'

'What child?'

George slowly turned his head to look at her. 'My single-parent stepdaughter. Haven't I ever told you about her?'

Sarah shook her head.

George took another handful of peanuts and washed them down with a large mouthful of Scotch before he continued. 'A sweet girl who lives with a community of New Age travellers. The last time we saw her was on *News at Ten*, being turned away from Stonehenge by the Wiltshire Constabulary.'

Sarah took a sip of her wine and then said, 'Well, what news have you got for me?'

'If I told you, you wouldn't believe me,' he replied. 'Read this.' He took a crumpled sheet of paper from his pocket and handed it to her. Sarah saw it was an official press announcement from LOC PLC, the parent company that owned the *Gazette*. She studied it for a few moments and then looked up in disbelief. 'They've actually made Simon Marr the editor?'

George nodded. 'That's what it says.'

'Simon Marr,' Sarah repeated incredulously. 'But he's not a journalist, he's a television game show host.'

George gestured to the barman for a refill. '*The Skeleton in Your Cupboard* is not a game show,' he said. 'It's a popular form of investigative journalism. At least that's what Sir Robert Hall said when he made the announcement this morning.'

'But people volunteer to go on the show because they *want* to tell the public about their dirty linen.'

'Sir Robert says it's a clear indication you can get the famous to tell the truth about themselves without having to resort to invasions of privacy.'

Sarah shook her head in disbelief. 'How long has Sir Robert Hall been in charge of the *Gazette*, George?'

He swallowed some more Scotch and raised his eyes to the tobacco-stained ceiling while he thought. 'Well, you were away from the paper for seventeen years,' he began. 'And the buy-out happened about five or six years after that, so it's got to be more than ten years now.'

'And he still doesn't understand the first thing about newspapers. It's quite incredible, really. I wonder if all of British industry is really like LOC PLC? It could explain why the Japanese are taking everything over.'

George shrugged. 'Perhaps it always was. Maybe the Empire was run by people like Sir Robert – generations of half-wits who convinced gullible shareholders they knew what they were doing.'

Sarah thought for a moment. 'I don't think Charles Miller is; I thought he would have made his move by now and brought back Brian Meadows.'

Meadows had been the editor of the *Gazette* when Sarah had returned to the paper. He had been fired by Sir Robert Hall, but there were strong rumours that the company was going to be taken over by Charles Miller, a city financier, with the intention of restoring Meadows as editor.

George agreed. 'We all thought that, but Sir Robert has kept the share price up rather well. It's too rich for Miller at the moment.'

A waiter passed them menus so they could order at the bar. 'And bring me a large Scotch and a bottle of Frascati,' George added when he had made his choice.

'I only want one glass of wine,' Sarah said. 'I've got to work this afternoon.'

'The rest of it's for me,' George said as he slid from the bar stool. 'You haven't heard the whole of it yet.'

'There's *more*?' Sarah said when they had taken their seats at a table that looked out on to the street.

'I'm afraid there is – wait for it – Alan Stiles is one of Marr's oldest friends.'

Suddenly the good humour she had felt since meeting George evaporated. Sarah loathed Stiles, and the idea that his star could be in the ascendancy was a major blow. The mood she had experienced in the garden that morning returned and suddenly the image of the lost child's face.

She looked into the Gray's Inn Road as if to find comfort among the grinding traffic that passed the window and George, sensing her unhappiness, reached out and covered her hand with one of his own. He gave an awkward squeeze and said in an unusually gentle voice: 'Why don't you get out – now, today – you don't need the money, Colin's rich enough to keep you both in comfort. Just go home and burn leaves. It's more fun than working on the *Gazette* these days.'

Sarah considered his words. He was partly right of course. Although Colin had never suggested it, he would be happy enough if she stopped work; and he did have a great deal of money. But she shook her head with sudden determination. 'I'm not quitting,' she said firmly. 'It wouldn't be the right thing to do.'

'Why?' George asked. 'What do you mean, the right thing to do? You don't owe the paper anything. What has it done for you lately?'

Sarah paused while the waiter served their food. 'I just can't,' she said when he had departed. 'I *do* owe the paper something, despite the gang who are running things at the moment. There's more to it than that. I met Jack on the *Gazette*, and there's still people like Harry Porter and Pauline Kaznovitch there – decent worthwhile people.' She looked up. 'And there's you, George. You saved my life when I needed the work. You're not going to quit are you?'

He laughed, although there was not much humour in the sound: 'I may not have any option if Stiles gets his way.'

Alan Stiles was George's deputy. A man whose only distinction was an overwhelming ambition to destroy everyone whom he saw as a barrier on his path to glory.

'And you say Stiles and Simon Marr are old friends?'

'Stiles says they were at the same college.'

'I didn't know Stiles went to university.'

'He didn't. But he likes to give the impression he

did. Actually they were on the same training scheme at a technical college.'

'So Simon Marr did start out as a journalist?'

George held out his hand and rocked it from side to side. 'Sort of. He certainly did the course with Stiles, then he went into local radio as a disc jockey.'

'Well I can't be snobbish about it,' Sarah said briskly. 'After all, I started out making the tea on a magazine.'

George smiled. 'To hear Stiles talking this morning, you'd think they'd begun their careers together on the *Times Literary Supplement*.'

'Where is Stiles now?'

'Gone to lunch in the boardroom with Sir Robert Hall, Fanny Hunter and the new man.'

'The chairman invited your deputy and not you?'

George smiled again, but there was an edge in his voice. 'Sir Robert knows how to cut a man to the quick – no, actually it was Marr who requested Stiles's presence. Apparently Sir Robert asked him if he wanted to invite any guests and Stiles was the only person he knew on the staff, apart from Fanny Hunter; so they were the chosen lunch guests.'

'So he knows Fanny too?' Sarah said and she watched George, who was now pretending to eat a veal cutlet. He hid some of the meat under a lettuce leaf, then looked up. 'She was one of the first people on *Skeleton in Your Cupboard*, don't you remember?'

'Yes, I do now,' she answered. Fanny Hunter was the *Gazette*'s star columnist and, like Stiles, no friend of Sarah's. 'Wasn't there supposed to have been something between them?'

George laid down his knife and fork as if relieved

22

of a tiresome burden and drank some wine before he answered. 'The story was, there was definitely something between them. It seems that Marr stayed on at Fanny's house after the interview, and when the crew left and her husband went off to bed, Marr gave her one on the fireside rug.' George poured himself some more wine and continued: 'So the skeleton in Fanny's closet turned out to be Marr's pork sword.'

Sarah sighed. 'George, spare me your sexual euphemisms, I am eating a pork chop.'

'Sorry,' he answered. 'It was a bit schoolboy.'

Sarah thought of her twins for a moment. Did they use expressions like 'pork sword' these days? She supposed so. It was an idea that brought her little comfort. Nor did the news that Fanny Hunter was an intimate of the new editor. Fanny was one of those individuals who used whatever power she could as a means of punishing those who opposed her. The information caused a certain pall to fall over the rest of the meal and they continued with a rather desultory conversation about happier days on the paper, when Sarah had been the youngest reporter on the staff.

'It must be strange – joining the *Gazette* today,' George mused. 'We've just taken on a new crime reporter. Did you know? I wonder if he finds it a funny place to work.'

'Why don't you ask him?'

'He's an odd bloke, Joe March,' George said thoughtfully. 'Not the sort you exchange idle chatter with – an ex-copper.'

'I don't know the name,' Sarah said. 'Where does he come from?'

'Scotland, he's been with a Clydeside news agency.'

'Is he any good?'

George nodded. 'I think so – he's no kid – a bit of a loner. He's already refused to go to the Features party.'

George was referring to an annual institution. Some of the revels in the past had entered the mythology of the *Gazette* and were passed on to all who joined as part of the paper's folklore.

'Do you remember the Features party when Cat Abbot dressed up as Carmen Miranda?' George asked.

'And led everyone through the editor's office doing the conga,' Sarah answered.

'Well he won't be at the party this year,' George added. 'He's gone to Spain to spend Christmas with his daughter.'

'I don't think I'll be there either,' Sarah said.

'Why not?'

'Oh, memories I suppose. They were great fun in the old days, when it was all singsongs and Harry Porter playing the piano. They've got a disco this year – it's just not my sort of thing any more.'

'Too old at thirty-nine, eh?'

Sarah considered the question. 'Well, maybe not,' she answered finally.

Chapter Two

3.05 p.m. Wednesday, 15 December

Travelling from north London to Scotland Yard Colin Greaves asked the driver to make a short diversion in Hampstead to one of the grander tree-lined roads close to the Heath. He stopped the car outside a handsome pair of wrought-iron gates and Nick Holland glanced up at an engraved brass plate set in one of the brick pillars which bore the words 'Saint Catherine's School'.

'I shall be about an hour,' Greaves said as he got out. 'Why don't you two get something to eat and pick me up later. The Flask in Highgate is open all day.'

'We'll be back at 4.15,' Holland said and he directed the driver to go on.

Greaves walked up the gravel drive and entered the main door of the building. He paused for a moment in the entrance hall to feel the atmosphere, although he knew his way about the premises. In his experience, there was something about the fabric of every school that told you more about the sort of establishment it was than any amount of conversation with the inhabitants. This one was happy enough, he could tell; but there was an underlying sternness that tempered any illusion of laxity.

Despite the grandeur of the building, there was a comfortable, genteel shabbiness about Saint Catherine's. Almost like a country hotel that had known other days. The panelled walls were scuffed near the main doorway and the large Turkish rug covering the polished wooden floor was well worn and frayed at the edges. A large stained-glass window above the curving staircase cast a good deal of light for a gloomy day. It did not depict a religious theme, but showed an eighteenth-century huntsman complete with game bag, gun and sporting dog. Greaves walked along a short corridor behind the staircase and knocked on the first door.

'Enter,' called a high, cultivated English voice. Greaves turned the brass handle, feeling like an undergraduate about to attend a rather daunting tutorial. The feeling was reinforced when he entered the cluttered little room that smelt of dust, old books and sweetish pipe smoke. Father Robson was seated at a crowded desk, working at a lap-top computer, frowning with concentration.

The priest completed the sentence he was typing and then looked up with a smile of pleasure. 'Superintendent Greaves,' he said, glancing at his wrist-watch, 'Is it three o'clock already?'

'A little after,' Greaves replied. 'I'm sorry I'm late.'

'Not at all,' the priest answered. 'Just let me save this and I'll be with you.' He returned his attention to the screen and made a few keystrokes, then sat back in his chair. Greaves took the seat opposite his desk and handed him a small leatherbound book that he'd taken from his raincoat pocket.

'How did you get on with it?' Father Robson asked.

26

'Fine.'

The priest nodded in satisfaction. 'I thought you might appreciate reading it in Portuguese. I have a copy in English, if you would prefer?'

Greaves smiled. 'No, I managed well enough.'

Father Robson laughed shortly. 'Better than I could've probably. It's been a few years since I needed the language. By the way, I've almost finished the one you lent me; tonight should see it out.' He stood up. 'I've been sitting here for too long. Do you mind if I stretch my legs for a bit?'

'Not at all,' Greaves answered and he followed as Father Robson led him out of the school once more and into the grounds at the rear of the building. As they walked, Greaves could hear distant noises: the sudden clatter of desks being closed, and from somewhere closer a group of young voices conjugating Latin verbs.

'Let's go down to the vegetable garden,' the priest suggested. 'It will be quiet at this time of year.'

They walked in silence for a time, then Father Robson said, 'Any further developments in the case?'

Greaves nodded. 'Another woman – but this one is still alive.'

'Thank God,' the priest said, meaning the words he had spoken.

'Does the name Victoria Howard mean anything to you?'

Father Robson stopped and closed his eyes. 'Yes it does,' he answered after a pause. They walked on a few paces and he added, 'A man called Joseph March wants to come and see me; he says he's a reporter on the *Gazette*. That's the paper Mrs Keane works on, is it not?'

'Yes it is,' Greaves answered thoughtfully.

3.15 p.m. Wednesday, 15 December

George Conway had a final large brandy to round off the lunch then, after swapping a few insults with Luigi, he and Sarah walked back along Gray's Inn Road to the shabby grey-stone building that housed the offices of the *Gazette*.

'Any news of when we're moving?' Sarah asked as they crossed the forecourt. For some months it had been general knowledge that LOC PLC and the *Gazette* were to be rehoused in a new building in the far reaches of Docklands. When Sarah had been a young reporter on the *Gazette* the other journalists had complained bitterly about the dreary, soulless area they inhabited. Now, with the prospects of moving to an unknown part of the city, they declaimed with even greater passion about the Philistines who were taking them from the delights of their beloved heartland on the edge of Bloomsbury.

George stuck out his lower lip and held his hands palms up as if to receive manna from heaven. 'Who knows if we'll go at all,' he replied.

'Sir Robert has cocked up everything else recently. Maybe he'll forget to order the removal vans.'

In the main hall they found two secretaries from the publicity department dressing a large Christmas tree that was bright with lights and tinsel. Scattered around the base were boxes of presents wrapped in expensive shiny paper. Standing to one side was a

28

thickset figure who carried a large leather photographer's bag. He wore a heavy overcoat and a brown racing trilby that appeared to be slightly too small for his head. As George and Sarah approached he looked up from watching the two girls and refocused his attention through the thick spectacles that dominated his beefy face.

'Trying to spot which present is yours?' Sarah said to Harry Porter, the doyen of the *Gazette*'s photographers.

Harry lightly tapped one of the boxes with his foot and it skidded across the marble floor. 'Huh,' he said contemptuously. 'Just as I thought; they're like all Sir Robert bloody Hall's promises – as empty as a Scotchman's porridge bowl.'

The two secretaries looked uneasily at Porter. It was a dangerous business to speak sedition around the office. Sir Robert Hall was known to value staff members who passed on the remarks employees made about him. Sir Robert called it 'keeping in touch'. Others simply thought of it as spying.

But Harry Porter was beyond caring for such matters. He was close to retirement and his pension was safe, so he spoke with the freedom others could only envy.

'Welcome back from Black Pudding Land,' Harry said, pecking Sarah on the cheek. 'Great stuff that – like the old days, when this bloody paper stood for something.'

'So what do you think about the new editor, Harry?' George asked as they walked to the lift. Harry sighed and punched the call button. He glanced up at the No Smoking sign and lit a small black cheroot. 'I don't know. I've worked for comedians before in Fleet Street – we might as well have a professional for a change.'

'So we can put you down as a Don't Know,' George said.

'More like a Don't Care,' he answered. 'Mind you, I did hear a whisper that he was a bit of a blue-arsed fly merchant,' Harry continued as they entered the lift.

'On what authority?' George asked.

'A friend of my granddaughter was a researcher on his TV show for a while.'

'So?'

'Well, it seems Mr Marr gives the impression of being a real dynamo. He gets everyone running around like blue-arsed flies, chasing his ideas, but they usually turn out to be rat shit. Then he leaves the last one holding his baby to carry the can.' Harry paused, then said, 'He should fit in here perfectly.'

At the third floor they walked through swing doors into the newsroom. Sarah still found it odd to enter a modern newspaper office. When she had begun her career, they were noisy places, resonant with the sound of clattering typewriters, ringing telephones and shouting men. Scattered with paper and filled with tension and cigarette smoke.

The vast air-conditioned room she now walked through was as hushed and sedate as the headquarters of an insurance office. Carpet softened their tread and most of the staff on duty sat silently before computer terminals, their eyes transfixed by the glowing words displayed on the green-tinted screens.

They parted as they moved through the vast room,

Harry heading for the photographer's room, George taking his seat on the news desk and Sarah walking on to her section, where Pauline Kaznovitch was talking to fellow reporters, Mick Gates and Tony Prior.

'Welcome back. Have you heard about the new editor?' Pauline asked when Sarah had logged on to her terminal and called up her own file to see if there were any messages.

'I have,' Sarah answered.

'It's all right for you two,' Tony Prior said in a chiding tone. 'You've got rich men to support you. I've got a wife and child to feed.' He tried to sound confident, but Sarah could hear the slight edge of worry in his voice, despite his jocular attitude. There was always a chill wind of fear when a new editor was appointed. Old alliances were suddenly without value until talents had been proven all over again.

'You're a good reporter, Tony,' Sarah said. 'And you're young. They'll hang on to you.'

'Do you really think so?' he asked, his voice now serious.

'Absolutely certain.'

Prior stood up and plunged his hands into his jacket pockets. He did not look old enough to have a wife and child. He still had a boy's body, thin and awkward. But she was right about his talent: he was a good reporter, with a quick, suspicious mind. 'If they give you ruled paper – write the other way,' Jack used to say. Prior was capable of understanding that. He walked over to gossip with a friend on the sports sub's table and Pauline chuckled when he was out of earshot.

'What's that supposed to mean?' Sarah asked.

'It was a noise not a comment,' Pauline answered.

'I know a noisy comment when I hear one.'

'Just laughing at the mother hen.'

Sarah sat back and folded her arms. 'That's the most depressing thing I've heard all day,' she said. 'I'll have you know I was as young as you are – about fifteen minutes ago.'

Pauline glanced quickly at her. 'I was referring to your attitude not your age,' she said. Then something else caught her eye. Sarah followed her gaze and saw Fanny Hunter and Alan Stiles walking through the newsroom together. All eyes were now upon them. Something of which they were totally aware, although they gave the impression they were wrapped in each other's company.

It was obvious where they had just come from. Stiles, who was still smoking one of the chairman's large Havana cigars, leaned towards Fanny, who listened to his whispered comment and then burst into raucous laughter. Harry Porter had once described Fanny as always looking like a retired villain's wife – just back from a long holiday on the Costa Brava. Sarah agreed with the accuracy of the observation. Although the silk dress and ample gold jewellery were as genuine as the South of France suntan, there was something strikingly vulgar about the general effect.

' "When Chloris to the temple comes, adoring crowds before her fall," ' Pauline quoted to Sarah as Fanny approached.

' "She can restore the dead from tombs and every life but mine recall," ' Sarah continued the game they played together.

Fanny, now close enough to hear, took up the verse:

' "I only am by Love design'd to be the victim for mankind." ' She stopped at Sarah's desk and said: 'I didn't know they taught poetry at grammar schools.' Fanny, despite her deliberately crude manner, was a graduate of Cambridge and liked to remind people of it from time to time.

'I went to a convent, Fanny,' Sarah replied sweetly, 'but you're right, they didn't teach us much poetry. Chastity and compassion were the major priorities. What were yours?'

Pauline gave a chuckle and lowered her head so that a cascade of bright red hair hid her face.

Fanny glanced at them both and said: 'You two bead-rattlers better say a few Hail Marys when you get home tonight. It could turn out to be bad times for you around here.'

'Thank you for the warning, Fanny,' Pauline called out as the columnist moved on. 'I'll light a candle for you on Sunday.' Then she turned back to Sarah. 'Isn't it strange how some things never change. Editors come and go; but Fanny goes on for ever.'

They gossiped for a few more minutes and then Pauline answered a telephone and Sarah began to read the agency copy that she called up on her terminal: another change from her early days on the *Gazette*. Before computers had become commonplace, reporters saw only the news agency copy that related to the specific stories on which they were working. Only key members of the news desk and executives on the back bench saw all the information that flooded into the office, handed to them by messengers who distributed the copy as they tore it off the telex machines in the wire room. Now Sarah could read reports from all over the world, on any subject that she wished to select from the lists she could call up on her screen. It was an endless source of fascination to her.

When she glanced up again she saw George Conway leave the news desk and make his way towards the editor's office at the far end of the room. When he had gone Stiles got up and sauntered over to the reporters. More of them were at their desks now and he had a largish audience. He stopped before Sarah and puffed on the remains of his cigar.

'Good lunch, Alan?' Don Bradley spoke as if asking the question at a press conference.

'First class,' Stiles replied as if he had been to an audience with a member of the Royal Family. He ran a hand across the sparse ginger hair that was carefully arranged across his freckled pate.

'How was the new editor?' Ian Bradshaw asked.

Stiles took another long pull at the remains of the cigar and studied the glowing tip for a moment. 'Same as ever,' he answered slowly. 'Old Simon never changes.'

'Nice bloke is he?' Bradley said.

'Nice?' Stiles repeated and paused again. 'I don't know if nice is the right word. He's as hard as fucking nails – always was. But he can sniff out buried talent like a magpie.'

'Don't you mean a truffle hound,' Pauline said.

'What?' Stiles said suspiciously.

'Truffle hounds sniff buried things out,' Pauline continued. 'Magpies like carrion.'

'Well he's not interested in smart-arsed remarks, that's for sure, so you'd better start looking for decent stories. Things are changing around here. And I mean decent,' he added. 'He's not interested in any sex trash – or bleeding-heart crap.' He looked at Sarah as he spoke the last part of the sentence.

'Can you translate that bit about "sex trash" for us, Alan?' Pauline asked.

Stiles heard her question, but turned away and addressed the others. 'He agrees with the chairman, there's too much fucking filth in newspapers these days. Women talking about orgasms and how they like their boyfriends to bang them. He thinks the paper's been obsessed with sex crimes. Simon says there's a whole category of journalism that's been forgotten – and we ought to get back to it, pretty damned quick.'

'What category is that?' Tony Prior asked.

Stiles pulled at the cigar again. 'The rattling good yarn – that's the sort of thing he wants to see more of.'

'Just exactly what does that mean?' Pauline said.

'Adventure stuff,' Stiles said vaguely. It was clear that in the discussion over lunch the new editor had not specified exactly what constituted a rattling good yarn.

'But can you give us an example?' Pauline persisted.

Stiles turned to her again: 'I'll tell you in Simon's own words,' he said: 'Asking what a good story is reminds him of the man who wanted a description of an elephant; and the guy he was asking said: "you'll know it when you see one." '

Pauline watched him walk away and said: 'Prat!' in a voice loud enough for him to hear. He didn't look back.

Sarah looked at her. 'You were a bit short with him, weren't you?'

'I can't stand the little prick,' she answered. Sarah was used to people about the office hating Stiles, but there was deeper feeling in Pauline's remarks.

'Oh, don't let him get to you. He's not worth that amount of effort,' Sarah said, then looked at Pauline's face. It was filled with loathing.

'Has he done something bad to you?' she asked quietly.

Pauline paused for a moment and then said, 'Come and have a cup of coffee with me.'

Sarah collected her bag and walked with her to the canteen. When they were seated at one of the Formica-topped tables, Pauline glanced around. They were far away from the other people in the room. She was gripping her hands together so tightly that Sarah could see red marks on the pale skin. Eventually she spoke. 'Stiles attacked me,' she said flatly.

'When?' Sarah asked quickly.

'A couple of months ago.' She looked down at the table. 'The night of 27 October, to be precise.'

'How bad was it?' Sarah asked. 'Did he actually rape you?'

Pauline shook her head. Then she looked up and smiled mirthlessly 'Not quite.'

'Were you hurt?'

'A few bruises.' Pauline spoke lightly now; but Sarah could tell how hard it was for her.

'Tell me exactly what happened.'

Pauline sat back and placed her hands palm down on the table. Sarah could see the marks on them clearly now. 'My husband was away for a few days visiting his family in Poland,' she began hesitantly. 'I stopped in the Red Lion for a drink a couple of nights running. The second night, Stiles offered to drive me home – he knew I was on my own.' She shrugged. 'I'd never made a secret of the fact that I didn't like him; but I thought: what the hell, there's no point in being ungracious. After all we do have to work together. So I agreed.' She turned to look towards one of the windows.

'Go on,' Sarah prompted.

Pauline looked back at her. 'On the way he suggested we stop for an Indian meal. I didn't want to, but he pleaded.' She paused. 'I suppose I should have insisted that he take me home there and then, but I didn't. In the restaurant he ordered champagne. I tried to talk him out of it but he started to get noisy. I refused to drink any. That was a mistake – he drank the whole bottle. Suddenly he was very pissed. I didn't want him to drive; I said I'd get a taxi. That seemed to sober him up and he apologised. He said he'd take me straight to the flat. He kept saying he was sorry, and begged me to let him take me home. I thought I'd get rid of him quicker if I agreed. When we got to the flat he asked for a cup of coffee. I was still a bit worried about how much he'd drunk.' She paused again. 'No, that's not really true – in fact I was worried about the neighbours. Anyway, I let him in.' She stopped and shrugged. 'When we got inside he tried to pull my clothes off.' She shuddered involuntarily. 'He had his hands everywhere – down the front of my dress; between my legs. I struggled and kept saying no. Then he got rougher and hit me a couple of times. I fell over and banged my head, I think that pulled him up a bit.

37

He let go of me and just called me names. He kept calling me a fucking little prick-teaser. I told him to get out, then he started again. We struggled for a bit more and I managed to kick him a couple of times. Then he really believed me. Suddenly it was all over.'

'Did you tell anyone? Your husband?'

She shook her head.

'Were you frightened?'

'Yes,' she answered, 'when he wouldn't stop I was suddenly terrified. He's a lot stronger than me. I just felt so bloody helpless.' Then her voice became lower. 'He even started to smell different.'

Sarah looked up. 'He *smelt* different?'

Pauline nodded. 'A heavy, animal smell. I suppose he was just sweating.'

Sarah thought for a moment. 'Why haven't you told me before now?'

'I suppose I tried to forget it. Stiles has kept well away from me for the last few months. Haven't you noticed he put himself on nights recently? No, of course not, you've been out of town.'

Sarah felt suddenly powerless, and at the same time filled with anger. She had thought her opinion of Stiles could not be pitched any lower, but apparently he had achieved the impossible.

'Is there nothing we can do?' she asked finally.

Pauline shook her head. 'No – thanks for listening, though. It's helped to tell someone.' She got up quickly and forced her voice to be cheerful. 'Come on, let's get back and look for some rattling good yarns.'

When they reached the newsroom, George was still missing from the desk. Stiles was making a lot of noise – snapping out orders and shouting instructions into the telephone. The stub of the cigar remained in his hand, like some talisman that reinforced his new-found position as 'friend' of Simon Marr.

From her position at the end of the reporters' section, Sarah was close enough to see what happened on the news desk and even hear conversations unless they were conducted in low voices. Now she saw a security guard in the company's blue-shirted uniform approach Stiles and hand him a yellow visitor's slip. Sarah had not seen the guard before; perhaps he had been hired while she had been out of town. She understood the transaction taking place. It was a common enough sight. Somebody had come to the building with a complaint or a story to tell. Members of the public frequently called at the offices of newspapers with a request to speak to someone, usually the editor. Quite often the callers were disturbed, sometimes dangerous; and occasionally the bearers of excellent stories. The commissionaires were fairly shrewd judges of character, and could usually sum up callers at a glance, but it was the policy of the paper that a journalist must speak to everyone that came to the *Gazette* who wanted to air a grievance or pass on a story. First, the visitor filled out a slip of paper with their name, address and the reason why they had called.

Stiles hardly glanced at the paper before saying, 'What's he like?'

The young commissionaire shrugged. 'Looks all right.'

Stiles studied the slip again, then handed it back. He glanced around and said, 'Give it to Keane.'

'Which one is he?'

'She,' Stiles corrected. 'She's the one sitting on the end.'

The young man walked over to her in a swaggering fashion and Sarah took the piece of paper with a re-signed smile. 'Where is he?' she asked.

'Interview room 2.'

'What's he like?'

The commissionaire shrugged again and Sarah got the feeling he resented being asked the question. He stood at the edge of the desk with hips thrust towards her, powerful arms folded casually, a half-smile of contempt on his face. Sarah was now sure she had not seen him before. There was something odd about his face that she couldn't quite place. His closely cropped, straw-coloured hair and hard, square features were regular enough – much like the other guards about the building. But Sarah didn't much care for the young men LOC PLC now hired to secure the premises. They all looked like members of some paramilitary organi-sation. Years ago the commissionaires had been cheerful, fatherly men who whistled and called her 'Luv', and she had not felt patronised or sex-ually harrassed by the endearment; but this man communicated with a body language that was ag-gressively suggestive.

'Do you want me to come and hold your hand?' he asked softly. It was a light voice that didn't match his bulky body. South London working class – despite his effort to sound the vowels and consonants of the sen-tence correctly. The innuendo was absolutely clear.

'No, thank you,' Sarah answered shortly. 'I'll be able to manage on my own.' She began to search in a

40

drawer for her notebook. When she looked up again he had gone.

She walked to the far end of the newsroom where there were a pair of offices close by the lifts which were kept for private interviews. Just before she entered the second, she read the visitor's slip. The handwriting was well formed and very legible. The name was Andrew Maclean and in the 'Reason for interview' box was written the single word: 'Apocalypse'. Sarah gave an inward groan. A religious nut, she thought, and prepared herself for a sermon on the imminent collapse of civilisation – or even the end of the world.

But Mr Maclean was not what she expected. He was about her own age, Sarah guessed. Average height; a slender build; carefully polished shoes; an expensive dark overcoat; short fair hair, flecked with grey; a long, plain face; intelligent eyes. He carried a slim briefcase, which he placed on the table in the bare little room, and he stood up when she entered.

When they had introduced themselves, Sarah gestured for him to take a seat and he tapped the empty ashtray on the table. 'This doesn't look as if it's ever been used. May I smoke?'

'Please do,' Sarah replied. She noted the accent: lowland Scot – and well educated.

He took a silver case from his pocket and lit a filter-tipped cigarette with an expensive lighter. 'A bad habit,' he said apologetically. 'But hard to relinquish.'

Sarah smiled and shook her head when he proffered the case. She felt relaxed now. 'My father is a doctor and he still smokes,' she said.

He smiled, which made his face seem more youthful. He had a very agreeable manner, Sarah thought, and she wondered if he might be a salesman of some up-market product. Such a trustworthy first impression would be invaluable for demonstrating the finer points of an expensive motor car or yacht.

'There's a coincidence, my father is a doctor as well,' he said with a grin. 'But he's a firm advocate for giving it up. Now, may I tell you why I'm here?'

Sarah opened her notebook and pointed with her pen to the visitor's slip, which she had placed on the table before them.

Maclean nodded, understanding the unasked question. 'I'm sorry for that melodramatic touch, but I thought it might get someone's attention.'

'I'm all ears.'

He gave a short bark of laughter and then became more serious. 'It may not seem such an exaggeration, Mrs Keane, when you've heard what I have to tell you.' He sat back for a moment and stubbed out the cigarette before he began. 'I'm an engineer – employed by the Camtech Oil Company, based in Houston, Texas. Have you heard of us?'

'No, but go on.'

Maclean ran a finger along the line of his jaw. Sarah noted that the hands were well kept, the nails shaped carefully. 'I've just returned from the Soviet Union – I mean Russia,' he continued. 'You may have heard that they've been having a hell of a lot of trouble with their oil industry?'

Sarah nodded but did not speak. Maclean went on: 'Camtech is not one of the big companies but it leads the field in technology. As you may know, the

Russians have vast deposits of oil, but half of it is dribbling away into the ground because their technical skills are so primitive and they just can't get vital spares. The infrastructure is unbelievable over there, God knows how long it will take them to get their act together. Don't get me wrong, there's nothing wrong with their theoretical work – they can put a man on the moon, but their refineries and pipelines have been starved of skilled workers and good technicians for years so the whole industry has run into the ground – it's incredibly ramshackle. That's why they called in Camtech. I was dispatched to a little town called Vialistock to meet with their representatives and take a look at the problems.'

Maclean lit another cigarette. 'They put me up in a dreadful little hotel and treated me with the usual hostility the Russians reserve for those who have come to help them. I had plenty to do in the daytime, but the Russians knock off quite early – I wouldn't say they were a hard-working race – and there was absolutely nothing to do in the evenings except sit in the bar drinking cheap vodka.

'On the sixth night I was in the bar reading a novel when I was approached by a very old man who saw my book and started a conversation. Well, hardly a conversation, his English was poor. But after a few minutes he discovered I could speak German. He was delighted and introduced himself as Doctor Otto Frichter. He seemed to me to be on his last legs, you know that curious fragile look some old people get when they're near death.'

Sarah nodded again.

Maclean continued. 'He wasn't a medical man, his

degree was in engineering – metallurgy, to be precise.'
He paused and was about to stub out his cigarette, but
changed his mind. He looked at Sarah until she raised
her eyes from her notebook. 'The story he told me was
incredible and quite terrifying, Mrs Keane.'

Sarah waited in the silence that followed, but Maclean just sat watching her, his grey eyes unblinking.
Finally she said: 'Are you going to tell me anything?'

Maclean reached out, unzipped his case and took
out two closely typed foolscap pages, which he passed
to her. Sarah expected it to be the information he had
promised, but was surprised to see that it was a confidentiality agreement obviously drafted by a lawyer.
It stated that anything he disclosed was to remain
strictly his copyright.

'Do you have any objection to signing?' he asked.

Sarah smiled slightly and shook her head. She
wrote her name at the foot of the second page and
pushed the sheets back to Maclean who placed them
carefully back in his case. 'You know, it would have
been enough to say you were speaking off the record,'
she said.

Maclean shrugged. 'Scots prefer a sound legal basis
for everything they agree upon, Mrs Keane. As a nation, we tend to follow the advice of Sam Goldwyn:
"A handshake isn't worth the paper it's written on." '

Sarah sat back and folded her arms. 'Are you going
to ask a lot of money for this story?'

'Exactly $807,000,' he replied crisply.

'That's a curious amount,' Sarah replied. 'Why dollars?'

Maclean lit another cigarette. 'Exchange rates
fluctuate. After I've paid Doctor Frichter his share I

must have a precise amount left – and I want it in dollars.'

'Can you give me any indication what sort of story is worth that kind of money?' Sarah asked.

He sat forward in his chair and tapped the ash from his cigarette, then began in a low, unemotional voice. 'According to Doctor Frichter, quite soon Britain is going to be devastated by a plague more terrible than the Black Death. Loss of life will be on an appalling scale. The rest of the world will quarantine Britain. The medical services will be overwhelmed, law and order will break down. As somebody once said about the aftermath of a nuclear war: "The living will envy the dead." I can provide documentary evidence that this is true, but first let me tell you Doctor Frichter's story.'

For the next thirty minutes Maclean recited what the German had told him. It was clear and concise. When he had finished, Sarah closed her notebook, thanked him and asked if he could continue to wait for a while. He answered that he was quite content to stay for as long as she wished and refused her offer of refreshments. Sarah went looking for Peter Kirk, the *Gazette* science correspondent.

She found him in the library, leaning on the counter, spectacles propped on his high domed forehead, consulting a textbook.

'Can you spare me a few minutes, Peter?' she asked. Kirk glanced up, slammed the book shut and nodded so that the glasses fell back on to the bridge of his nose. 'Of course, my dear,' he answered with a smile. Kirk liked Sarah. He was one of the oldest members of the *Gazette* staff and had known her since she first worked on the paper. 'Will it take long?'

'A bit.'

'Why don't you come to my room? I'll even give you a cup of tea.' He led her to the little office he occupied on the floor above the main newsroom. Apart from the computer terminal, it had not changed since Sarah had first seen the inside of it many years before. Kirk belonged to the 'no décor' school of journalism. Some people tried to make their offices comfortable or homely with potted plants, hoarded furniture, pictures on the walls, carefully filled bookcases. Kirk preferred the opposite. The only contents in the bare-walled room were a plain gun-metal grey desk, scruffily piled with old newspapers; three filing cabinets; some cheap shelving that contained back numbers of the *Lancet* and a few reference books on subjects so obscure that no one had bothered to steal them.

Kirk cleared an overflow of magazines from the spare chair then left the room for a few minutes to return with two plastic cups. He handed one to Sarah and said, 'I thought your series was excellent. Tell me, in spite of the misery you so powerfully described, do you believe the world is an improving place?' Now he sat facing her, eyebrows raised in anticipation.

'I suppose it's all relative,' Sarah replied. 'In general, the poorest people today would have been considered fortunate in Dickens's time. But not the children I interviewed.'

Kirk held up his cup and examined it closely. 'My father was the editor of a Fleet Street paper, you know.'

'I didn't,' Sarah answered.

'Oh, yes,' he said wistfully. 'It's long gone now of

46

course – closed down, sold off, amalgamated with other dead newspapers. But do you know, before the war, when I was a child, we had five servants at home. Our nanny used to serve us tea in the nursery each afternoon.' He held the plastic cup even higher. 'Life has gone down for me a bit. I wonder what Nanny would have thought of this incredible concoction?' Then he turned to face her. 'But I digress – what is it you want to know, my dear?'

'Do you know about the German V weapons in the Second World War?' Sarah began.

Kirk nodded. 'Of course. The V-1, commonly known as the Doodle-bug, was essentially a pilotless aircraft packed with explosives. It wasn't all that fast; in fact we shot quite a lot of them down. The V-2 was a far more formidable weapon: a supersonic rocket that flew faster than sound and therefore gave no warning. The first thing you knew about it was a bloody great bang when it exploded and knocked down an entire street.'

Sarah consulted her notebook. 'Were the Germans good at metallurgy?'

'Excellent. Better than us or the Americans, by all accounts.'

'What about germ warfare?'

Kirk nodded. 'That too. Clever buggers, the Germans. It's always puzzled me why they didn't get the atom bomb first. Good job we beat them to something.'

'Did you ever hear of them making a V-3?'

Kirk thought for a moment then shook his head and began to brush the front of the ratty brown cardigan he wore under his dark grey suit. 'Can't say I have,' he said in a preoccupied voice.

Sarah looked at the notebook again. 'The V-2 buried itself in the ground before exploding, didn't it?'

'Correct.'

'Do you think they could have constructed rockets with germ warheads?'

Kirk nodded.

'Could they have made a container that would take fifty years to erode?'

Kirk thought for a moment then he spoke. 'I would say quite possibly yes – why, where's all this leading to?'

Sarah closed her notebook and looked at Kirk. 'There's a man downstairs in one of the waiting rooms who says the Germans built V-3 rockets and bombarded our reservoirs with them in 1945. Does that sound possible?'

Kirk raised his glasses to his brow again and looked at the ceiling. 'It's a good plot for a thriller, but there's a pretty big flaw.'

'What's that?'

'The rockets had no degree of accuracy at all. They were a weapon for terrorising civilians, not hitting military targets. Plenty fell on London but the Germans couldn't pinpoint the spot where they would land. Hitting something as specific as a reservoir would have been out of the question.'

'But if they'd managed to solve the problem of accuracy?'

He shook his head. 'They just didn't have the technology then – no microchips, no lasers, no electronics to speak of, just primitive directional beams, that sort of thing. No – I just can't believe it.'

'Why?'

Kirk raised the palms of his hands upwards. 'If they could hit something with that accuracy why bother with a reservoir, why not drop one down Churchill's chimney?' He stood up. 'Who is the source for this man's information?'

'Doctor Otto Frichter.'

Kirk rummaged in the packed shelves behind his desk and finally located a thick book. He flipped through the pages for a time, stopped, read for a moment and then said, 'Hmm, Doctor Otto Frichter. Metallurgist. Staff of Peenemunde Rocket Research Establishment. Captured by the Russians in 1945.'

Sarah returned to her desk in the newsroom where she typed a memo into her terminal that gave a complete précis of Maclean's story and stated that he'd insisted on a confidentiality contract. She added a paragraph pointing out Peter Kirk's doubts and included the fact that Maclean wanted more than half a million pounds for the story. Then she typed the commands that made an electronic transference into Stiles's personal file in the system.

The amount of money was large, but papers had paid more for big stories in the past. Maclean had struck her as being sincere enough and the story almost plausible, in a nightmarish sort of way. It would take a lot of checking; and in the end, Sarah expected they'd find some kind of flaw or half-truth. In her experience, people were often quite inaccurate when they talked to journalists. Although there certainly were unscrupulous reporters who would invent quotes and 'bend' stories, Sarah could remember plenty of occasions when people had flatly denied they had made certain statements, then, when they'd had tape recordings played back to them, would say: but surely the reporter had known they meant something completely different? Somehow the words had been 'put into their mouths'.

Sarah became aware that there was some kind of activity taking place on the news desk. Stiles was sitting in George Conway's desk, despite the fact that George was still about the office, and people were shaking Stiles's hand. With a sinking heart, she drew the obvious conclusion. She heard Stiles say, 'Drinks at 6.30, back to work now.' He turned back to his terminal and Sarah saw George entering the small office off the newsroom which he used for private work. She made her way there. He looked up when she entered and she could see that he had been hurt but was putting on a brave face.

'They've fired you,' she said.

George shook his head: 'Not quite – you're looking at the new assistant editor in charge of forward planning.'

'What does that mean?'

George sat back and folded his arms. 'It means I'll say: "What about doing a series on the coming threat of killer rabbits in the West Country", and they say, "Good idea, give me a memo", and I do a memo and nothing else happens.'

Sarah looked at him, but she could think of no words of comfort. 'I'm sorry, George,' she said finally, but it sounded inadequate.

George smiled a little sadly: 'I know you are,' he replied, looking down at the piles of papers scattered on the desk. He slowly swept them on to the floor with his forearm, looked about him at the scruffy little room and said, 'Not much to show for twenty-seven years is it?' He smiled with a certain difficulty. 'I should have married you – we could have been happily divorced by now.'

Sarah decided to leave him alone for a while. Pausing at the doorway she said, 'I'll buy you a drink later.'

He nodded. 'Perhaps not in the Red Lion, I'll go along there later. Give Stiles time to enjoy his fifteen minutes of fame before I turn up.'

As she walked back to her desk, Alan Stiles beckoned her over to the news desk. When he spoke it was in a surprisingly civil tone. 'I've read your memo. How many people have you told about the rocket story?' he asked in a low voice.

'Just Peter Kirk.'

'Good. Don't say anything to anyone else.'

'Do you believe it?' she asked.

'Why?' he answered, looking suddenly suspicious.

'Peter Kirk doesn't think they had a guidance system that would have worked with the degree of accuracy needed. I have other doubts as well.'

'What are they?'

She thought for a time. 'If he believed the story and thought there was going to be a real Apocalypse, he would have gone to the government – not tried to sell it to us for half a million pounds.'

'Well it's not your worry any more,' Stiles said, still in a pleasant voice.

'You don't want me to follow it up?'

Stiles nodded. 'That's right – forget about it. By the way,' he added, 'do you know Simon Marr?'

'Only from the television show.'

Stiles looked at her for a moment as if doubting her word; then he indicated her dismissal by a flick of his head and returned his gaze to the terminal screen.

Sarah walked back to the interview room, composing some polite words of thanks for Mr Maclean, but when she opened the door he was gone, leaving nothing but the smell of his cigarettes.

Chapter Three

After the evening conference finished at six o'clock, the *Gazette*'s night shift came on duty. The day staff briefed them on the day's stories and those still to be filed before they stood down. Stiles left the news desk and led those members of his staff that were now free to the pub for the traditional celebrations. Sarah would have gone – hostilities were usually suspended on such occasions – but she had been asked to make a few check calls on an agency story about a runaway girl.

It didn't take long and she had just finished filing the information when she became aware of someone standing before her. She looked up and saw the familiar figure of Simon Marr smiling down at her.

Sarah's first thought was that he was bigger than he appeared on the screen. He had handsome fleshy features and a mane of iron-grey hair. The cloth of his sharply cut tan-coloured suit seemed to be made of a fibre that resisted wrinkles. Somehow he gave the impression he was composed of brighter colours than other human beings: the flesh pinker, eyes clearer, teeth whiter than washing powder. Sarah had encountered the same phenomenon with other people in show business.

'Hello, Sarah,' he said warmly. 'Long time no see.' His voice had a booming resonance with a mid-Atlantic intonation.

Sarah smiled in confusion. She was baffled by his familiarity.

'I was sorry to hear about Jack,' he said. 'He was one of the all-time greats.'

'Yes he was.'

'I'll never forget how good he was to me. Only the real stars remember what it's like to be a nobody. That's the sign of real class.' He nodded at his own sagacity. Then he looked at her sharply and winked. 'You were nice to me too. I don't forget that.'

Suddenly Sarah began to recollect a night long ago, when Jack had won some television award. She had not been able to attend; but later, when she was asleep, he had arrived at the house in Hampstead in the middle of the night, with a crowd he had accumulated at the celebration dinner.

Sarah had got up and cooked them all bacon and eggs. There was a slim, dark-haired young man in the party, she recalled, unimportant but anxious to be one of the crowd. Now she realised it had been Simon Marr. She had spent some time talking to him, for which he had seemed grateful. The following afternoon flowers had arrived with an indecipherable signature. She guessed they had come from him.

'I'm sorry you couldn't come to lunch, Alan told me how busy you were,' Marr continued. 'Perhaps we can do it some other day. By the way, I thought your articles on the lost kids were terrific. Just the sort of stuff we need to do . . . now and again.'

'Thank you,' she said. 'It was George Conway's idea, you know.'

He seemed to be about to say something else then turned with a sudden urgency, as if he had remembered a pressing appointment, and hurried away.

'Thank you for those flowers,' she called out to the retreating figure. Marr did not turn back, but he held up a hand in acknowledgement.

Sarah told the news desk she was going to the Royal William public house and gave them the telephone number.

'Not going to the Lion?' said Arthur Swann, the news-desk assistant on duty. 'They say the drinks are on Alan Stiles.'

'I'll call in there later,' Sarah replied. She crossed the Gray's Inn Road and made her way to the public house in Bloomsbury where George had told her he would be waiting.

Sarah enjoyed walking through the quiet streets of elegant brick houses. Most of them were offices now, but occasionally she would pass one that was still a private residence and would look into the living rooms, trying to imagine the sort of people who lived there. She had always liked Bloomsbury. It wasn't just the reputation of its literary past, there was something else, probably to do with the proximity of the British Museum; she had happy memories of visits during childhood. Sitting in the shadows of the great pillars, eating her lunchtime sandwiches, chattering with her classmates.

Despite the decorations in some of the windows, it did not feel much like Christmas. She still had most of her shopping to do and had not yet decided on a present for Colin. Then there was the food to be ordered and the tree bought and trimmed. When they had decided to go to Oxfordshire, Sarah had tentatively suggested they should dispense with the tree this year. It was as if she had told the children she was going to sell the house and move them all into a squat she had found in an inner-city slum.

'It just wouldn't be like home, Mum,' Emily had pleaded.

'But we'll be in Oxfordshire,' Sarah repeated.

'But we'll *know*,' the boys said.

They should declare a special Christmas for mothers, she thought – about the middle of June would be a good time. She tried to remember her own mother's face again, but the features still would not form. If only she had a photograph; but there were none. Her father had destroyed them all when she was a child – it was an irrational attempt to come to terms with his grief, she now understood, but for years it had caused her a great deal of pain.

The public house she approached had once been very familiar to her. In the days of her youth, when she and Jack Keane had first met, he had often taken her there. Then he had referred to it as 'The Lovers' Pub'; a place frequented by those embarking on office romances who wanted to avoid the prying eyes of colleagues. When Jack had first taken her there he had pointed out couples in the bar who were acting out the various stages of their personal dramas.

'They're just starting up,' he had said, indicating a

pair close by, eyes locked over a bottle of champagne. Then he had nodded in another direction. 'Those two drinking white wine are having a difficult time.' She followed his gaze and saw a couple who sat in silence, looking about them at different parts of the room.

'And he's just told her it's all got to end,' he had added. The last pair he'd pointed to were obviously cloaked in misery, the woman on the verge of tears and the man on the edge of his stool, looking at his watch, thinking of a train he had promised to catch.

But it had not worked out that way for Sarah and Jack: their affair had not come to an end. Now it was all a lifetime away.

When she entered the familiar door, Sarah found that the interior had been altered beyond recognition. The once sedate saloon bar, furnished in the style of the Thirties, had been transformed into a mock-Victorian alehouse. It was crowded with young people who seemed to be holding an office party. George was wedged at the end of a counter, next to a group who were singing Christmas carols in competition with the blaring music of a jukebox.

'Welcome to hell,' George shouted, and passed her a glass of white wine that he'd already bought. They attempted a conversation but the roaring noise about them made it impossible.

'I don't think I can stand it in here,' George said after a few more minutes of effort. 'Shall we join the odious Stiles?'

Sarah agreed. She'd taken one sip of the wine, which was lukewarm and tasted as if it had been made from crab apples. George finished his Scotch in one swallow.

As Sarah put down her glass on the crowded counter, she glanced across the angle of the bar and saw a figure watching her. It took her a moment to realise it was the young commissionaire she had met earlier in the day. He wore a leather jacket now and was staring at her intently, his gaze made somehow sinister by his ill-matched eyes. When he caught her attention he half-smiled in the same patronising way then ran his tongue around his half-opened lips before making a wiggling motion. It was a crudely suggestive action and she found it repulsive. Ignoring his gaze, she turned away and followed George from the bar.

'I suppose I shall be a spectre at the piss-up,' George said as they walked towards the Red Lion.

'Nonsense,' Sarah said, linking her arm through his. 'Even Stiles must have enough grace to show some good manners.'

'We'll see.'

The crowd in the saloon bar of the Red Lion was almost as noisy as the carol singers. Stiles was standing at the counter with Fanny Hunter, surrounded by reporters and a fair amount of people from the other departments. The level of conversation suddenly dropped by several decibels when George and Sarah stood before them.

'Drink, George?' Stiles asked, waving to Tony Prior who was opening a bottle of champagne. He was flushed and sweating but it was hard to tell if the intoxication in his voice was from elation or alcohol.

'Whisky please,' George replied.

'Bucket of Scotch for our new assistant editor in

charge of . . . what was it, George?' interjected Fanny, not bothering to conceal the contempt in her voice.

'Future planning,' he answered softly.

Sarah watched him closely. He appeared to be in a good mood, but that was misleading. When George was happy he was usually irascible; gentleness was a sign of danger. But Fanny did not read his temperament very well. She assumed his quiet manner was a symptom of defeat. 'So you'll be thinking up ideas for us all from now on?' she said and winked at Stiles. 'Giving us the benefit of your wisdom and experience – but not after lunch.'

George took one of the glasses of champagne that Tony Prior had just poured and handed it to Sarah before he answered.

'Oh, I don't think I'll be bothering you, Fanny,' he said amiably. 'You and I haven't been in the same business for years.'

'Now you're not going to start accusing me of being an old whore, are you?' Fanny said with a laugh. 'I've admitted to that plenty of times.'

'Oh, I wasn't referring to your personal life,' George replied. 'What you do in your own time is between you and your gynaecologist.' He shook his head. 'No, I was talking about what you've done to the *Gazette*.'

Fanny stood up straighter and the smile had almost gone from her face. The rest of the group waited for her to reply.

'And just what have I done to the paper?' she asked tightly. 'Apart from put on circulation.'

George nodded his thanks and sipped some of the Scotch. 'Now that's an interesting point, because cancerous growths are often mistaken for weight gain.'

59

'Cancer?' Fanny said in a barely audible voice.

George raised his glass to her. 'Yes, Fanny. That's what you've become. Not the honest whore you like to imagine you are. Nor do you make the valuable contribution of a jackal or a vulture in cleaning the environment of carrion. You and your kind are just malignant growths, attaching yourselves to newspapers, thriving at the expense of healthy tissue. You don't practise journalism, you just peddle cheap prejudice.'

Fanny clenched her fists as if she were going to hit George. Her face had become as hard as beaten brass. 'You drunken old failure,' she said in a rising voice. 'Do you know how many readers I have? Ponces like you have been riding on my coat-tails for years, clinging on to the jobs I made secure for them. How many people do you think would be buying the *Gazette* today, if all there was to read in it was the crap you've been shovelling out for the last twenty years?'

George smiled, and Sarah saw how easily Fanny had fallen into his trap. He gestured with his glass to the crowd that stood around them. 'Take a good look at the crap shovellers, Fanny. The reporters who stand on the doorsteps and knock on the doors while you sit back earning five times their salaries and pronouncing judgment from afar on the people they meet face to face.'

Sarah saw that George's tactics had been a blatant piece of crowd pleasing, but devastatingly effective for all that. Reporters always saw themselves as the poor bloody infantry: doing the dirty jobs in the worst conditions at the most testing times. Fanny's dismissal of their work struck to the heart. Suddenly they were on George's side and Fanny was the old enemy:

one of the soft-living office wallahs that always under-valued them.

Knowing she had lost, Fanny decided to make a strategic retreat. She turned to Stiles and said, 'Alan, thank Christ the reporters have now got the sort of leadership they deserve. If you don't mind I want to get some fresh air.' She kissed him swiftly on the cheek and swept out of the bar.

The brief silence that followed was broken by a bar-maid calling out, 'Telephone for Mr Conway.'

George went to take the call and slowly the conversation started up again.

'And you, Sarah,' Stiles suddenly said. 'Are you going to manage without your boyfriend holding your hand?'

Sarah was not above using a low shot when the opposition was cheap enough to warrant it. 'I think I've got enough friends, Alan,' she said. 'Simon seems to want to continue our old relationship. He mentioned the invitation to lunch.'

Stiles's expression wavered uneasily: 'I thought you said you didn't know him.'

Sarah nodded to Prior, who was offering more champagne. 'Yes, I did, didn't I,' she said airily. 'Well I didn't want to seem boastful, but I realised it would have to come out eventually.' She shrugged. 'So there we are – all old friends together, Alan.' She turned away and began a new conversation with Charles Trottwood, the head of the Legal department, who had just entered the bar.

'Have I missed anything?' he asked. 'I just passed La Belle Hunter wearing a face that would melt granite.'

Sarah was about to relate the exchange when

George returned looking preoccupied. 'Everything all right?' Sarah asked.

'It was a call from a contact. A copper, actually. They had a rape victim in their nick, giving a statement. He thinks she'll talk to a reporter about the attack.'

'Why is this one special?' Trottwood asked. It sounded like a callous question but Sarah knew rape was a common enough crime that would not usually call for more than a routine follow-up.

'The contact is pretty sure the attack was by the same one who's been murdering the women.'

Trottwood nodded his understanding. Murder gave it another dimension.

'Could it be prejudicial to write about it before it comes to trial?' Sarah asked.

Trottwood shook his head. 'No one's been charged yet.'

'We wouldn't want to name names or take photographs in any case,' George added. He looked around him with a determined expression that suddenly changed to one of uncertainty as the realisation came to him that he could not automatically give the job to one of the reporters in the bar. It was Stiles's responsibility now. He looked towards the news editor and said, 'Alan, have you got a moment?'

Stiles was listening to a rambling compliment from Sinclair, one of the reporters, who was drunk and had suddenly become emotional. He was declaring his undying loyalty, and Stiles – who was enjoying the experience – held up a hand for George to wait. When Sinclair's oath of loyalty was completed, Stiles turned his head. 'What can I do for you, George?' he said in a condescending tone.

'A contact has just rung me with a story,' George said quietly. 'A girl has been raped; the police believe it's the man who's been killing those women. My contact thinks the girl may be prepared to talk to us. It might make a good one for Joe March.'

Stiles made a sucking noise with his teeth and looked up at the ceiling. 'I don't know, George . . .' he answered. 'March is covering the news angle, it's not his kind of thing, more like a feature – what are we going to get at the end of the day? Just another victim telling us how horrible it all was and how she wanted a bath afterwards. Anyway, Simon's not too keen on sex stories – haven't you heard that yet?'

Sarah could see that George was fighting to hold his temper. He now forced himself to speak in a reasonable tone. 'This isn't just a sex story,' he said tightly. 'Can't you see that? It's a woman prepared to tell us what it's like to be attacked by a madman. Bloody hell, Alan – it could do some good for someone. Maybe warn a potential victim.'

Stiles shrugged and turned back to Sinclair. He glanced over his shoulder to George again. 'Tell you what, let's give it to Sarah – for old times' sake,' he said, as if suggesting they throw a scrap of meat to a begging dog. For a moment, Sarah thought that George might begin a character reading of Stiles, but instead he indicated for her to move down the bar.

When they were out of earshot, George pushed a sheet of paper torn from a notebook to her. 'That's the address. The girl's name is Victoria Howard.' George beckoned the barmaid and asked for another drink. Then he said, 'There's something else. The other women who were murdered in the last couple of weeks – they had similar marks on them. The police asked us not to write about it.'

'Are they sure this is the same man?'

'Who knows? Maybe it is. Why don't you check with Superintendent Greaves?'

'Is Colin working on this case?' Sarah asked in sudden surprise.

'Didn't you know?'

Sarah put down her half-finished glass of wine. 'We haven't seen much of each other recently. Remember, I've been away.'

'Give me a call when you're done,' George said.

'Where will you be?'

He smiled. 'In the office – where else?'

Sarah looked down the bar to where the noisy group still crowded around Stiles. 'Why don't you go home?' she said softly.

George looked around and raised his shoulders. 'I am home,' he answered.

Chapter Four

7.15 p.m. Thursday, 16 December

Sarah's car was parked in the forecourt of the *Gazette* building. By the light on the dashboard she read again the address on the piece of paper George had given her, and consulted a street map. It was just off the North Circular Road, close to Golders Green. The drive didn't take long; it was home territory to Sarah so her subconscious mind guided the car through the familiar streets. She arrived close to her destination without being able to recollect the greater part of the journey. Most of the time she had been wondering what to buy Colin for Christmas.

She soon found the block of flats and parked nearby. They were typical of a sort, built in the 1930s, that could be found in all the suburbs of London: a low stone-topped brick wall at the edge of the pavement, backed by a fringe of trees and shrubs before a wide lawn, then plain brick-faced apartments, three storeys high, sparsely trimmed with plain white stone set with iron-framed windows.

Sarah felt a sense of relief: blocks of flats were not always the best places for a woman to visit alone at night. But this one looked safe enough. There were two elderly men on the asphalt pathway that led to the entrance, standing close to each other while they talked. Each had a small dog on a lead. Sarah could tell from their gestures that they were Jewish, which brought her more comfort; it meant families lived here, people concerned about their neighbours. A cry in the night would not go unheeded.

The two men watched her pass, pausing in their conversation. She bade them good-evening and entered the building. The flat she wanted was on the third floor. Sarah rang the bell and after a moment a woman's voice said: 'Who is it?'

'My name is Sarah Keane,' she replied. 'I've called to see Victoria Howard.'

The door opened slightly, but there was no light in the inner hallway. Sarah could just see a face partially hidden by shadows. Then the door opened wider.

'I'm from the *Gazette*,' Sarah said. 'Are you Miss Howard?'

Now Sarah could see the young woman clearly. She was taller than Sarah had anticipated from the smallness of the voice: a strong, athletic-looking girl, barefooted, wearing a loose, polo-necked sweater and jeans. Her dark hair was cut short and framed a striking heart-shaped face. Pale skin and large blue eyes gave a dramatic quality to her features. As she turned to gesture for Sarah to enter the hallway, the light caught a bruise the size of a fifty-pence piece on her right cheek.

'Go to the left,' the girl instructed and she stood aside in the narrow passageway so that Sarah could pass. Sarah found herself in a square little living room, furnished in a style that had once been referred to as 'modern' in the years following the Festival of Britain:

tables and chairs supported on spindle legs, a radio-gram against the wall beneath the bookshelves. There were ornaments from the same period on most surfaces. Sarah stood waiting for an invitation to sit down and glanced at the books; she noticed they were mostly on the theatre.

'I've just made some coffee. Would you like some?' the girl asked.

'Yes, I would, thank you,' Sarah answered. The girl brought two mugs in and placed them on a low table. She pulled up a metal chair and sat down, inviting Sarah to do the same, then lit a cigarette which she inhaled deeply.

'Did you collect the furniture?' Sarah asked. Victoria smiled for the first time. 'No, this flat belonged to my grandmother, she left it to me – this is how it always was.'

'They say this period is valuable these days.'

'I suppose a lot of things get more valuable when they're old – except people,' the girl said.

Sarah drank some of her coffee, which was very good. Victoria noticed her surprise and smiled again. 'My only extravagance,' she said. 'I can't stand instant coffee.'

'Miss Howard,' Sarah began, 'may I call you Victoria?'

'Vickie,' the girl said quickly. 'Everybody calls me Vickie – spelt with an I and an E.' Her voice carefully enunciated the vowels. 'Aren't you going to write it down?'

Sarah shook her head. 'I can remember.' She had a sudden strange feeling they were being watched. It caused her to glance quickly around the room, but they appeared to be alone. 'Can you tell me something about yourself?' Sarah went on.

Vickie shrugged quickly and flicked up her head in what seemed to Sarah like a studied mannerism. 'What sort of thing do you want to know?'

'Anything you want me to know,' Sarah answered easily.

Vickie repeated the mannerism. 'I'm an actress, twenty-one years old, an only child. I was educated at a private school in Hampstead where I was brought up.'

'Which school?'

'Saint Catherine's.'

Sarah did not say she knew the school, that her own children went there. 'Your parents still live in Hampstead?' she asked.

Vickie shook her head and then reached forward to stub out the cigarette. 'My father is dead, my mother lives in Canada with her second husband.'

'Do you want to tell me what happened to you ?'

She looked up again. 'Do you want to hear everything – what I told the policeman?'

'Which one?'

'A Superintendent Greaves.'

Sarah wrote Colin's name down without comment. 'Do you mind telling me what you told him?'

'Will you pay me for the interview?' the girl asked with sudden interest.

Sarah sat a little straighter. 'Were you expecting to get much money, Vickie?'

'I'm not really bothered,' she answered. 'I was just curious. The money's not important.' She sounded as if she meant it.

68

'You're working at the moment?' Sarah asked.

She smiled again. It made her even prettier. 'I'm working but I couldn't live on the pay. My grandmother left me a bit of money.'

'Do you really want to tell me what happened?' Sarah said gently.

Vickie nodded, there was no doubting her determination. 'Where do you want me to start?'

Sarah opened her notebook now.'Wherever you like.'

Vickie took cigarettes and a plastic lighter from the pocket of her jeans. She waved the packet in Sarah's direction as both a question and an offer. Sarah smiled and refused. Vickie lit one and held the coffee mug to the bruise on her cheek.

'I was home here in the afternoon,' she began. 'Gerry and I – that's Gerald Trench, my boyfriend – are performing each evening at the White Hart, a pub at Barnes.' She reached out to the floor beside her and picked up a large folder which she opened on the coffee table before them. She passed Sarah a photograph taken under harsh theatrical lighting. It showed Vickie, wearing a blonde wig, shouting at a young man who was made up to look older.

'You can keep that,' Vickie said, 'That's us in the play we're doing at the White Hart. Gerry wrote it for us. It's about a publican and his daughter.'

Sarah put the photograph in her handbag. 'You were here alone?' she prompted.

'That's right,' Vickie said quickly, then she drank some coffee and held the mug to her face again. The action was becoming mannered. Sarah supposed it was a necessary part of the girl's profession to find gestures and affectations that could be used before an audience.

'It was about four o'clock, not quite dark,' she continued. 'I'd just had a bath, so I was only wearing a towelling robe while I put on my make-up. The bell rang and I opened the door without thinking.' She paused to look at Sarah through the smoke that curled from her cigarette. 'He was inside the flat before I could even think. The next thing I knew he was holding a knife at my throat.' She pulled down the polo neck of her sweater and Sarah could see three small pieces of sticking plaster.

'He had the knife with him?' Sarah asked.

'Yes, a kitchen knife. They seem different when somebody holds one to your throat.' Vickie held a hand to her neck and said, 'He kept the knife here and pushed me into the bedroom. Then he started on me.' She spoke the last sentence flatly, which somehow gave it even more power. Sarah could not be sure if Vickie's timing and intonation was natural or had been rehearsed – but there was no doubting the power of their effect. Sarah felt them almost physically.

'Was it your bedroom where it all took place?'

'No, the spare room off the hall. This is my room.' She stood up and gestured for Sarah to follow her into the narrow hallway again, where she opened another door. Sarah looked in and saw a wardrobe, double bed and a dressing table with a mirror surrounded with light bulbs, the kind used in theatre dressing rooms.

'Did he steal anything?' Sarah asked.

She shook her head.

'Did you fight him?'

Vickie looked up. 'He hit me twice, then held a knife to my throat. I was too terrified to fight. It was as if I didn't have any strength in me at all.'

'What was he like, Vickie, did you see his face?'

She answered without hesitation; it was clear she had now told the story several times. 'He was tall, taller than me and I'm five feet nine. In his twenties, or early thirties. Well-built, dressed in casual clothes. Fair short hair. Very fair, I can remember the blond hair on his forearms.'

'What colour were his eyes?'

'I couldn't see them, he wore dark glasses.'

'Sunglasses?'

Vickie shook her head. 'They weren't really sunglasses, just heavily tinted.'

'Did he smell?' Sarah asked, suddenly remembering what Pauline Kaznovitch had told her.

Vickie shook her head. 'No, well yes – he smelt of soap actually. He was quite clean. I think he may have showered or bathed quite recently.'

'What makes you think that?'

Vickie hesitated and looked at her almost defiantly. Then she said, 'He had baby powder on his penis.'

'You noticed that?'

Vickie gave a twisted smile. 'I did when he made me put it in my mouth.'

'I'm sorry,' Sarah said after a slight pause. 'It must have been terrible.'

Vickie shrugged. 'Strangely, I think it was worse later. While it was happening I was in a state of shock, I think. I just kept telling myself: I'm going to survive this. I said it to myself over and over again.'

'Did you think he was going to kill you?'

'He *was* going to kill me. He made that quite clear.'

'What exactly did he say?'

Vickie thought for a moment, as if preparing herself then she took a deep breath and began to speak in deeper and harsher tones than her own. 'I'm going to kill you, you fucking whore,' she said savagely. 'First I'm going to fuck you in your mouth and up your arse and in your cunt, and then I'm going to cut out your fucking heart.'

The words chilled Sarah; she could feel the skin on her neck crawl, so powerful was Vickie Howard's imitation. It was as if the man was still there in the room and the terror all around them.

'Why didn't he kill you, Vickie?' Sarah asked after a few moments.

The young woman stood up quickly and said, 'Come next door.'

Sarah followed her into the little bedroom closest to the front door of the flat. Vickie switched on a single weak overhead light, stood beside the bed and gestured to a metal reading lamp that stood on the bedside table. 'That saved me,' she said. Sarah glanced at her, puzzled, and Vickie said, 'Look closely at the flex, where it joins the base of the lamp.'

Sarah did as she was instructed and saw that at the junction the old woven cloth cover was frayed away and the rubber on the metal wires perished.

'I knew it was dangerous,' Vickie said, 'and I kept meaning to have it repaired. I never guessed it would save my life.'

'What happened exactly?' Sarah asked.

Vickie stood in the doorway looking down at the bed. 'When he'd finished sodomising me . . . he pulled out and then punched me here.' She touched the bruise on her cheek. 'Then he knelt over me and said: "Now I'm going to make *you* come." I thought he was going to kill me with the knife, but instead he began to masturbate to get back his erection.'

'You're sure of that?'

'It was happening right in front of my face.' She stopped and looked away from the bed for a moment. Then she seemed to recover and looked at Sarah again. 'As his penis got harder he held me by the throat with his left hand and reached out to put the knife on the bedside table. He must have touched the bare wire with the knife blade. Suddenly he was thrown off the bed. He smashed against the wall and just slumped down.'

'So he didn't actually attack you with the knife?'

'No, only these little cuts' – she touched her neck once again – 'I think they were more by accident. He said he was going to fuck me to death, but he electrocuted himself before he could get back inside me.'

Vickie lit another cigarette and drew deeply. 'Do you know what he meant – that he was going to fuck me to death?'

Sarah nodded, she knew the reason why.

Vickie looked at the glowing end of the cigarette while she spoke. 'The policewoman at the rape centre told me that people have an orgasm when they're strangled.'

'That's right,' Sarah answered.

Vickie continued. 'He was going to choke me to death while he had it inside me.'

'You must have felt pretty close to the edge,' Sarah said.

'Well, pretty close to something,' Vickie said, and Sarah recognised the remark as an attempt at humour. Good for you, girl, she thought. You've certainly got guts.

'What happened then?' Sarah asked. 'When he was lying on the floor?'

'He seemed stunned – I didn't wait to examine him. I managed to get upstairs to Mr and Mrs Brinkley's flat and they called the police. Of course, by the time they arrived he was long gone.'

'I take it the police tested everything here,' Sarah asked.

Vickie was speaking in a matter-of-fact voice now. 'Everything, including me. They think they've got a good sample of him. I would have washed, but Mrs Brinkley told me not to – she'd seen a programme about rape on the television. Women always want to wash themselves, but if you do, it gets rid of vital evidence.'

They returned to the living room and Sarah thanked Vickie for her patience. 'It must have been difficult, going over it all again,' she said as she prepared to leave. Vickie shook her head. 'It wasn't so bad. Being an actress is repeating things again and again.'

'I suppose so,' Sarah replied. She looked around the little room. 'Are you all right to be alone – it must take some getting over, a shock like that?'

Vickie leaned against the wall. Her head lowered, she looked smaller now. 'Sure,' she answered. 'Gerry is coming over later. He's been working alone for the past few nights. I'm starting again tomorrow.'

'I must come and see you perform.'

'It's easy to get a ticket,' Vickie said with another wry smile. 'You won't have to book.'

'I'll remember,' Sarah answered and she said good-night.

The drive back to the office did not take long, and while she passed through the streets, Sarah went over Vickie's story in her mind. There were Christmas decorations in the shop windows, and houses were bright with festive lights. But Sarah kept thinking of the horror that had taken place in the little flat near the North Circular.

When she reached her desk, there were a few reporters on duty, but Stiles's celebratory drinks had taken their toll. Sinclair, Prior and Bradshaw had finally returned from the pub and were playing a noisy game of spoof, while Mick Gates was making a placatory telephone call to his wife, explaining why he had not come home at 7.30, as he had promised.

'He's the new boss, Mandy,' he pleaded. 'I couldn't just piss off when all the others were there . . .' It was a conversation Sarah had overheard a thousand times before.

She logged on to her terminal and began to write rapidly. When she'd first had to use a computer Sarah had found the experience daunting, but now she could not imagine going back to an old-fashioned typewriter. The ease with which she could make corrections to her copy still gave her pleasure: not that it was necessary with the piece she was working on now. Sometimes writing a short, simple prose about a complex matter, with the pressure of a deadline, could be an infuriating business that filled her with frustration, but Vickie Howard's story flowed without effort. She was just writing the pay-off line when George Conway came and stood behind her.

'Can you print it out?' he asked. 'I want to make sure Marr reads it and he hasn't mastered the computer system yet, I'll have to give him hard copy.'

Sarah entered the commands and a machine at the side of the room began to chatter out her story on to a spool of paper. George stood by, waiting until it was finished and then walked back to her, reading the piece. He nodded once when he had finished, said 'Good', then headed for the editor's office. While this had been going on, Arthur Swann on the news desk had been reading her copy from his own screen. He looked up in irritation as the reporters' game became even noisier and eventually called out, 'Why don't you lot fuck off back to the pub, you're no bloody use to me here.'

The four were pleased by the suggestion and after vainly entreating Sarah to join them, shambled away. Swann watched them depart and then went to the back bench, where he had a short conversation with the night editor, who was now working on the third edition. Sarah saw him walking in her direction. 'That piece is terrific,' he said. 'I just told Stenton he should lead page five with it.'

'Thank you, Arthur,' Sarah answered. 'And what did he say?'

Swann smiled. 'He told me to mind my own sodding business, but at least he called it up. He's reading it now.' He hesitated for a moment and then said, 'I'm leaving the *Gazette*.'

Sarah looked at him carefully. There was more to come. 'I'm sorry, Arthur, I shall miss you. Is it a good offer?'

Swann nodded. 'Night news editor. I can't say which paper yet, but it's a good one – the thing is, they're interested in hiring new reporters as well. Would you consider moving?'

Sarah smiled. 'I don't think I'd qualify as a new reporter, Arthur. Some would say I'm coming up to my sell-by date.'

'Only clowns like Stiles,' Swann continued. 'I wouldn't ask his opinion on what date to put on a paper.'

Before she could answer, Reg Stenton called out her name. She walked to the back bench, where Stenton sat in a huddle with two of his assistants.

'This piece is great stuff,' he said, indicating the screen where Sarah's copy was still displayed. 'Are there any pictures?'

'No,' Sarah replied. 'The girl doesn't want her real name mentioned.'

'It doesn't matter, we can get a stock picture of some bird silhouetted against a window, there's plenty of shots in the library. I want to use the piece in the last edition. Have the lawyers seen it?'

'I don't think so,' she answered. 'I've only just finished.'

'Forget it,' said a sharp voice behind them and Stenton turned to see Alan Stiles.

'What do you mean, forget it?' Stenton replied after a pause in which he directed a contemptuous stare at Stiles. 'You're just the fucking news editor, Alan. I still run this end of the paper.'

Stiles realised he had exceeded his authority in issuing the command so tactlessly. 'Sorry, Reg,' he said quickly. 'It wasn't me who made the decision, it was

Simon. He doesn't want sex stories in the paper. It's a directive straight from the chairman.'

Stenton paused for a moment. Telling the exact truth wasn't one of Stiles's abiding characteristics. He got up and said, 'I think I shall have a word with Mister Marr myself.'

'He's talking privately to George Conway at the moment, Reg,' Stiles called after him.

'That's all right,' Stenton replied. 'George and I are old friends.'

Sarah returned to her desk and the phone rang. It was her daughter, Emily. 'Granddad's been on,' she said. 'I think he's had a few. He wants to know if we're having goose on Christmas Day and turkey on Boxing Day, or the other way around.'

'What possible difference could it make?' Sarah said.

'He says he knows we're having clear soup on Christmas Day and it will affect the selection of wines if it's followed by turkey or goose.'

'Tell him what you like, darling, you choose,' Sarah decided.

'Oh, and Colin called,' Emily said. 'No message, he just sent his love.'

'To me?'

'No, to me, silly. Of course you. He said he wishes he was home. He had to visit a gay club last night and the pianist actually sang them a song.'

'I hope he wasn't with a woman.'

'He was with Nick Holland. He says he thinks the pianist thought Nick was his boyfriend.'

Sarah laughed. 'Well, Nick is very attractive.'

78

'I suppose he is, if you like the beefy type.'

'Is Ric with you?' Sarah asked. Emily's boyfriend was as slim as a clothesline.

'He's just gone. He won't watch *The Sound of Music*. The boys have gone up in disgust, there's just me and Pat sitting here with a box of chocolates.'

'I might be home in time to see Julie Andrews win through,' Sarah said and hung up. A few minutes later she saw Reg Stenton and George, deep in conversation, walking slowly along the newsroom, which was now half deserted. They stopped outside George's office to finish their talk and then Stenton hurried back to his desk. George paused, looked towards her and then beckoned. Sarah joined him in the stuffy little room where he sat with his hands laced behind his head. The floor was still covered with the papers George had scattered earlier.

'The editor won't use the story,' he said in quite a cheerful voice.

Sarah felt only a slight sense of disappointment. Like all reporters, she was accustomed to having work spiked.

'Does it bother you?' George asked.

Sarah shook her head. 'Not particularly. It isn't the first time a woman's spoken about being raped, George.'

Conway looked at the wall beside him. 'He said Christmas was coming, and that was what people wanted to read about, the festive season. That and rattling good yarns.' He yawned. 'It's quite strange in there, his desk is piled with paper – it reminded me of the old days. And copy baskets, he's even got them labelled: In, Out, Pending and Top Priority.'

'Does losing this one bother you, George?' Sarah asked.

'Yes, it does. Not because of pride, though. I think this is a bigger story than he realises.'

'Why?'

George picked up her copy. 'Because of what happened to your girl. The two women who were murdered over the last couple of weeks were strangled after being threatened with a knife. The police asked us not to reveal any of the details.'

Sarah suddenly became interested. 'How do the police know about the knife if the women were dead?'

George looked up from her copy. 'There were tiny nicks on all of the victims' throats; the second woman had a deep cut on the palm of her left hand as well.'

George leaned back again. 'I just persuaded Marr to let me stay with the story. He doesn't much want to, but he also doesn't want trouble from what he calls "the old guard".' He paused and watched her carefully. 'I asked if you could be seconded to me. He said yes if you are prepared to work on this in your spare time. Stiles says he can't release you from the reporters' rota.'

Sarah did not hesitate. 'Of course I'll do what I can.'

He smiled. 'Good girl.'

She got up to leave and George said, 'By the way, what's this rubbish about Nazi secret weapons?'

Sarah thought for a moment, then the interview with Andrew Maclean came back to her. 'Oh, just someone who came in with a tall tale this afternoon. Stiles told me to drop it.'

George smiled. 'Well, the new editor has it in his Top Priority basket.'

80

'How do you know?'

He smiled again. 'I read through the contents when he went out for a piss.'

'George!' she said in mock outrage.

He chuckled. 'I used to be a bloody good reporter in my day, you know.' Then he waved her off. 'Go home – unless you want another drink in the Lion?'

'I'll pass on that one,' Sarah answered, and closed the door behind her.

The Sound of Music was coming to an end when she got home. Pat and Emily were seated before the embers of a fire, with the dog chewing on the empty chocolate box. Sarah dumped her bag on the sofa next to Emily and went into the kitchen to heat the remains of the shepherd's pie in the microwave. When she returned a few minutes later the film had finished, but Pat was still watching the credits. 'Lovely,' she sighed with contentment.

Sarah sat down with a tray on her lap and was about to begin her food when Emily said 'Why have you got a picture of Victoria Howard and Gerald Trench?' She was holding up the photograph she had taken from Sarah's gaping bag.

'Do you know them?' Sarah asked in surprise.

'They came to us at the beginning of term. They go around all the schools doing scenes from Shakespeare.'

'They're appearing at a pub in Barnes,' Sarah replied evasively. 'I might go and see them for the paper.'

'They're good,' Emily said. 'It must be frustrating to be an actor and not be able to get any work.' She yawned and stood up. 'I'm going to bed,' she said.

'Thank you for bringing the film, Pat. It's always love-ly to watch. Good-night.'

Sarah did not want to eat all of the food but felt guilty about leaving too much, as Pat had prepared it. 'Delicious pie,' she said, then felt further guilt because of her hypocrisy. The food was stodgy and tasteless, but she managed a few more mouthfuls before Pat rose to leave. When she heard the sound of Pat's car starting Sarah took the remains of the pie into the kitchen and scraped it into the dog's bowl. He sniffed it for a few moments and then walked away. 'Spoilt creature,' Sarah scolded. 'Eat it up, there are children starving in the world.' Then she smiled: they were words she had heard Sister Veronica use many times in her days at boarding school.

She climbed the stairs and prepared for bed, all the time thinking of the story Vickie Howard had told her. Then she looked in on the boys, who lay deeply asleep in the dreadful disorder of their room. Emily was still reading, her door ajar. She kissed her good-night and glanced down at the book, expecting something suit-ably weighty that Ric had recommended. It was a Jilly Cooper novel. Sarah felt a sudden moment of appro-val. Sometimes, she thought her daughter took life too seriously.

'Is this good?' Sarah asked, tapping the book.

'Great,' Emily replied. 'Ric says my brain is soften-ing, *The Sound of Music* and Jilly Cooper: he says he's going to buy me a Rupert Bear album for Christmas.'

Sarah sat down on the bedside for a moment and brushed the hair from her daughter's forehead. 'I haven't seen much of you for a bit,' she said. 'How are you?'

'I'm fine, Mum – how are you?'

'Mustn't grumble,' Sarah answered.

'Is everything all right with you and Colin?'

'Yes, of course. Why do you ask?'

'I wondered if you'd thought about the future any more.'

Sarah smiled. 'Do you mean if we're going to get married?'

'Well, are you?'

'Would you like that?'

Emily didn't hesitate. 'Yes, I would. It's time you settled down again. After all, me and the boys won't be here for ever.'

Sarah felt a sudden lump in her throat. She leaned forward and kissed her daughter again, then said, 'I'll bear that in mind, but remember it's up to the gentleman to ask.'

'Colin wants to.'

'How do you know? Has he said anything?'

'He doesn't have to, I can tell.'

Sarah tapped the book again. 'Too much Jilly Cooper, my girl. You'd better get back to Thomas Hardy.'

She got up and said good-night again. Further along the landing, her own room was full of reminders of Colin. When he had come to live with her she had moved from the old room she had shared with Jack throughout her marriage. Colin had brought some of his own possessions: a leather sofa, lamps, books and a small military desk, so he could use the room as a study.

While she prepared for bed, Vickie Howard's words kept coming back to her. Then she did something she had not done in a long time; she knelt beside her bed

and prayed. During the night she awoke to the sound
of heavy rain and was aware that Colin was now beside
her. Comforted, she slept on.

Chapter Five

8.05 a.m. Thursday, 16 December

The following morning Colin had gone out before she woke up. It was still raining hard so Sarah decided to drive the children to school, despite the protests of the boys, who, strangely, had wanted to set off even earlier. The dog looked distressed when they were all preparing to leave the house together so the boys pleaded for him to come with them. Sarah relented finally and he climbed on to their laps in the back seat. Once they were under way he roamed from window to window and at one point tried to get into the front passenger seat with Emily.

'I knew this wasn't a good idea,' Sarah said, when all she could see in the rear-view mirror was the face of a panting Labrador.

'Think what he'll be like on a long journey to Oxford,' Martin said.

'Oh, that's all right,' Sarah said briskly. 'If Grand-dad slows down occasionally, you and Paul can take it in turns to hold on to his lead while he trots beside the car.'

There was a fraction of a second of shocked silence before the boys began a barrage of 'Garrrrmns' and 'you wouldn'ts.'

Even her children were not always prepared for Sarah's humour. She seemed such a proper and sedate type of Englishwoman that few people suspected her of possessing a rather surreal sense of fun that she could not always control. Solemn moments would bring on a sudden fit of giggles; as did pompous behaviour. Luckily it was an aspect of her character that Colin Greaves found endearing.

After a short journey, Sarah drove into a curving tree-lined road that descended from the Heath towards Saint Catherine's. The mansion that housed the school had once been the home of a Swiss arms dealer, who had taken up residence in England at an earlier part of the century. It stood in neo-Gothic splendour behind high iron railings, and banks of laurel screened a wide gravel drive from the roadway. In 1926 – when he was very old and repentant about his trade – the arms dealer converted to the religion of his mother and upon his death he left the vast property and a substantial sum of money to the Roman Catholic Church. But only on the understanding that a school would be established on the premises and suitable prayers offered at appropriate times for the salvation of his soul.

Sarah drew close to the gates now. Other cars delivering children filled the road, but she was lucky and managed to pull into a space that had just been vacated next to the entrance. When Emily opened her door, she saw Father Robson on the pavement, sheltering under a large black umbrella while he talked to another man.

'Good morning, Mrs Keane,' he called out with a

wave. The other person then said something to him, and after nodding Father Robson leaned towards the open door and called out, 'Do you have a moment, there's someone here who wants to talk to you?'

Sarah got out of the car and Father Robson held out the umbrella for her protection. Her first thought was what an odd contrast the two men made. Father Robson wore his usual old black suit, which hung shapelessly on his tall, stooping frame. All the colour in him showed in his long face, which was always a wind-burnt red. A lock of yellowish white hair, longer than the rest, hung over his forehead, and he occasionally brushed it out of his pale blue eyes.

In contrast, the man he stood beside wore a blue waterproof trilby with matching raincoat and a bright red tie, but his pale, pinched face seemed to be without any colour at all. He wore steel-rimmed spectacles that slightly enlarged his grey eyes, and his thin lips were set in a line that gave his features a cast of grim disapproval.

The children said good-bye to Sarah and good-morning to Father Robson before they entered the school gates. Father Robson said in his soft voice, 'Mrs Keane, may I introduce a colleague of yours, Joseph March.' The reporter offered his hand and she felt the quick dry grip for just a moment before it was withdrawn.

Sarah had not yet met the *Gazette*'s new crime reporter. It was not uncommon on newspapers, where people worked at different hours and some often didn't come into the office for weeks at a time.

'Do you know Superintendent Colin Greaves?' he asked, in a flat London accent. It was a simple question, but somehow Sarah felt that much more was implied; maybe even an accusation.

'Yes,' she answered, suddenly also aware that Father Robson knew she was living with a man out of wedlock. Now she was no longer a grown woman but a little girl who had committed a punishable sin.

Father Robson realised her discomfort, but he came from a worldly order of priesthood. She knew he would not condone her behaviour, but would apply the skill of a fly fisherman rather than the threat of fire and brimstone.

'And how is the dear man?' he asked.

'He's very busy at present,' she answered, surprised. Until that moment she hadn't known that they had met.

Father Robson continued: 'Tell him I've now finished the book we discussed yesterday, will you?'

'I didn't know you'd seen him recently,' Sarah answered.

Father Robson was about to answer when a slight, elderly figure, carrying a brightly coloured umbrella, tugged at his sleeve. Sarah recognised her: it was Helen Hathaway, Father Robson's secretary.

'Oh, good morning, Mrs Keane,' she said. 'I wanted to remind Father Robson to ask you about the Christmas toy appeal.'

'I'll sort something out, Mrs Hathaway.'

She smiled and turned to Father Robson. 'The Bishop's office is on the line, Father.'

'For me? How long have they been waiting?'

'A few minutes,' she replied vaguely.

The priest smiled briefly to Sarah and said, 'Duty calls,' then hurried away. It was still raining hard and Sarah was about to lose the protection of the umbrella.

'Can I give you a lift anywhere?' she asked March. 'If you don't mind dogs, our Labrador is in the car.'

'I like dogs,' March answered, as though she had accused him of some character flaw. He got into the passenger seat and took a moment adjusting the seat belt.

'I'm afraid that's a bit tricky,' Sarah said apologetically, and felt further guilt. 'I keep meaning to get it seen to.' What an extraordinary man, she thought as they drove away; he makes me feel as if I've committed some crime that I'm not aware of yet.

They drove in silence for a while, until Sarah gave in. 'Father Robson said you wanted to talk to me.'

'That's right,' he answered. The dog was now thrusting forward again to nuzzle his neck. 'Get down,' he said without any force in his voice, and the dog immediately retreated and curled up on the back seat.

'I wish I could get him to do that,' Sarah said, impressed.

'You have to make dogs want to please you, not you them,' he said. Then, after a pause, 'You interviewed Vickie Howard last night.'

'Yes, I did.'

'The paper didn't print it.'

'That often happens, I wasn't trying to burgle your story, you know. Stiles put me on it.'

'I heard it was Conway.'

'You heard wrong,' Sarah said firmly. 'George Conway got the story from a contact but Stiles suggested I do the interview.'

'Can I read what you wrote?' March asked and she

could detect his reluctance. It was clear he did not like asking anyone for favours.

Sarah thought for a moment. Co-operation between journalists could sometimes prove tricky – even when they were on the same paper.

He misread her pause and said, 'I suppose they'll want you to take over this one, what with your contact with Greaves.'

Sarah shook her head, laughing as she did so. 'You couldn't be more wrong,' she answered. 'Living with Colin Greaves is a positive disadvantage. I promise you, he hasn't mentioned a word of this case to me. The tip-off on Vickie Howard came entirely from George Conway.'

March remained silent but she knew he was unconvinced. Few people believed how scrupulous Greaves was in his professional dealings with Sarah. But George Conway knew that Sarah had requested that she should not be given crime stories that might cause her path to cross with Greaves; and usually they were lucky.

The relationship between police and journalists had always been a complex one. Close links between certain individuals existed and occasionally deep gulfs of antipathy. Often the police could not understand when journalists refused to co-operate in giving them information that they saw as part of their public duty. But journalists claimed they had to draw the line somewhere. If reporters and photographers were seen by the public as an extension of the police force no one would ever give confidential information to them. On the other hand, the police could withhold information from the press. It was an ever-changing market, where bartering took place and relationships varied from hatred to deep friendship.

Sarah was aware that in certain eyes she and Colin Greaves had crossed the line. In reality, they were scrupulous about keeping confidential information to themselves; but not everyone was convinced – so they could only be satisfied that they preserved their own code of ethics. Others would have to make up their own minds.

They were close to Sarah's home by now. She had to make up her mind whether to drive March to Hampstead High Street, where he could catch a taxi or get the underground. She glanced at his grave profile and said, 'I live near here, would you like to come in for a coffee?'

March accepted the invitation after a slight pause and Sarah took the turning for home. When they arrived, he got out of the car and looked up at the vine-clad exterior. 'This is a big house,' he said, once more making the statement sound like an accusation.

'It's got a big mortgage too,' Sarah replied briskly. 'Where do you live?'

'Fulham. In a council flat.'

'Are you married?'

'Divorced,' he answered shortly.

Sarah still felt awkward with this spiky man. It was cold and there was no fire in the living room when she ushered him in; usually she would have asked a visitor into the kitchen, where it was more cosy, but she was concerned that March would take it as a slight, almost as if she were asking him into the servants' quarters. When she returned with the coffee, he was standing by one of the bookcases, where Sarah kept the gramophone records.

'Who collected these?' he asked.

'My daughter, the classical stuff.'

'No, the 78s.'

'They belonged to Jack, my husband.'

March took one from the shelf. 'This is a Mugsy Spanier,' he said, and for the first time she heard warmth in his voice. 'It's almost priceless. I used to have a copy.'

'What happened to it?'

March put the record back. 'It got broken,' he said.

Sarah picked up the phone and dialled George Conway's direct line. 'Hello,' she said when he answered. 'I'm with Joe March. He's working on the Vickie Howard case. He wants to see my copy.'

'So?' George said.

'Will you fax it to me?' she asked. 'I'm at home.'

While Sarah talked to George, March had continued to examine the 78s.

'Would you like to borrow any of those?' she asked when she'd hung up.

March took a moment to reply. Sarah could tell that he was considering if the offer could be construed as any sort of bribe. Eventually he shook his head. There was the sound of the front door opening and Colin came into the room. He looked grey with fatigue and his clothes were soaked through.

'Hello,' he said to Sarah. 'I was caught in the storm. Just popped home to change.' Then he saw March. Sarah could feel something pass between the two men. Not exactly hostility; but far from any sort of empathy.

'You know Joe March?' she said.

Colin nodded.

'Did you know that Vickie Howard performed at the children's school?' Sarah asked him. March looked sharply at her while he was drinking his coffee.

'Yes,' Colin answered.

'And the woman who was murdered in Branshaw Gardens – she was connected as well.' Sarah made it a statement of fact rather than a question. Colin said nothing, but suddenly Sarah knew that all the victims had something to do with the school. She didn't understand if it was to do with Colin's attitude, or if it was simply intuition; but she felt a mixture of dread and a rush of adrenalin, as if a horse race had just started on which she had placed more money than she could afford.

March remained silent and placed his mug on the table beside him.

'How did you get this information?' Colin asked coldly.

Sarah resented his tone. 'Emily told me about Vickie Howard. Pat Lomax knew about the other women,' she answered. Then her anger became more personal. 'My God, why haven't you alerted everyone to the danger?'

Colin hunched forward in his wet clothes, his face suddenly bleak. 'We couldn't be sure, maybe it was just coincidence. I didn't want to start a panic. We warned the public to be careful.'

Sarah shook her head. 'I have a sixteen-year-old daughter at that school, Colin. Do you think a general warning is enough?'

'Look at the facts,' he said. 'The first victim was a supply teacher who was only there for two weeks nearly a year ago. The second was briefly working for a catering firm that prepares school dinners, the third was a landscape gardener and this latest attack was on an ex-pupil who had only visited the place for one morning. Think of all the other connections those people made in their lives. How could we be sure St Catherine's was the link?'

Sarah's anger subsided; she saw the logic in his argument. 'Will you warn everyone now?' she asked.

'Yes. I think the evidence is convincing enough.'

She got up. 'I'll go and see if that copy you want has arrived,' she said to March.

The fax machine was in her bedroom. She found the sheets of paper spilt out in the container and brought them back to March; then she turned to Greaves. 'If I tell you something that may prove to be important,' she said carefully, 'will you help us on this story?'

'You know the rules – as far as I can,' he answered.

'There's something I know that may be of use to you – and I'm prepared to trade.'

He thought for a moment and in the silence the dog came and licked his hand. 'All right,' he said reluctantly. 'What have you got to tell me?'

'Read the story first,' Sarah said, and March handed him the pages. After a few minutes he looked up. 'This is exactly what she told me. What is it you know?' he asked.

Sarah now stood by the fireplace in the cold room, as if warming herself at the dead grate. 'Vickie Howard knew the man who attacked her,' she said without looking up. 'In fact she may have invited him to the flat.'

94

Greaves studied her profile for a moment, then returned his attention to the sheets of copy.

'There's no indication here,' he said after a few minutes. 'The story's the same as the version she told us.'

Sarah sat down next to Colin. 'Was there any woman there when Vickie Howard was interviewed?'

'No,' Greaves replied. 'We offered to provide a woman police officer, but it meant calling one on duty. She said she was comfortable talking to me.'

Sarah consulted her own copy for a moment. 'Vickie Howard says she was putting on her make-up when he rang the doorbell.'

Greaves nodded. Sarah took her copy again and read: 'It was four o'clock and just getting dark.'

'So?' March interjected.

'I just think there's something wrong with that,' Sarah said to the two men, who exchanged puzzled glances. She continued. 'Vickie Howard is young, so young she's not all that bothered about her appearance. When I called she was wearing scruffy clothes and nothing on her face, and she looked good.'

The two men still could not see what she was getting at. 'What point are you making?' March asked.

Sarah shrugged. 'Having met her, I just doubt Vickie Howard would bother to put on make-up to go to a pub, then take it off and put on stage make-up.'

Greaves nodded. 'But if a man was going to call she might.'

'Exactly.'

'In my experience women do some bloody strange things,' said March. 'There's not always a logical explanation for their actions.'

'There's something else,' Sarah persisted. 'Vickie

would have been sitting before a good light when she was putting on her make-up. The dressing table was in her room, not the spare bedroom where the rape took place. That room and the hallway would have been in semi-darkness, and he pushed her into there as soon as he was in the flat.'

Greaves sat up straighter. 'Vickie Howard said she could remember every detail of the man, even the pale hairs on his arms.'

'Yes,' Sarah said. 'If you go straight from a bright light shining in your eyes into a gloomy corridor, you can hardly see anything – I know.'

'So you do think she knew him?' Greaves said after a few moments.

'Yes,' Sarah answered. 'But I still think it was rape,' she added.

'Do you?' March replied. 'A woman asks a man to her flat and all she's wearing when he arrives is lipstick and a dressing gown. Some people would say she was asking for it.'

'What about her bruises? It was obvious he'd been violent.'

'Like I said before, there's not always a logical explanation for the behaviour of women. A lot of them like violent men, I've seen it plenty of times. They like to be clouted, it makes them feel good if they can rouse that amount of emotion in a man. And some women like to set their men on to others: seeing people beaten up gives them a thrill.'

Sarah was not happy with his response, but she knew he was telling the truth.

Greaves stood up. 'I think I'll talk to Miss Howard again.'

'May we come with you?' said Sarah.

He thought for a moment, then said, 'Only if you give your word that you'll keep anything you learn to yourself if I ask you.'

'You'll accept my word?'

Greaves studied her, his eyes bleak for a few moments, then he smiled and nodded briefly. Sarah suddenly felt pleased, as if she had passed some difficult examination.

Greaves changed from his wet clothes, then telephoned Vickie Howard's flat to check she was at home. He told her Sarah and March were coming with him. Before they set off, Sarah had another duty to perform. 'I'll just pop next door,' she said to March. 'I want to leave the dog with a neighbour. My housekeeper doesn't arrive until later.'

March waited in her car while Sarah performed her errand and Greaves went first, in the police car that he had waiting for him. It was curious not to be travelling with Greaves, Sarah felt; it almost made her association with March seem slightly disloyal.

When they were on their way, March said, 'It must be difficult to cope with work and children, with your hours.'

'It's not so bad,' she answered, straining forward to see through the rain which still pounded against the windscreen. 'I've got Pat, my housekeeper, and some new people have moved next door who are really nice. Jenny, the wife, is at home all the time and she loves the dog, so I can leave it with her in an emergency. It must be hard for women who can't afford help. My only difficulty is remembering to make the proper arrangements.'

March was thoughtful. 'My mother brought up four of us on her own. I was a man before I realised how hard it had been for her. When I was a kid I just took it for granted.'

'What about your father?' Sarah asked.

March spoke without emotion. 'He was killed the month I was born. He was in the Merchant Marine.'

'My mother died when I was young,' Sarah said. 'I still miss her.' For a moment she tried again to recollect her face, but it still remained shrouded in the same mist. March interrupted her chain of thought. 'You don't miss what you never knew.'

There was a silence for a time and then Sarah said, 'I always think of you crime reporters going about in pairs.'

'I like working alone,' he replied.

Chapter Six

10.22 a.m. Thursday, 16 December

When they arrived Sarah parked in a side road. Greaves was waiting close by. He got out of the police car where he had been sheltering and they hurried to the entrance together. They paused when they reached the doorway and stopped to look back at the rain.

'Where's Nick Holland?' Sarah asked.

While he answered Greaves looked at Joe March, who was shaking the rainwater from his hat and coat like a fastidious cat.

'Following up a lead – at least I hope it's a lead.'

He rang the bell of the flat and when Vickie Howard opened the door she stood back without answering his greeting. They entered the living room; Sarah noticed that it looked shabbier in the daylight. The fabrics were worn and there were patches of bare wood on the furniture where varnish had flaked away. A bowl of flowers stood on the mantelpiece, their blooms drooping in the browning water of the vase.

Vickie Howard was dressed as she had been before, in the same sweater and jeans. This time there was no offer of coffee.

'I hope this isn't inconvenient, Miss Howard,' Greaves began.

'I was just going out,' she said, gesturing towards the window with a hand that held a half-smoked cigarette.

'I'm sorry,' he said. 'It shouldn't take long.'

When they were seated, Vickie curled her feet up beneath her on the sofa. Greaves produced a notebook and began. 'I'd just like to go over a few details about what you did before the man broke in.' Sarah noticed that March, beside him, sat in rather a stiff fashion, his raincoat still draped over his arm, as if he were in a station waiting room. It was clear to Sarah that he was not particularly comfortable in Vickie's presence.

Greaves opened the notebook and continued. 'Can you tell us exactly what you were doing in the twenty minutes or so before he rang the bell?'

'I've gone over all this – I can't remember anything else,' Vickie replied in a sulky voice. 'I've told you over and over again.'

'Maybe we overlooked something, Miss Howard,' Greaves replied easily. 'I'm sorry but it really is necessary.'

She sighed and glanced towards the windows. 'Like I said, I'd been taking a nap, I always do in the afternoons before performances.' She looked towards Sarah. 'We do two shows, you know, one at six o'clock for the early crowd, and again at 8.30. I'd set the alarm because I suffer from insomnia so if I fall asleep during the day, I might go on for longer than I want. It wasn't quite twilight when it went off. I got up straight-away – I have to do that or I might go off to sleep again. Then I went to the bathroom and ran the bath.'

'And were you wearing your dressing gown at this point?'

She shook her head. 'No. The only good thing about this place is the central heating. It's always warm. I sleep naked.'

'Go on.'

Vickie didn't have to think. She began to speak in a singsong voice as if she were talking to children. 'First I brushed my teeth, then I got into the bath. After that I dried myself.'

'Then?'

'Then I started to put on my make-up.'

'Were you wearing your dressing gown by now?'

Vickie had to think. 'I'm not sure.' Then: 'No, I wasn't. I remember, I had to put it on when the door-bell rang.'

'You're quite sure you were wearing your dressing gown when you answered the door.'

'Quite sure.'

Greaves interrupted again, but his voice was soft. 'And is the make-up you use in the street the same sort you wear on the stage?'

'No, that's quite different. No one wears greasepaint in the street.'

'Do you wear make-up very often – in everyday life, that is?'

'Sometimes. It depends . . .'

'Depends on what, Miss Howard? I notice you're not wearing any now – but you said you were about to go out.'

'Only to the shops.'

Greaves looked at her with a steady gaze. 'But you put on your make-up the other evening – just before you were going out to work, where you would have to remove it once again to prepare for your performance?'

She hesitated and shot an uncertain glance first at him and then at Sarah. Her expression changed slightly; and Sarah knew she was silently being accused of betrayal. 'Not usually,' Vickie said in a low voice, still looking at Sarah.

Greaves consulted his notebook. 'So you put on street make-up, then the doorbell rang,' he stated.

She looked back to him, defiant now. 'That's right.'

'And that's when you put on your dressing gown.'

'I didn't go to the door naked, if that's what you're implying.'

'You opened the door,' Greaves went on, 'and you then say: "he burst into the hallway and held a knife to my throat while he pushed me into the bedroom – then he attacked me".' Greaves glanced up. 'That's the bedroom closest to the front door – where the rape took place?'

'Yes.'

'There's no window in the room, Miss Howard. Did he stop to put on the light?'

'I can't remember.'

Greaves's voice was hard now. 'Surely you must. You can remember every other detail so clearly. Think – did he put on the light?'

'No, I don't think so,' Vickie Howard continued. She was clearly distressed. Sarah wanted to comfort her. She leaned forward, but without taking his eyes from Vickie Howard's face, Joe March reached out and held her forearm in a powerful grip. Sarah had never seen Greaves in this role before; it seemed hateful now that he appeared to be bullying a defenceless girl. She regretted giving him the information.

'There was no light in the room, but you recollect

him so vividly,' Greaves continued, quoting from his notebook again. 'The hair on his forearms was blond. He had put baby powder on his penis.'

Vickie lowered her head. 'He raped me,' she said almost inaudibly. 'I didn't want him to make love to me, I fought with him.'

Sarah could feel her throat constricting. Once more she wanted to reach out and comfort the girl who seemed to be reliving the pain as she remembered her ordeal.

Greaves spoke again, in a gentler voice. 'I know he raped you, Vickie – but you knew him, didn't you?'

There was a long silence in which Sarah could hear the rain gusting against the windows.

'Yes,' Vickie answered finally; and so softly they could barely hear her reply. Now her shoulders began to shake and tears streamed down her face when she looked up again. 'I knew what you'd think . . . I knew what everyone would think. How could I tell Gerry? I didn't encourage him. He *did* attack me.'

'Tell us what really happened, Vickie,' Greaves said. Sarah could feel the compassion in his voice now. She fumbled in her handbag and handed Vickie some tissues with which she wiped her face; then she stood up and hurried to the bathroom. Through the thin door they could hear the sound of retching.

'Did you have to be so hard?' Sarah said to Greaves, who now looked out of the window, his face expressionless.

'Yes, he did,' March said quietly.

After a few minutes Vickie returned. She looked very young. Her face was stamped with misery, but she was more composed.

'How did you come to know him?' Greaves asked when she had taken her seat once more.

'I met him last Tuesday in the public library,' she answered, her eyes looking down into her lap. 'I was in the theatrical section. I reached out for a book I wanted and our hands touched. He was reaching for it too. He apologised and we just started talking. He was interested in the theatre, we just chatted. He seemed nice . . . gentle. After a time, he told me he was an out-of-work actor, but I didn't believe him, I think he just said that to impress me. Somehow it made him seem even nicer. He said he really wanted to read the book, so I told him I was a fast reader and I could let him have it in a few days. He took my telephone number and I thought that was that.'

'Did he tell you his name?' Greaves asked.

She looked up. 'He said it was Clive Roman.'

'Why didn't you tell me this before?'

Vickie lit another cigarette, her hand trembling as she raised the plastic lighter. 'If he'd raped me he was hardly going to give his real name was he?'

Greaves nodded. 'So he rang you and you invited him to come here.'

'Yes.'

'What made you believe he wasn't an actor?' Greaves asked.

Vickie shrugged. 'His voice –' she held her hand to her throat – 'it was all up here. Actors are taught to speak from the diaphragm.' She moved the hand to her solar plexus. 'Here – even the ones with working-class voices learn to do that.'

'Did he have a working-class voice?' Greaves asked.

'South London.'

'Are you sure?'

'Pretty sure, I've a good ear.'

'Where am I from?' March asked.

'West London, Hammersmith area.'

March looked impressed. 'Near enough,' he said.

'What about Mrs Keane?' Greaves said.

'Boarding school,' she replied immediately. 'A convent, I would think.'

'Why do you say a convent?' Sarah asked.

Vickie smiled, suddenly more confident. 'My old drama teacher always said it takes a convent to make a real lady – or a real tart.'

Greaves looked up from his notebook again. 'Which public library were you in when you picked him up?' he asked, and once more his voice was hard.

Sarah sat forward as if to protest, but he shot her a warning glance.

'I told you, I didn't pick him up,' Vickie replied, her voice uncertain once again.

Greaves shrugged. 'Where did you meet by accident?'

'Holborn Library.'

Sarah sat forward again. 'The one in Theobald's Road?' she asked. It was just around the corner from the offices of the *Gazette*.

Greaves's glance told Sarah to be silent. He then turned to Vickie. 'That's a long way to go from here. Isn't there a closer branch?'

Vickie looked at Sarah as if seeking support before she answered. 'I used to share a flat near there with two other girls. Then I was left this place. I still visit them occasionally – that's when I change my books.'

'And what time of day was it?'

'The afternoon, about three o'clock.'

Greaves thought for a moment, and as he did he rapped his teeth with the plastic pen he held. Suddenly becoming aware of what he was doing he stopped abruptly. 'What did you talk about – precisely?' he asked.

'The theatre,' Vickie answered.

'And did you get the impression he knew what he was talking about?'

Vickie considered the question. 'I thought he'd spent time around actors. He'd picked up a lot of the jargon. That's not difficult.'

'What was he wearing?'

'Casual clothes: jeans, a dark blue shirt and a dark green bomber jacket. They were expensive – designer stuff.'

Greaves sat back and closed his notebook. 'You'll have to change your statement,' he said flatly. 'I'll make the necessary arrangements.'

Vickie looked at him bleakly, her face puffy from crying. 'This will make things difficult if you catch him, won't it?'

Greaves did not answer.

Vickie continued. 'His lawyer will say I invited him here and seduced him, won't he? Then he'll say I lied to the police.'

'Yes,' Greaves replied flatly. 'There's no point in telling you otherwise. This will damage your case.'

'Oh, God,' Vickie said despairingly. 'This is a nightmare. I wish I'd never reported it now.' She lowered her head and her shoulders began to shake once more.

'Will you be all right?' Sarah asked. 'Do you want me to stay with you?'

She looked up, her face strained with misery, and shook her head. 'Just leave me. I'd rather be alone for a while.'

The three of them walked back to the cars in silence. The rain had eased to a steady drizzle, bringing a cold drabness to the day.

'I must be off,' Greaves said and Sarah could hear the weariness in his voice.

'See you later,' she replied. She wanted to kiss him, but it would have been somehow inappropriate. He got into the police car. Sarah waved, but he didn't look back as they drew away.

'Where can I take you?' Sarah asked. March, who had been preoccupied with his own thoughts, took a neatly folded handkerchief from his coat pocket and polished speckles of rain from his glasses. His face looked incomplete without them, and curiously vulnerable.

'Any tube station will do,' he replied.

Sarah looked at her watch. It was just after eleven o'clock. 'I'm in no hurry,' she said. 'I'm not due in the office until three.'

He still hesitated as if reluctant to ask for further favours, then said almost as a challenge: 'Well, Shepherd's Bush, as long as it's no bother.'

Sarah set off along the North Circular while March made a long call on a mobile telephone which he had produced from the pocket of his raincoat. He was filing the new information about Vickie Howard's attacker on to the *Gazette*'s computer. It seemed an incongruous piece of equipment for March to use; there was something about him that seemed to keep him rooted

107

firmly in the past. Sarah felt he would be happier making calls from a red telephone box shrouded by swirling fog.

Once he'd finished, March began to pay close attention to Sarah's driving. He moved uneasily whenever she overtook a lorry or came close to any other traffic. It was clear he did not enjoy being driven by others, or perhaps it was because she was a woman.

'Are you happy with this route?' Sarah asked eventually.

'If you come off this road at the next intersection on the left,' he instructed, 'I'll take you a quicker way.'

She followed his suggestion and he guided her across Dollis Hill and into the streets of Willesden.

'You know this area well?' she asked as he directed her through unfamiliar territory. March looked out on to the wet dismal streets and nodded. 'I used to work over here when I was first on the job,' he answered, but there was no nostalgia in his voice.

Sarah recognised the slang. 'I heard you'd been a policeman.'

'Seventeen years,' he replied.

'No happy memories?'

March shook his head. 'See this pub we're coming to on the right?'

Sarah looked towards a massive Edwardian building.

'I was called in to break up a fight in there on a Saturday night twenty years ago,' he said evenly. 'Paddies against Spades. Not a good mix – but it turned out they hated coppers more. They stopped punching each other and set on me. I was in hospital for six weeks.' He watched the pub as they passed its grim, tiled exterior. 'Nobody loves a policeman,' he added, without noticeable rancour.

'Some people do,' Sarah replied with a smile.

'You and Greaves?'

'That's right.'

'He's better than I thought,' March said. 'He was good with that girl. He didn't learn that at Oxford.'

'When did you start as a policeman?'

'Twenty years ago,' he repeated. 'I suppose you were still at school then.'

Sarah laughed. 'How old do you think I am?'

'Thirty-nine,' he answered.

'That's right. Why would I still be at school when I was nineteen?'

'I meant university.'

Sarah shook her head. 'I went to work as an office dogsbody when I left school.'

'Why – didn't you want to go to university?'

Sarah stopped at a set of traffic lights before she answered. The rain started to fall heavily once again. 'I did, but my academic record wasn't good enough. I tried for science subjects – but I just wasn't up to it.'

'You should have switched to something else.'

'My father is a doctor. I thought it would please him if I became one as well. He'd wanted a boy, I started off as a disappointment.'

'But even then you walked into a cushy job.'

Sarah bridled.'I wasn't beaten up regularly, if that's what you mean; but it was hard work. I wasn't handed it on a silver platter.'

'What kind of a magazine was it?'

Sarah paused slightly before she answered: 'For young gentlewomen.'

March didn't say anything.

'Where exactly are we going?' Sarah asked as they headed towards Shepherd's Bush Green.

'The market,' he answered. 'Do you know where it is?'

Sarah nodded. She parked off the Uxbridge Road and glanced up at the sky. The rain had stopped when they reached the maze of market stalls set beneath an elevated section of the underground system. March walked purposefully through the milling crowd and eventually they arrived at his destination: a stall piled with old gramophone records. A fat man with a carefully tended beard and an anorak sat beside the stall.

'Mr March,' he said. 'Always a pleasure to see you. I've got your parcel.'

He handed March a flat package wrapped in a plastic carrier bag and March handed him some money. 'Nice stuff that,' the fat man said. 'Four Al Bowleys and two Roy Fox.'

'You haven't seen a copy of "Tiger Rag" by Mugsy Spanier, have you?'

The fat man shook his head. 'Not since Elvis Presley was in the hit parade.'

March turned away from the stall. 'I want to get something to eat now,' he said. Sarah looked at her watch: it wasn't yet twelve o'clock.

'I was going to offer to buy you lunch a little later,' she said.

'I don't eat lunch unless I have to,' he answered, as if she had suggested something slightly shocking, like mixed nude bathing.

'What did you have in mind?' she asked. 'It's a bit late for breakfast.'

110

'It's never too late for breakfast,' March replied with conviction.

A few minutes later they were seated in a dingy café where the windows were streaked with condensation. The humid air was filled with the smell of cigarette smoke, damp clothes and fried food. Sarah looked at the other customers. They were mostly elderly couples, surrounded with bags of shopping. At the table behind March was a group of noisy workmen, their clothes caked with mud.

A gaunt woman smoking a cigarette came to serve them. She ignored Sarah. 'The usual?' she asked March, in the same accusatory tones Sarah was accustomed to hearing from March himself. Expressionless, he nodded his agreement.

'Do you want the same?' she now said to Sarah with equal hostility.

'What is it?'

'Eggbaconsausagebeanschips,' she answered.

Sarah did not want to appear ungracious, but she didn't think that good manners were worth that amount of cholesterol.

'Just coffee, toast and a soft-boiled egg for me,' she replied.

'We only fry eggs here,' the woman said. 'Hard or soft.'

'For Christ's sake boil her an egg,' March said irritably. 'Len can stick it in a saucepan. I know he can't tell the time but I'll shout out when it's done.'

The woman called their order to a portly, balding man behind the counter who waved a hand in acknowledgement and stayed at the table.

'Are you coming to see Mum tomorrow afternoon?' she now asked.

'I can't,' March replied edgily. 'Fulham are playing at home. I'll try and get over in the evening.'

The woman shook her head. 'You always were a spoilt bastard – you know it's you she wants to see.' She looked at Sarah as if to draw support. Sarah smiled uneasily. The woman looked at him again with hostile intensity for a few seconds and then walked away with a shrug.

'My sister, Marge,' he said in a disinterested voice.

'I gathered she was a relation.'

'I'm the first one in my family to wear a suit to work,' he said. 'They think I'm a bit of a snob.'

'In which sense?' Sarah asked.

March looked at her suspiciously. 'How many senses are there?' he asked.

Sarah looked up as March's sister banged down white china mugs of tea and coffee before them.

'Well, there's the sense of someone who attempts to suck-up to those they consider their social superiors. It can also mean to avoid or patronise people regarded as inferiors. It can also mean someone who has an air of superiority in matters of knowledge and taste.'

'The last, I suppose,' he said gloomily. 'Mind you, I do have better taste. None of them would know Mugsy Spanier from Barry Manilow.'

Suddenly Sarah had to suppress an urge to giggle. It was like trying not to sneeze. There was something deeply comical about March's melancholy acknowledgement that his family were right to regard him as a snob.

When the food arrived he ate quickly, so that he was finished before Sarah had hardly started on her boiled egg. Marge cleared away his plate, saying in a scolding voice, 'You're still bolting your food. No one's going to pinch it, you know.'

'Are you as close to the rest of your family?' Sarah asked when Marge had moved away.

March nodded. 'You only get one family, you know.' Sarah realised that his curious manner disguised a complex man.

'What did you think of the interview with Vickie?' she asked.

March spooned sugar into his mug of tea and slowly stirred. 'It's the best stuff I've got so far,' he answered. 'Up till her story, I didn't have a damned thing. Greaves didn't even know if they were looking for someone who was black, white, big or little. All the other victims were shortish women, did you know that?'

Sarah shook her head. 'I don't know much about the case at all, I've been out of town for the last few weeks. Tell me about the others.' March took out a small notebook and flipped through the pages with a slight frown of concentration. 'The first victim was Heather Beattie, married, aged 41, a supply teacher. She lived in a big house in Golders Green, didn't have to work, her husband owns a local restaurant. The second was Judith Kenworth, aged 37. She lived in a maisonette in Dollis Hill, her husband works as a tool fitter in Willesden. The third victim was Marjorie Patton, aged 48, divorced, employed by a landscape gardener.'

He closed the notebook and placed it carefully in an inside pocket. 'In each case the body was discovered by the victim's children.'

Sarah thought of each terrible scene for a moment and then made an effort to block out the horror. 'They all worked part-time?' she asked.

'They were always home early enough to be there when their kids got home from school,' March replied, then he drank some tea and made a face. 'This is stone cold,' he protested to his sister. She took it from him with a tutting sound and brought another.

'How many sisters do you have?' Sarah suddenly asked.

'Three,' he replied. 'I was the only son.'

'Did they all wait on you when you were at home?'

'I suppose so,' he answered as if baffled by her question. 'I was the man.'

Sarah thought for a moment about the wife from whom he was divorced, but she made no comment. Instead she asked, 'Why did you switch from the police to journalism?'

He turned round to stare coldly at one of the workmen who had been kicking the back of his chair in time to a record playing on the wireless kept on the counter. To Sarah's surprise the brutal-looking youth said, 'Sorry, mate, got carried away.' March turned back to her and said, 'Why did I want to be a journalist?'

'Yes.'

'I always wanted to be a reporter. When I left school I wrote to just about every local paper in the country.'

'No luck?'

'Oh, I got a job – three quid a week as a junior reporter in east Lancashire. I was there nearly three years.'

'What happened?'

'I met Betty.'

'Betty?'

'My wife. She worked in a local factory.'

Sarah noticed that he didn't use the prefix 'ex'. She wondered if it signified anything. Colin rarely mentioned his first wife – who had now remarried – but when he did, he also just referred to her as his wife. Sometimes it made Sarah feel he hadn't accepted their divorce.

'Didn't she want you to be a reporter?' she asked.

'I don't think she cared,' he replied. 'After I'd been going out with her for six months she told me she was pregnant. I couldn't support a family on the money I was earning so I joined the Liverpool Police.'

'Was the money that much better?'

'A house went with the job. Betty had never lived in a house, just council flats – they were bloody awful places in those days.'

'You have children?'

March shook his head. 'It was a phantom pregnancy. Once she got a house that was enough for her. And that's all she cared about, really. If you'd asked Betty what she wanted, a baby or a new sideboard, she'd have been down at Times Furnishing before you could put the cat out.'

Sarah decided to change the subject. 'You say the previous victims were small?'

'It wouldn't have taken a Samson to hold them down.'

She thought about the attacker Vickie Howard had described. 'Do you think he's clever?' she asked.

'I *hope* he is,' March said with conviction.

Sarah was surprised. 'Why?' she asked.

'Clever ones often like to play games, show off – then you have a chance to out-think them. It's the animals who are the hardest to catch, they can be completely unpredictable – especially if they're just operating on instinct.'

115

'Can you explain that a little more?'

March drank some tea before he answered. 'How did he come to choose Vickie Howard?' he said. 'They're now pretty sure it's got some connection with your children's school.' He looked towards the streaming window and rapped on the Formica-topped table with his teaspoon. Then he turned back to her. 'The trouble is, your man Greaves still can't work out the reason he's picked on Saint Catherine's. If it was just kids at the school or their mothers it would be easier. But the victims seem to have a random connection – there's definitely a pattern in there somewhere. Now he knows who he's looking for he may still be able to find a particular link. When he does, he might find the pattern. The clever ones usually work to a logical shape. Sometimes it's a pattern on a map; other times in the mind.'

'What time of day did the attacks take place?' Sarah asked.

'All in the afternoon,' he replied. 'And all in north London.'

'Perhaps he's unemployed.'

March continued to look at the window while he answered. 'Maybe, that would have been easier to check once upon a time.' He looked back at her. 'Do you remember London in the Fifties?'

Sarah shook her head. March reached out and wiped the window with his hand. 'Look out there,' he said. Sarah watched the crowd passing.

'All those people,' he said softly. 'When I was a boy you hardly saw anybody on the streets during the daytime. If you did you recognised 'em. Milkman, insurance man, barrow boy. Everybody worked then.

116

When I was a kid if we played truant from school, we were noticed. Every day is like a Saturday now; the streets are crowded.' He looked at Sarah again. 'Still, he's made a mistake, letting Vickie Howard live. At least they've got something to go on.'

Sarah looked at her watch. 'I'm going to go into the office, do you want a lift?'

March shook his head. He produced a wallet and took out a card. 'This is my mobile telephone. If anything happens you think I should know about give me a call. I try not to go in the office much.'

Sarah put the card in her bag and they rose from the table. March gave a half-wave to his sister and they left the café.

'You really want them to catch this man, don't you?' Sarah said when they stood on the wet pavement again.

'Yes, I do,' March answered; and she could hear the depth of his conviction.

'You make it sound personal,' Sarah said.

March explained: 'I owe everything to women – my mother and my sisters. I want this man inside.'

'So does Colin,' said Sarah. 'Are you sure you don't want a lift?' she offered.

He said he would walk to the underground, so they parted in the Uxbridge Road. From her car, Sarah now noticed the pavements of Shepherd's Bush and Holland Park. March was right – there seemed so many people. How can Colin hope to find a man hiding out here? she wondered, then the heavy traffic regained her attention.

There were still a couple of hours before her shift started when Sarah parked in the vanway of the *Gazette* building. She did not want to go into the office quite so soon and the rain had started again. She was still hesitating at the entrance when George Conway and Gordon Brooks, the deputy editor came out. 'Hello,' George greeted her, 'I didn't expect to see you until later.'

'It's a surprise to me too,' Sarah answered.

'Come and join us for lunch,' George suggested. 'Unless you've got something better to do.'

'I've already eaten,' Sarah replied. 'I've been with Joe March working on the rape story.'

'That's all right,' George said. 'You can come along and just get pissed. It'll make a nice change for you.'

Sarah considered the options. It was raining quite heavily now. The only alternative to sitting at her desk was standing in the Lion and she did not relish the thought of being jostled and harangued by arguing reporters for the next two hours. 'Well, if I'm not intruding . . .' she answered.

'My dear Sarah,' Gordon Brooks said, smiling. 'Your presence will lend tone to what otherwise promised to be a vulgar brawl.'

'Where are you going?' Sarah asked as an office driver held open the door of the car that waited for them.

'The White Tower,' Brooks replied, when they were seated in the roomy interior. She felt a stab of regret for the boiled egg, but knew her appetite had gone until later that evening.

While the car battled through the slow-moving traffic, her companions continued with the conversation they had been engaged in before Sarah joined them.

118

'We had four men in New York when I joined the paper as foreign editor,' Brooks said mournfully. 'Two in Washington, three in Paris, two in Rome. Two in Berlin, one in Bonn, one in Moscow, stringers all over the globe. Look at it now; no staff men anywhere. Foreign news is dead. We won't be replacing Hopkins when he retires next month. I never thought I'd see the day when the *Gazette* wouldn't have a staff man in Paris.'

'I never thought we'd see the day when the editor of the *Gazette* would be a game show host,' George said drily.

Gordon Brooks shot a glance at the back of the driver's head. It was Alf Thomas in the seat, a man who had overheard more than a thousand private conversations in the years he had driven executives on the paper, and never gossiped afterwards. Brooks knew it; but he was still discreet. 'What do you think, Sarah?' he asked quickly.

'I suppose I'd have more than an academic interest in the subject if the *Gazette* had ever appointed women abroad, Gordon,' she answered. 'But I am sorry – in an abstract way.'

'Do you know what the management said when I protested,' Brooks continued. 'Take it from the telly – I asks you. We're supposed to be a great newspaper; and if we're covering a major story taking place outside the United Kingdom, the bloody reporter just sits in the office and turns on a satellite television news broadcast.'

Conversation lapsed for a time and they looked out of the window.

'God, the traffic is appalling these days,' Brooks

said. 'It only used to take half the time to get to the West End a few years ago.'

'There was only a quarter of the cars on the roads during the Sixties,' George said in a distracted fashion.

Brooks seemed fretful. 'When I was young, I thought everything would get better,' he said. 'But these days it all just seems to get worse and worse.'

George turned and slapped him on the knee. 'That's because you're getting old, Gordon.'

'Bollocks,' he answered with some feeling. 'My generation got a lousy deal. Just when they invented teenagers I had to do my National Service. Two years in a scratchy uniform with my head shaved bald, while you were hanging about in coffee bars, rock 'n rolling with girls. Then I got married and the next year they started the permissive society. Another desirable boat that I missed – as usual.'

'You're lucky to have only one wife,' George said. 'Unbridled sex brings its own penalties – I should know.'

Sarah was beginning to wonder if she had made the right decision. She wasn't really in the mood for Gordon's gloomy introspection.

Eventually, Alf Thomas pulled up outside the restaurant and Gordon paused on the pavement to say what time they wanted to be picked up. George, first inside, said he wanted a drink before they went to their table. He led them to an area furnished with comfortable chairs. To their surprise and pleasure, they found Brian Meadows, the previous editor of the *Gazette*, sitting with Charles Miller, the financier who was reputed to be interested in taking over LOC PLC.

120

Meadows greeted them enthusiastically and insisted they join him and Miller for champagne.

'So how do you like coming off the desk, George?' he asked.

'It's an acquired taste, Brian,' he answered drily.

Meadows turned to Miller, who was clearly not up on the latest gossip from the *Gazette*. 'The new editor has appointed George's deputy to be news editor,' Meadows explained. 'George is an assistant editor now.'

Miller raised his eyebrows; a useful reaction, Sarah thought, if you wish to signify nothing. He turned to Sarah and asked, 'What do you do on the paper, Mrs Keane?'

'I'm a general reporter,' she answered.

'Do you approve of the new editor?'

'It's early days yet, but I still think I prefer Brian.'

'And is that the view of the rest of the staff?'

Sarah had noticed before that the powerful often cultivated the irritating manner of asking questions that would seen unpardonably rude if they came from the mouths of lesser mortals – but she was determined not to be intimidated.

'The only thing I've ever heard the entire staff of a newspaper agree on is the demand for a pay rise all round,' she said easily.

'So some of them think Marr's OK?'

Sarah nodded thanks to the waiter who was pouring her champagne. She looked at Miller again. 'If Lucifer was appointed editor of the *Gazette*, some people would say he was a wonderful choice – and others would yearn for the good old days.'

Miller laughed. 'And you prefer the good old days?'

121

'Only because they really were better. That's not nostalgia – it's fact.' Oh dear, she thought, and on the way here I was bored with Gordon's nostalgia.

'And what do you think of Simon Marr's appointment?' Miller continued.

Sarah reached for her glass of champagne as she answered. 'I wouldn't be too quick to write him off; he got to the top in television and that's a tough business.'

The others were now glancing over her shoulder. She turned and was startled to see Simon Marr standing inches away, smiling down at her. He and Alan Stiles had just entered the restaurant. Clearly they had heard her remark.

Chapter Seven

After exchanging strained pleasantries that sounded to the diners on nearby tables like the good-natured joshing of old friends, the parties were called to their separate tables by the proprietor: Sarah, Brooks and George at ground level; the other two groups on the floor above.

'Christ, that was a bit awkward,' Brooks said when they were seated. 'Do you think Marr will suspect us of plotting with Meadows and Miller?'

'What would you think, Gordon?' George replied in a bored voice.

The deputy editor looked harassed. 'Well, at least we're not lunching together, Marr will see that,' he replied and mopped his forehead with his napkin.

George took pity on him. 'Why don't you suggest that you go back in the car with them?' he said gently. 'That will be a declaration of loyalty; and then you can explain the meeting was a coincidence.'

'Should I ?' Brooks said with sudden hope. Then he relapsed into gloom. 'Mind you, by that time all the damage will be done. That weasel, Stiles, will be filling his ear with poison right now.' He cast an almost desperate glance above him, as if willing his thoughts to penetrate the ceiling and convince his new master of his innocence.

George was beginning to weary of Brooks's self-pity. After all, the intention of the lunch had been to console *him* for being kicked upstairs, not to exorcise the deputy editor's demons of anxiety.

'For God's sake snap out of it, Gordon,' he said, only just managing to disguise his irritation. He turned to the waiter: 'Bring us mixed pâté and two ducks. And make sure the one for Mr Brooks is well and truly dead.'

'I'm sorry, sir?' the puzzled waiter asked.

'Never mind,' George said. 'It was a joke for my friend – dead duck, get it? No? Well, forget it. I'll have a large Scotch.'

Conversation lagged throughout the meal, and Sarah wished she had taken her chances in the Lion. Brooks was about to go upstairs when a waiter appeared and handed a note to Sarah. Puzzled, she took it and then looked at her companions. 'Marr wants me to go back to the office with him in his car. He's asked me to join them upstairs – if you two will excuse me.'

'Just you?' Gordon asked, anxiously.

Sarah handed him the note. He scanned the few lines as if hoping to divine a deeper meaning, then handed the scrap of paper to George who didn't bother to read it.

'Off you go,' George said gently. 'The editor's decision is final.'

'Tell him about the coincidence if you get a chance,' Brooks called after her as she climbed the stairs. After a glance around the long room she sat down at Marr's

124

table. Meadows and Miller were at the far end of the restaurant, well out of earshot. Marr had risen when Sarah first stood beside them; following his example Stiles also got to his feet.

'What would you like to drink?' Marr asked. 'A brandy, or perhaps something lighter, a glass of champagne?'

'I'd really like some coffee,' she replied.

'Our Sarah doesn't like alcohol,' Stiles said, making it sound like some perversion that decent people could barely tolerate.

'Is that so?' Marr asked.

'On the contrary,' Sarah replied briskly. 'I enjoy a drink; but I'm working this afternoon and I have a limited capacity.'

'How does it get you?' Marr asked grinning. 'Do you pass out or dance on the table tops?'

'It happens the other way around,' she replied, returning his smile.

Stiles stirred in his seat unhappy at the ease of their rapport. 'Miller and Meadows seemed to have a lot to talk about,' he said, changing the subject.

Marr followed his gaze. 'Didn't I hear some gossip about those two and Miller's wife?'

'They're living in a *ménage à trois*,' Stiles answered. 'That's the talk. I'm surprised at old Meadows, I would never have thought he had it in him.'

'That's a good story,' Marr said. 'Why haven't we read about that in the paper?'

Stiles grinned knowingly. 'Mrs Miller is in the government – Sir Robert Hall wants his peerage. Need I say more?'

'It's not quite like that, Alan,' Sarah said quickly.

'The Millers have separated. They're getting a divorce; and Meadows *is* living with Miller's wife. After the divorce, Charles Miller is going to marry someone else. It's all very amicable.'

'The girl's pregnant,' Stiles offered. 'He got his secretary up the stick.'

'That hardly counts as a *ménage à trois*,' Marr said.

'Doesn't it?' Stiles said with surprise. 'I thought it was, when two men fucked the same woman.' Like a lot of journalists, Stiles had received only a rudimentary education. But he made up for it with malice.

'Mr Miller is a lucky man,' Marr said. 'I wish my estranged wife would find someone else, the alimony is killing me.' He turned to Stiles. 'How about you, Alan? She's very beautiful, you know.'

For a moment, Stiles's face was such a portrait of conflicting emotions that Sarah nearly laughed aloud. It almost seemed as if he were going to take up the offer – if it would please his new master. Then he caught the spirit of the remark and gave a flustered giggle. 'That would be taking friendship too far, Simon. I don't believe in mixing business with pleasure.'

'I do,' Marr replied. 'I couldn't bear the idea of not gaining pleasure from my work. How about you, Sarah? Don't you like being happy at work?'

It was too good an opportunity to miss. She nodded firmly. 'I do. I think reigns of terror in Fleet Street are detestable – and bad for papers in the long run.'

'I'm not sure I follow,' Marr said and he gestured for the waiter to make the brandy he was pouring a larger measure. 'Explain what you mean by "reign of terror." '

126

Sarah took a deep breath, knowing she was entering the dangerous region of office politics – territory she had avoided in the past. 'There's always been two conflicting theories about running papers,' she began. 'One school of thought believes in treating journalists like adults and creating a happy atmosphere where talent is encouraged. The other school works on the premiss that an atmosphere of fear produces the best work.'

'Don't people get sloppy if executives are too lenient?' Marr said. 'They do in television.'

'I suppose I believe that good journalists respond to good leadership,' Sarah continued. 'Mostly they're pretty bright; treat them badly and they'll find ways to evade responsibility or take difficult decisions – especially if they know they won't be backed up by their executives.'

Marr drank some of his brandy. 'Won't some of them take advantage, though?'

'Fire them,' Sarah said. 'I'm not advocating a holiday camp. But if somebody is working flat out and they make a genuine mistake, exercise some tolerance. Don't set up an inquisition.'

Marr nodded as if he agreed. 'So what's the best way to achieve the atmosphere you desire?'

Sarah took another deep breath and glanced at Stiles, whose eyes were on the tablecloth.

'I'd start with the executives. Make sure they know you expect them to be loyal to their staff – and to each other – as well as to you.'

'And you think this will work?'

'There'll always be a few who'll take advantage; but you'll soon be able to spot them and weed them out.

I'm sure the high morale will bring enormous bene-
fits, and attract the best talent.'

Marr was now selecting a cigar from the box proffered by the waiter. His hand hovered over the
different compartments for a moment, then he chose a
Havana. Now it was Stiles's turn. Sarah saw that he
went for the same selection as Marr without hesitation.

'Tell me about what happens when you have a reign
of terror,' Marr said as he carefully clipped the end of
his cigar.

She drank some coffee and continued. 'That turns
the office into something like the court of the Borgias.
Advocates call it "creative tension". Spies flourish and
warring factions divide the paper. People are appointed so that their responsibilities overlap with others.
Favourites jostle for power. Executives are deliberately encouraged to undermine each other. In that kind
of atmosphere the staff go in constant fear of their jobs.
The newspaper simply becomes a by-product. Their
real efforts are concentrated in destroying rival members of the staff.'

'Just like television,' Marr said thoughtfully. Then
he looked up. 'Ah, and here's our star columnist. She
said she'd try and join us for coffee.'

Fanny Hunter was approaching; she was only mo-
mentarily put off her stride by the presence of Sarah.

'Jesus Christ, protect me from whingeing cabinet
members,' Fanny said as she sat down. 'This one was
so wet you could sail boats on him. Sometimes I grow
weary of doing these little jobs for the chairman. Why
can't he keep his own appointments instead of sending me?'

128

Neatly done, Sarah thought. Now Mr Marr can be in no doubt about how close you are to the *real* power on the paper.

'Come on, Fanny,' Marr said soothingly. 'You know they'd rather have lunch with you. The chairman really did have another engagement, which I happen to know took precedence. Only you could bridge the gap.'

Touché! Marr's detail about the chairman's private movements was nicely done.

But Fanny smiled smugly at the compliment and accepted a drink.

'So what did the soggy cabinet minister want?' Marr asked.

Fanny paused; she had spotted Meadows and Miller and was waving a greeting. Then she leaned forward conspiratorially: 'Can't speak, here, darling, too many loose tongues. Come back in my car and I'll spill the beans.'

Marr put a hand to his chest in mock regret. 'I shall have to pass that invitation, I've already arranged to travel with Sarah. But if you can share the secret with her . . . ?'

Fanny shot Sarah a bitter glance, then smiled at Marr. 'If it were up to me I'd say yes; but it really wouldn't be fair for her to know. If word got out –' her voice became even more serious' – It really is top-level stuff. You understand, don't you Sarah?'

'Of course, Fanny.'

'Then I shall have to wait with breath bated until we meet in my office,' Marr said.

Fanny glanced along the room as Charles Miller and Brian Meadows rose to leave. 'Hello,' she said softly, 'the wife-swappers are on the move.' When the two men paused at the table, she smiled and said: '*Brian*, good to see you. And Charles, when are you going to buy us from Sir Robert? I need a pay rise.'

Miller did not smile at the remark. 'I'm sure when that happy day comes, all of Fleet Street will be knocking at your door with offers, Fanny. How could we afford to keep you?'

They passed on and Fanny shrugged, but she was disconcerted by his remark. Usually the powerful treated her with deference, and prospective employers, courtly charm. 'He's right about the rest of Fleet Street, I'm tired of being made other offers,' she said tightly.

'No one could possibly appreciate you as much as the *Gazette*, Fanny,' Marr said lightly. Sarah noticed he slid the bill towards Stiles as he spoke. Then he stretched. 'I suppose we should be getting back.' He smiled at Stiles, who had placed his credit card on the bill. 'Why don't *you* go in Fanny's car, Alan, it would be ungallant to let a lady travel alone.'

But Fanny wasn't going to allow Sarah time alone with the editor if she could help it. 'My driver can go back on his own,' she said as she followed Marr and Sarah downstairs. 'It'll be cosier in one car – we can all have a singsong.'

Marr didn't seem to hear the remark. He whisked Sarah into the back of his car and waved as they drove away. 'Phew,' he said settling back in the upholstery. 'I wonder what song Fanny had in mind – probably the "Horst Wessel".'

Sarah laughed and looked about her. 'This is a new car isn't it?' she asked.

'Yes,' Marr replied. He pushed a button so that a window slid up between them and the driver. 'And one in which you can have a private conversation.' He lit a cigarette and turned back to her. 'Fanny doesn't like you, does she? Why is that?'

Sarah spoke carefully. 'It's personal, and it goes back a long way.'

'Something to do with Jack?'

Sarah didn't answer. Marr stubbed out the cigarette after a few puffs.

'Stiles and Fanny,' he continued. 'They believe in the Borgia school of journalism you described, don't they?'

'Yes,' Sarah answered without elaboration.

'Have you ever thought about doing a column?' he asked.

'I'm not the right type,' she smiled. 'You need someone with lots of spleen. I don't get angry often enough to keep up a column.'

'Maybe that's what we need,' Marr said thoughtfully. 'A less strident note in the paper. I'm all for robust opinion but the readers may like something less hysterical.' He reached for the cigarettes again and then stopped himself. 'The reason I wanted to talk to you was about this German story,' he said.

Sarah was bewildered for a moment, then she recollected Andrew Maclean. 'What about it?' she asked.

'It seems the man selling it took a shine to you. Can't blame him. He says he'll only deal with you.'

'Are you really keen on it?' Sarah asked.

Marr leaned forward and took her hand. 'This could be a big one, Sarah. The television possibilities are enormous. I could see a cracking documentary being produced simultaneously with the newspaper series. Think of the publicity in a multi-media package such as this. We'd get a book out of it too. It's all there for the taking.'

'I don't know anything about television work,' she answered. 'I'm a newspaper reporter.'

'I can take care of all that,' he said enthusiastically, still holding her hand. 'You put the words together.'

'I'll see the man again, if that's what you want,' she said. 'But don't expect too much.'

Marr squeezed her hand before he let go. 'Great, that's wonderful,' he said. He leaned forward and picked up the car telephone. 'Let's have some fun.' He dialled a number and Fanny answered. Sarah could hear her quite clearly.

'Fanny darling,' he began. 'I've just dropped Sarah. Why don't you tell me what the cabinet member said.'

'That's funny, Simon,' Fanny replied. 'I'm in the car right next to you and I can see Sarah quite clearly.'

Marr was not disconcerted at all. 'Just testing, my dear,' he replied with a laugh. 'The chairman is worried about security in this organisation. I told him we could trust you.'

He lowered the partition and told the driver to go faster. The car accelerated into a gap ahead, and Sarah just caught a glimpse of Fanny looking from the window of her own car. The stare of hatred reminded her of the head of the Medusa.

When they reached the front entrance hall of the *Gazette*, a group of reporters was just returning from their lunch break in the Lion. Marr, aware of their presence,

132

kept up a stream of friendly small talk with Sarah while they all waited for the lift together. Sarah felt slightly embarrassed by his attention and her gaze moved away for a moment as she smiled politely at one of his remarks. Beyond the reporters, who were steadfastly ignoring Marr's interest in Sarah, stood the young commissionaire whom she had seen in the pub the night before. He stood with folded arms, and as their eyes met he smiled unpleasantly and looked her up and down, as if undressing her. She turned back to Marr and shivered suddenly, even though the hallway was quite warm.

When they reached the editorial floor, Marr invited her into his room and told his secretary to ask Alan Stiles to come in the moment he arrived at the office.

'Doesn't this place give you the creeps?' he said, gesturing around the room. 'It's like a scene out of Dickens. I'm going to have it redecorated in something modern and bright. What do you think?'

Sarah looked around the room. It had only been changed in recent months by Brian Meadows. She liked the bookshelves, dark wood and leather furniture. 'I suppose it's best to have it the way you like, seeing how much time you'll have to spend in here,' she replied diplomatically.

Marr was hanging up his jacket behind the door of his private bathroom. 'I don't intend to spend much of my time in here,' he said. 'I told Sir Robert I think that's death for an editor. How can I keep in touch with the real world if I'm stuck in an office day and night? Gordon Brooks will take over after the evening conference and I've given the broad brushstrokes on

133

how I want the paper to be. Do you think he's up to it?'

'Gordon is a good journalist,' Sarah replied. 'You couldn't leave the paper in better hands.' She had been about to add: providing you tell him exactly what you want, but managed to stop herself.

Marr came and stood very close to her with a look of concern on his face. 'You know, Sarah, I really value your advice,' he said with soft sincerity. 'I intend to lean heavily on my friends. I hope you'll always be there with your support and wisdom.'

'I'm sure you'll be able to rely on all our loyalties,' she answered carefully.

'There's one thing you could do for me right now,' he said; and for a moment she thought he was going to make some sort of advance.

'What's that?' she answered slightly nervously.

'Show me how this damned thing works,' he said, pointing to the computer terminal on his desk.

She gave a short laugh of relief. 'It's not that complicated,' she said quickly. 'The trickiest part is learning how to input your own material.'

He waved dismissively. 'I won't be writing on it. Show me how you call up the stuff other people have done.'

Sarah stood before the keyboard and he crowded close to her again, his leg brushing hers. She could smell his aftershave, a musky and expensive scent. Trapped against the edge of the desk, she could not move away from the pressure of his thigh against her own.

'These are the command keys you have to remember,' she said briskly. He leaned forward and rested

134

his hand on the table top so that his arm half encircled her. 'Show me again,' he said, his face so close that she could feel his breath on her cheek.

'This keystroke starts up the equipment,' she said.

'Stroke,' he repeated. 'Equipment – it all sounds very suggestive.'

Now she felt very uncomfortable. My God, I'm blushing, she suddenly thought. This is ridiculous. Unsure how to extricate herself from what was almost an embrace, Sarah was contemplating standing on his foot when there was a sharp rap on the door and Stiles entered.

'Oh, I'm sorry,' he said quickly and was about to back out of the room.

'It's alright, Alan,' Marr said easily. 'Sarah was just showing me the tricks of the trade.'

'Of which she knows many,' Stiles said. Sarah could now see that Gordon Brooks was also hovering at the edge of the doorway.

'Come in, Gordon,' Marr called out.

When they entered he looked from one to the other as if weighing the balance between them before he spoke. 'Sarah's just been telling me what a splendid chap you are, Gordon,' he began. 'From now on, I want you to take over the running of the paper after evening conference.' He glanced at Sarah. 'What do you think of that?'

A look of enormous relief came over Brooks and he beamed at her. 'I shall be delighted, Simon. Of course I shall consult before making any important changes.'

Sarah wasn't so happy. She was pleased for Gordon, but Marr had managed to convey the impression that she had been instrumental in the decision. Stiles now stared at her almost in apprehension, as if she were the king's mistress.

'Now, about Mr Maclean,' Marr continued. 'You say he only wants to talk with Sarah?'

'That's right,' Stiles answered.

'Where is he now?'

'The Staffordshire Hotel. I've got Pauline Kaznovitch minding him.'

'That's a bit pricey, isn't it,' Gordon interjected. 'Are we picking up the bill?'

Marr held up a hand. 'Leave this to me, Gordon,' he said. 'I'm handling this one personally.' He turned to Sarah. 'Why don't you go round there and buy him tea. Keep him sweet for a few hours and I'll join you later. We can talk to him together.'

'As you wish,' Sarah replied, and took this opportunity to leave. She was halfway along the newsroom floor when Stiles caught up with her. 'Where are you off to?' he asked. 'Simon told you to go straight to the hotel.'

'I'm just calling on George Conway,' she answered. 'It won't take long.'

Stiles took two steps ahead of her and barred her way. Hands on hips, he bristled like a playground bully trying to re-establish his hold over a rebellious child.

'The editor said straight away,' he muttered almost menacingly. Sarah could see his eyes flicker in an alarming fashion. Clearly he was only just clinging to his temper and further defiance would pitch him over the edge. He shot out an arm and pointed over her shoulder towards the exit. 'I order you to go straight to the Staffordshire Hotel,' he hissed and now she could

136

see the muscles along his jawbone quivering from the force with which he clenched his teeth. Sarah replied in even tones, as if to an hysterical child. 'If you don't get out of my way,' she said quietly, 'you have my word that I shall turn around and walk out of this building and never enter it again.'

Stiles fought to control his temper and his flushed face drained of colour. He was about to speak but changed his mind and stalked over to the news desk.

Sarah entered George's office and found it empty. She quickly wrote a note telling him of her meeting with March and the subsequent interview with Vickie Howard, then sealed it in an envelope. She was going to leave it on his desk but then changed her mind. Instead she walked to the area of the editorial floor referred to as the tape room and handed it to the messenger on duty. 'Give this to Mr Conway in person will you, Fred?' she said.

'Will do,' he answered cheerfully.

Outside she stood for a moment, contemplating whether to take her car, but decided against it because of parking difficulties. Usually she would have asked to be dropped off by one of the office drivers, but they were controlled by Stiles and she was in no mood to ask favours of him. So she stood in the rain and at last managed to hail a taxi.

Colin Greaves stood by the window as the last light faded from the weeping sky. The room was overheated and the rain blurred the coloured lights of the city, changing the shapes of neon signs to abstract patterns of colour. For a moment he could imagine he was in Hong Kong once again, then he became aware of

Holland standing beside him. He took the paper cup of coffee the sergeant offered and sipped the scalding liquid. 'All done?' he asked.

'Done or in the pipe line,' Holland replied. 'As we suspected, there's no one called Clive Roman in the computer. But they're checking the new information she gave us against anyone with form. I've also fixed up for her to give us a photo-fit.'

Greaves grunted, he was not sure that composite pictures were any real help in matching a likeness. Privately he believed they served more as a public relations exercise to give the impression of police activity rather than a reliable method of catching the wanted. 'What about the stuff she told us about his knowledge of actor's jargon?'

Holland look up from stirring the contents of his own paper cup with a plastic spoon. 'As soon as we get the photo-fit snaps I'm sending DCs Birch and Craig around the Shaftesbury Avenue area to check the pubs and clubs. They should start about mid day tomorrow.'

Greaves looked back to the wavering patterns of colour. 'Why did they open their door to a madman?' he said softly.

'Vickie Howard said he just smashed his way in,' Holland answered.

Greaves turned from the window and looked at Holland. 'That was just her, the others all had chain locks on the doors.'

'Perhaps they thought it was their children home from school,' Holland suggested.

'No,' Greaves said, almost to himself. 'The children all had door keys.'

Wearily, Holland sat on the edge of a desk. 'Maybe he'd made dates with them, like Vickie Howard.'

'I don't think so,' Greaves answered. 'I think there must be another reason. They opened the doors because they trusted him.'

Chapter Eight

The Staffordshire Hotel was located in an elegant cul-de-sac in St James's. Its modest entrance gave little indication of the discreet elegance within. Sarah asked for Mr Maclean and after a telephone call she was shown to the doorway of his suite. Pauline Kaznovitch answered her knock and looked relieved to see her.

'Stiles rang me to say they were changing the guard,' she said in a low voice as they stood in the hallway.

'Where is he?' Sarah asked.

Pauline looked over her shoulder. 'In the bathroom.' She reached out and touched Sarah's arm. 'There's something wrong with this one,' she said softly.

'How do you mean?' Sarah asked.

Pauline nodded towards a closed door. 'He doesn't know I speak German. He's been having some very odd telephone conversations.'

'I didn't know you spoke German.'

'I'm Polish,' Pauline answered. 'I understand Russian as well.'

'What kind of conversations?' Sarah whispered.

'Trying to talk someone into something. If he's selling a story, he hasn't got it buttoned up yet.'

'Don't you know what this is all about?' Sarah said.

Pauline shook her head. 'I was just told to baby-sit him. Stiles forbade me to ask any questions.'

The door to the bathroom opened and Maclean, in his shirt-sleeves came out. 'Ah, Mrs Keane,' he said. 'I'm delighted to see you again. Two beauties from the *Gazette*, I am being spoilt.'

'I'm afraid you'll have to make do with just one, Mr Maclean,' Pauline said. 'I'm going back to the office now.' She collected her possessions and bade them good-bye.

Sarah entered the living room and sat facing Maclean in an armchair next to the window.

'Lovely hotel, this,' Maclean said. He sat down in the chair opposite her.

'I'm not all that familiar with it,' Sarah answered, 'but it seems very nice.'

Maclean nodded. 'A lot of big deals go down here,' he said authoritatively. 'Powerful meetings. Politicians, top businessmen, the cream. They all use it.'

'It seems very suitable,' Sarah answered, unable to think of any other response.

Maclean looked about him, as if pleased that she appreciated his choice of ambience. 'Shall we get down to brass tacks?' he said, suddenly leaning forward with such an intense expression that Sarah sat further back. For one moment she looked into his eyes, and they danced crazily in exactly the same way Stiles's had earlier.

This man is unbalanced, she told herself, yet did not feel threatened. The realisation came to her quite calmly. Whatever emanations he gave out, physical danger was not among them.

141

'What sort of brass tacks do you refer to, Mr Maclean?' she asked soothingly.

'I want to get the money sorted out,' he answered. 'To be frank with you, I'm worried about my man's health. I think he could drop off the perch at any time. I think I told you he's got a dicey heart.' Maclean stopped and looked towards the window. 'And there's another problem.'

'What's that?'

'Mossad,' he replied flatly.

'Mossad?' Sarah repeated.

He nodded. 'They want him.'

'Why?'

'War crimes. He was a pretty important Nazi, you know.'

'I thought you told me he was an engineer.'

'That's right, but a top one; he controlled a whole department of the programme – and his section was using slave labour from the camps.'

'Why?'

'Don't forget there were no computers in those days, they had to use human beings to work out the mathematics. They used Jews, promising that their families would be safe if they co-operated.'

Sarah paused; what he said sounded plausible.

'What about that Jewish girl that was just here?' he asked. 'She pretended she didn't know German. I tested her.'

'I don't think Pauline is Jewish, Mr Maclean,' Sarah replied carefully. 'In fact I know she's Catholic.'

'Is that what she told you?' he asked. 'Take another look at that red hair.'

Sarah felt a sense of misgiving. When she was a girl,

142

there had been a pond near her parents' house. The shallow water froze if the winter was severe enough and Sarah was permitted to skate there without supervision. One year, she remembered, ice had formed overnight and she had wanted to skate so badly, she had hurried there and launched herself on to the smooth expanse. Most of the surface was strong enough to bear her weight, but occasionally she would glide over thinner parts of the pond. Then the ice would groan and buckle, causing her to wobble.

Listening to Maclean was like skating on that unsafe surface once more. His conversation sounded plausible, but some instinctive memory told her that certain areas would not bear weight.

'Do you know why I'm asking so much for this story?' Maclean suddenly began.

She smiled. 'I supposed it's the usual reason.'

'Greed, you mean?' he said quickly.

She did not answer. Maclean shrugged. 'It's curious how people put value on different sorts of information,' he began. 'If I'd been selling gossip about a famous film star or peddling some hot political memoirs you wouldn't have considered my demands excessive, would you?'

Sarah remained silent. Maclean lit a cigarette and waved the smoke away from his face with a swift motion. 'Tell me, why do you disapprove?'

'It's not for me to make personal judgments, Mr Maclean,' she said finally. 'Your motives are none of my business.'

'Call me Andrew,' he said. 'May I call you Sarah? You know I especially asked for you to work on this story?'

'I did – Andrew.'

He smiled fleetingly, hunching forward in his chair, then reached into a hip pocket and produced a wallet. 'This is my family,' he said, offering two coloured snapshots. Sarah took them and looked down at a pretty, plump young woman sitting on a sofa with a little boy and holding a baby in her arms.

'That's Jeannie with Andy. She's holding Janet,' he said. 'Jeannie's thinner now; that was just after the baby was born.' He took the snapshot from her and carefully placed it back in his wallet. 'They're the reason why I need the money.'

'There are millions of families. What makes yours different?' she asked.

Maclean drew deeply on the cigarette. 'Millions of other parents don't have a son with a defective heart, Sarah,' he said softly. He stood up and turned to look out of the window, then he spoke again.'You can call me a coward if you like, but I want to get my family out of the country. Surely that's understandable?'

'Yes,' she answered.

'I can transfer to Camtech's offices in southern California,' he continued, then turned and smiled at her again. 'The trouble is, there's no National Health Service in America. I don't have any insurance. If we move there, my son dies. It's as simple as that. If I sell Frichter's story, I can buy him a new heart.'

'Where does your family live?'

'Edinburgh,' he said in a distracted fashion.

'What hospital is treating your child?'

'The Royal Free Infirmary. The irony is, they say he's high on the list for a transplant – but I just can't wait.'

144

Sarah thought for a time. 'You do realise, if we do believe your story we shall have to tell the government. It's our duty. Then they may put a D notice on the story. It would be irresponsible to just go ahead and print it. There could be all sorts of panic.'

Maclean sat down again. 'Look,' he said earnestly. 'This is not my problem. I believe Frichter, therefore I want to get my family out of the country. Once I've sold his story, and given him his share, I'm off. What the *Gazette* and the whole bloody British government does is up to them.'

Another thought occurred to Sarah. 'Why does Frichter want to tell all this now?' she asked. 'If he's a war criminal, he could still have charges brought against him.'

'He just wants the money, Sarah. He's been living in the Soviet Union for nearly half a century. He wants to end his days in luxury.'

'But if he tells all this he could end up in jail.'

Maclean nodded. 'That's why he's in South America.'

'South America?' Sarah repeated. 'You mean he's in South America now?'

'That's right.'

Sarah sat back in her chair; she could feel the ice splintering beneath her once again. The telephone rang and Maclean answered. After listening briefly he said: 'Show them up,' then looked over at Sarah. 'Simon Marr, Barrie Loam and Charles Trottwood. I know Marr is the editor, who are the other two?'

'Charles Trottwood is the head of our legal department,' she replied. 'I don't know the other name.'

'Do you think he's brought the contract with him?'

She shook her head. 'I think there'll have to be a lot

more checking before we reach the contract stage,' she said.

Simon Marr entered the suite with his arm draped around the shoulder of a thickset, middle-aged man wearing an expensive leather jacket and a red silk shirt. The man wore an expression of boredom on his puffy face. Charles Trottwood followed. He glanced at Sarah with rigid features and then, almost imperceptibly, raised a questioning eyebrow. It was enough to convey his contempt for the venture.

'Mr Maclean,' Marr said. 'I want you to meet Barrie Loam: he's the best TV director in Britain.'

'How do you do, Mr Loam,' Maclean said. 'I'm afraid I'm not too well up on the names of directors. What work of yours might I have seen?'

Loam shrugged. 'Morocco perfume, the girls at the oasis. My advert for Zip trainers won an award as well.'

Maclean looked uncertainly towards Marr, then back to the director. 'So you're not a documentary film-maker?'

'All the best creative work is done in TV commercials these days,' Marr said. 'We want this programme to knock their eyes out.'

'Mr Maclean tells me that Otto Frichter is in South America, Simon,' Sarah said drily.

'South America – great!' Marr exclaimed. 'What do you think of that, Barrie?'

'Whereabouts?' Loam asked with a flicker of interest.

'São Paulo,' Maclean answered.

'Shit,' Loam said in disgust. 'São Paulo is just like Dallas. Can't we move him into the fucking jungle?'

'I'm sure that will be possible,' Marr said quickly.

The telephone rang again. Maclean picked it up, listened and then covered the mouthpiece. 'There's a Mr Crowther and Lawson downstairs. They say they're expected.'

'That's my lawyer and agent,' Loam said. 'I told them to meet me here.'

'Ask them to come up,' Marr said. Sarah noticed Charles Trottwood's eyebrow move fractionally once again.

A few minutes later, the two new arrivals entered and were quickly introduced. Sarah began to feel the room was getting crowded.

'How about some coffee?' Marr asked. He was about to suggest that Sarah get it, but changed his mind. 'Would you like to fix that, Charles?'

Trottwood was in one of the armchairs, studying a sheaf of documents he had taken from his briefcase. 'Room Service will do that for you, Mr Marr,' he answered easily, without looking up. Marr, slightly disconcerted, was unsure how to extricate himself without losing face.

Sarah took the opportunity she wanted. 'I won't be any help with these negotiations,' she said quickly. 'I want to go out for a few minutes. I'll tell them to bring something up.' She found her coat and by the time she reached the door, all the men were assembled around the table, exchanging papers. The air was already beginning to thicken with cigarette smoke.

Sarah descended to the lobby where the reception desk took her order for coffee then directed her to a telephone. Sarah rang her father and he immediately began to tell her about the wines he had ordered.

'That all sounds fine, Dad,' she said, cutting into his

recital of vintages. 'I wonder if you can find something out for me?'

'What sort of thing?' he asked warily.

'I want to know if a certain baby, a boy, is being treated for a heart condition at Edinburgh Royal Free Infirmary.'

'Is this for your newspaper?'

'It is but I promise you it will remain confidential. It really is important, Dad.'

'To whom?'

'More than just the readers of the *Gazette*,' she replied.

'Why don't you check in the usual way?'

'I don't have time; hospitals can be difficult with reporters. I know what a mafia you doctors operate. It'll only take you a few minutes.'

He paused for a moment and then said, 'Call me back in half an hour.'

Sarah hung up when she had told him the name and glanced at her watch. Not wanting to wait in the bar or reception rooms, she left the hotel and walked to St James's Street, turned and began to stroll down towards Pall Mall. She stopped for a moment to look into a shop window and caught the reflection of a man walking behind her who had also paused. Suddenly she felt menaced. It was pure intuition – but Sarah trusted her hunches. He had stopped at the same moment she had. On an impulse she crossed the road quickly, having to hurry to avoid oncoming traffic. Checking in the window of a gunsmith's she saw the figure had also followed her: he was tall and wearing a dark overcoat, a hat pulled down over his eyes. Sarah hurried on; it was dark and a cold wind whipped into her face, making her eyes water. Hurrying along Jermyn Street, she noticed the elegant front of a gentleman's outfitters. She entered and immediately there was something comforting, almost ecclesiastical, in the hushed confines of the cosy little shop. Immaculate sales assistants stood behind their counters like priests prepared to bestow benediction on customers seeking absolution.

'May I be of service, ma'am?' an elderly man asked.

After a fractional hesitation, Sarah decided. 'I want to buy a dressing gown for a tall, slim gentleman,' she replied.

'Certainly,' he said. 'We have silk or wool, which would you prefer?'

'Something warm and very expensive.'

The man turned to a rack. 'This is recommended for warmth, ma'am,' he said; he laid a long padded garment on the counter before her. It was the sort of thing a Victorian actor-manager might wear while entertaining in his dressing room. Beautiful; but quite unsuitable for Colin Greaves.

'Do you have something a little more conservative?' she asked.

The assistant returned a few minutes later with a plain, dark blue offering.

'This is cashmere, ma'am; and lined in silk,' he said with reverence.

'I'll take it,' she answered. The wrapping took longer than she could have imagined. After paying with her credit card, she left the shop and turned towards St James's Street again. She felt a hand on her arm. Startled, she turned to face Alf Thomas, the office driver.

'Alf,' she exclaimed with relief.

'Who was you expecting?' he said with a grin. 'Jack the Ripper?'

'Did you follow me here from the hotel?'

'Yeah,' he answered.

'Did you see anyone else behind me?'

He shook his head. 'Mind you, I wasn't looking hard. I wanted to ask what time you thought the meeting would be over. Mr Marr didn't give me any indication and I haven't had me dinner yet.'

'I don't know, Alf,' she answered. 'It might be some time. Why don't you come back with me and we'll order something from the hotel that you can eat in the bar while you wait?'

'Will it be all right?' he asked as they hurried back to the Staffordshire.

'Don't worry,' she said. 'I'll sign for it.'

'That's nice of you,' he said. 'I'll do you a favour some time.'

'Actually, you can now,' she said. 'May I put this shopping in the office car? I'm always forgetting things I've just bought and I don't want to leave it in the hotel.'

'Give it to me,' Alf said, taking the carrier bag from her. 'I'll put it in the boot.'

In the hotel once more, Sarah arranged a sandwich for Alf in the bar, then called her father again.

'They're treating a boy called Andrew Maclean, son of Andrew and Jean,' he said.

'Any address?'

'You didn't ask for that.'

'No, I didn't. Thanks, Dad. I'm very grateful. I'll tell you what I can about all this when we meet.'

150

Sarah could hear raised voices when she knocked on the door of the suite. Marr answered in his shirt-sleeves. Instead of standing back so she could enter he came out into the corridor. 'Contractual wrangling,' he said with a smile. 'There's no need for you to get involved.'

'Shall I go back to the office?' she asked.

'Yes . . . er, no. Look, why don't you have an early night? I'll ring you at home later.'

'Are you sure?'

Marr nodded. 'Certain – I'll call you later.' Then he clicked his fingers. 'By the way, did you know what the cabinet minister told Fanny?'

Sarah shook her head.

'That they're thinking of changing the law over your lost kids articles. God knows why she didn't want you to know, I think she's losing her touch.' Sarah smiled without replying. She was about to turn away, when she remembered Alf Thomas. 'What about the office car? Will you need it soon?'

'Why don't you take it and send it back for me,' Marr replied. 'He'll have to wait a long time. This could take all night.'

Sarah found Alf still in the bar, sitting next to an elderly American lady to whom he was giving his opinion of the Royal Family.

'The old king will be turning in his grave,' she heard him say. He got up when he saw Sarah.

'It's going to be a late one,' she said as they walked towards the car. 'I hope you enjoyed your sandwich.' She glanced towards the entrance to the cul-de-sac as she was about to get into the car, and for a moment thought she saw a figure waiting in the gloom.

But when they approached the turning no one was there.

Alf kept up a non-stop conversation on the way back to the office, mostly about the old days on the *Gazette*: names that she had half forgotten and some that were as bright and sharp as needles. When he dropped her at the front entrance in Gray's Inn Road, it was still raining. She decided not to go up to the newsroom. The chance of an unexpected early night was suddenly very appealing and there was always the possibility that something would delay her departure. She rang the news desk from reception and told Arthur Swann she would be at home if there were any emergencies. Alf bade her good-night, and she started out for Hampstead. She was almost at Camden Town before she remembered Colin's Christmas present still in the boot of Alf's car.

Chapter Nine

When she opened the front door the dog bounded towards her, rising on his hindlegs to be fondled. Sarah had to pat him with one hand while protecting her tights with her bag. There were sudden shouts of 'Don't come in here!' from the direction of the kitchen. Pat emerged, shutting the door behind her. 'They're wrapping your Christmas presents,' she explained. Then she looked at her watch. 'You're early, we weren't expecting you until much later.'

'Maybe there is a Father Christmas after all,' Sarah replied, suddenly realising how tired she felt. Pat sensed her weariness. 'I've just lit the fire in the living room. Why don't you put your feet up?' she asked. 'I'll make you a cup of tea – or would you like me to mix you a nice whiskymac?'

Sarah considered the options. 'Both,' she said finally. 'I'll have a cup of tea in the bath, then a drink when I come down.'

Sarah undressed in her old bedroom and had just slid into a deep bath, extravagantly laced with scented oils and salts, when her daughter Emily entered the room with her cup of tea. 'What's the new boss like?'

she asked, handing over the mug and sitting on the edge of the tub.

'Nice enough, I suppose,' Sarah answered. 'But different.'

'How do you mean?'

Sarah thought while she lay back luxuriously in the brimming water. 'He's not like a journalist at all. He seems to have quite another set of priorities.'

Emily picked up Sarah's mug and took a sip of the tea. 'Ric says he looks like a market trader.'

Sarah glanced at her daughter. 'That sounds a bit élitist, darling. I do hope you and Ric aren't catching the old Hampstead disease.'

'What's that?' Emily asked.

Sarah took the mug from her. 'A kind of high-minded self-regard by people who think of themselves as being progressive, but it's really just another form of snobbery.'

Emily laughed. 'Ric wasn't being snobbish, he was talking about a market trader in the City, where his father works. He meant Simon Marr has that glossy, expensive look.'

After a moment, Sarah agreed. 'He's right there, Simon Marr is glossy.'

There were sudden shouts of 'Good-bye, Mum' from downstairs and the crashing of the front door; the boys had departed for the evening. Sarah remembered that they were due at rehearsals for the school concert that was to be performed on the following evening.

'Aren't you and Ric going with them?' she asked. Emily looked at her watch. 'The choir is practising first, we're not due for another hour. Still, I'd better get ready.'

154

She left the bathroom and Sarah soaked in the hot water for a while longer. Then she dressed and came downstairs. Ric Daggert, Emily's boyfriend, was in the living room playing with the dog.

'Hello, Ric, I didn't hear you arrive,' she greeted him.

'I came in as Martin and Paul went out,' he answered.

'What time will you be home?' Sarah asked.

'A bit late,' he answered. 'Some of us are going for a pizza afterwards.'

Sarah nodded. She did not worry when Emily was with Ric. Despite his French film-star looks, he was a steady boy. Sometimes Sarah wondered if he might be too steady for Emily. She understood how attractive rats could be to romantic-minded teenage girls, and occasionally she would indulge in a mother's dread, imagining her daughter ditching Ric for a degenerate heart-breaker. Emily had a capacity for self-sacrifice and she could all too easily picture her slaving to support a wastrel.

Pat brought her the promised drink and taking advantage of Sarah's presence, declared she would have an early night herself. When they had all departed, Sarah stretched out on the sofa with the dog and switched on the television. A warm lassitude descended and she began to drowse in the comfort of the fire. Then the telephone rang. It was Colin.

'I called the office but they were vague about where you were,' he said.

'Who did you speak to?'

'Stiles,' he said. 'He thought you were in an hotel with Simon Marr. Were you interviewing him?'

155

'He's the new editor,' Sarah said. 'I was doing a job with him.'

'That's a bit unusual, isn't it? I didn't think the editor went out on stories.'

'Are you jealous, Superintendent Greaves?' Sarah chided.

'Of course I'm jealous,' Colin replied. 'I know how susceptible young women are to the sexual blandishments of glamorous television personalities.'

'I like the idea of sexual blandishments,' Sarah giggled. 'All he did was offer me power and fame.'

'Aphrodisiacs as well,' Greaves said drily. 'I think it's time I came home.'

'I wish you would,' Sarah said. 'I miss you.'

'Won't be long now.'

'What did you think of March?' she asked.

'I've known Joe March for a long time,' Greaves replied. 'How did you come to be working with him?'

'A story I was doing. He's working on the *Gazette* now – do you know him well?'

'Not well,' Greaves said. 'No one does. He has the reputation of being a loner. Terrible chip on his shoulder – both shoulders, in fact. Some people think he's a pain in the neck, but he was a good policeman.'

'Do you know why he became a journalist?'

'Some personal problem I think,' he said, then changed the subject. 'Where are the children?'

'Last night of rehearsals, the school concert is tomorrow.'

'Of course. I'd forgotten the holidays start at the weekend. Have you heard the boys practising?'

'Incessantly – actually they're not bad, I didn't realise

156

they had any musical talent. Guess what they've asked for as Christmas presents?'

'Oboes, electronic organs, violas, trombones, flutes, cornets, harps . . . stop me if I get warm.'

'No, silly, nothing to do with music.'

'I should have known. You are, as ever, the mistress of the *non sequitur.*'

'Don't start any of that haughty Oxford nonsense with me or you won't get your own present.'

'Just end this agonising suspense. What *do* the boys want?'

'Those full-size paper cut-out skeletons that you assemble yourself.'

'. . . What's so extraordinary about that? I would have thought they were reaching the age of blow-up, life-sized plastic women.'

'That's an awful thing to say – you don't think they're old enough to be interested in girls yet, do you?'

'Steel yourself for this piece of news,' Greaves said gently. 'Why do you think they volunteered for the choir?'

'Why?'

'Emma Harris and Amanda Phillips are also taking part.'

'How do you know this?'

'I'm a detective.'

'I'm their mother – and a trained reporter – they haven't mentioned these Jezebels to me yet.'

'You don't help them with logarithms. The names of the young ladies are engraved several times on their rough notebooks.'

'Is that all the evidence you have?'

'Would you say your sons were known for being

early for appointments, Mrs Keane?' he asked in the mock tones of a questioning lawyer.

She paused. 'Not really.'

'Then why do you think they have taken to leaving for school fifteen minutes earlier in recent weeks?'

Sarah thought. 'You're right, they are going earlier. They even complained when I drove them this morning.'

Greaves chuckled. 'That's because the girls walk to school together past the ponds. The twins wait for them and effect a chance encounter each morning.'

'I shall look out for these temptresses tomorrow night. What are you doing now?' Sarah knew that there was a high-level police conference in London at the moment. Greaves was expected to help out with hospitality in the evenings as well as carrying his usual workload during the day.

'Dinner with a Portuguese delegation; I've become something of a favourite with them. Few of our European colleagues speak their language so I'm considered a catch.'

'Aren't there any Chinese policemen there? Then you could get the double-up.' Greaves had spent his childhood in Hong Kong and was good at languages.

'As a matter of fact there are two observers from Shanghai. They speak French as well as Mandarin, so the boys from the Gendarmerie were delighted. They bitterly resent having to speak English all the time. When they heard me chatting to the Shanghai delegation in their native tongue they practically had apoplexy. I fear we're many generations away from a united Europe. Still, it makes the Americans laugh. They really hate the French.'

158

They bade each other good-night and Sarah contemplated putting more logs on the fire. The rain was gusting against the french windows; it was a foul night. She began to think about the boys. Sometimes she felt guilty that she seemed to play such a small part in their lives these days.

With Emily it was different: there were female things they shared that drew them close. Even shopping together deepened the bond. At times she felt they were growing more like sisters. But the boys were receding from her. It was as if they had boarded a different train that had run parallel to hers for a time but at some unnoticed junction had parted for a quite different destination.

The rain blew against the windows again and she made up her mind that she would go and pick them up from the choir practice. Give them a surprise – and maybe get a chance to catch sight of Emma Harris and Amanda Phillips.

'Fancy a trip out, young man?' she said to the dog, who was lying with his head in her lap in a state of blissful abandon.

He blinked up at her and sighed.

Later, Sarah found an old raincoat and a waterproof hat in the clothes cupboard in the hallway and led the dog to the car. The wind had dropped, but the rain continued. It did not take long to reach the school where the road was lined with parked cars. She had to leave hers some distance away and walk back through the deserted streets.

Rain fell heavily through the bare branches of the trees along the roadway and the dog walked close to her. She thought for a moment about entering the school gates and sheltering in the porch but decided against it, knowing that the sudden appearance of parents at unexpected times could cause paroxysms of embarrassment. So she stayed close to the trunk of a horse-chestnut tree that gave some protection. The sound of the choir singing 'Once in Royal David's City' came softly to her: it sounded beautiful, yet made her feel strangely melancholy.

It must have been the last carol, because suddenly cars began to double park in the street and a trickle of children emerged from the school. Some hurried off alone and others dawdled, laughing in groups. The cars clogging the road took aboard some of the waiting children and there were shouts of good-night and the slamming of doors. Sarah saw Emily and Ric Daggert with four others hurry past. She didn't call out, sensing that they were occupied in a time of their own that didn't have a place for parents.

Then she spotted the boys, walking sedately beside two girls who had their arms linked. She was about to call out when she saw that they were all making for the last car. It obviously belonged to the parents of one of the girls, she realised, when they all got inside. The car drove away, and the road was deserted again.

Suddenly Sarah felt very lonely. The dog brushed closer to her legs and a voice nearby said, 'You shouldn't be out on the streets alone, Sarah Keane.' Startled, she turned quickly and saw Joe March standing just a few feet away from her, back against the next tree.

'What are you doing here?' she asked.

March stepped nearer and rainwater ran from the brim of his hat on to the sheltering Labrador.

'Just a long shot,' he answered. 'I wanted to see if anybody was hanging about the school. I didn't expect to find you.'

'I thought I might give my children a lift, ' she said, 'but it seems they're all taken care of.'

'Isn't that ending a sentence with a preposition?' March said.

'Is it?' Sarah replied. 'I can never remember.'

'I'll come with you to your car,' he said.

They turned and began to walk down the hill. 'Do you think they'll find him soon?' Sarah asked. 'The murderer, I mean.'

'There's a good chance,' March replied. 'They've got a full description – and they know his blood group.'

Sarah realised he was referring to the sperm sample they had obtained from the examination of Vickie Howard. 'Didn't they have anything to go on from the other victims?' she asked.

'That's a puzzling fact,' March replied. 'They think he wore a condom with the other women. Usually rapists stick to the same pattern in their behaviour, but Vickie Howard was quite sure he wasn't wearing one when she was attacked – and she should know.'

'Strangely fastidious behaviour for a madman anyway,' Sarah said. 'Wearing a condom, I mean.'

March shook his head and rainwater fell from his hat. 'That's the thing about madmen – they do crazy things. Even the clever ones invent their own kind of logic.'

'Would it be possible to put on a contraceptive with

one hand if he was holding a knife to her throat with the other?'

'I couldn't say without trying,' March answered with no hint of irony in his voice.

Sarah was suddenly struck by the incongruity of their conversation. Here she was, discussing a violent sexual act with a man who was a virtual stranger. She guessed that the darkness and the rain made it easier, much easier than facing each other in a warm, well-lit room. They had reached Sarah's car and the rain drummed on the roof with even greater force.

'Why don't you come back to the house and ring for a cab? I'll give you a drink while you wait.'

March nodded. 'A cup of tea would go down well,' he said. A car swished towards them, headlamps on full beam against the torrential downpour. March's face was brilliantly lit for a moment; he looked ghost-like and exhausted in the harsh light.

When they reached the house, he followed her into the kitchen after hanging his hat and coat in the hall.

'Give me something and I'll dry the dog,' he offered. Sarah handed him an old towel and watched with interest while the kettle boiled. She had seldom seen someone perform a simple task with such intensity. When he had finished, March looked down at his handiwork with satisfaction and carefully folded the towel into a neat square, which he then placed on the draining board. The dog looked reproachfully at Sarah and departed.

'I'll bring the tea into the living room,' she said. 'Why don't you warm yourself by the fire?'

A few minutes later she found him examining the

records once again. He took the tea but refused the offer of a brandy.

'I talked to Colin earlier,' Sarah said when they were seated. She had no reason for mentioning Greaves, it was just that March seemed to have the ability of causing discomfort and she chose a topic of conversation that might establish some common ground between them.

'How's the London conference?' he asked. 'Expensive?', in that one word somehow managing to imply riotous extravagance on the part of those gathered there.

'He didn't say,' Sarah replied. 'I think he'd prefer to be at home.'

March looked around for a moment. 'I don't blame him,' he said flatly. Then, as if regretting his words, he stood up suddenly. 'I'd better ring for the taxi.'

'I'll do it,' Sarah answered and reached for the telephone next to her. While she was making the call the living-room door crashed open and the boys tumbled into the room, coming to a sudden stop when they saw March.

'You're early,' Sarah said when she had replaced the receiver. 'This is Mr March, he's a colleague of mine. These are my sons, Martin and Paul.'

'Mr Harris gave us a lift home,' Martin said, still looking at March. 'How do you do, sir – aren't you Chief Inspector Joe March?'

'How do you know?' March asked.

'Colin says you were one of the best coppers at the Yard,' Paul answered quickly. 'You broke up the Trenton Gang, didn't you?'

'I helped,' March replied.

163

'Is your leg better now?' Martin asked.

'Good as new.'

'What happened to your leg?' Sarah asked, mystified by the knowledge the boys shared.

'He got shot,' Martin informed her.

'Why did you stop being a policeman?' Paul asked.

'Sometimes it's a good thing to have a change in life,' March answered.

Sarah looked at him; she could see he was pleased by the recognition but there was some other emotion that showed in his face. He's shy, she suddenly realised.

The taxi arrived quickly and Sarah showed him to the door. The boys were watching a film that had just come on the television when she returned to the living room. She wanted to ask them about the two girls, but could not think of a way of raising the subject so went to the kitchen and started to make them hamburgers. After a few minutes they followed her.

'Movie no good?' she said when they were seated at the table.

'Rubbish,' Martin answered. There was no conversation for a time, but a lot of muttering. Then Paul began. 'Mum?'

'Yes.'

'When you first met Dad, did you let him know you fancied him?'

'Certainly not.'

'Why?'

'I didn't fancy your father all that much when I first met him. He had lots of girlfriends and I didn't want to be one of a crowd. He had to win me.'

'Win you?' Martin asked.

'Prove that he was worthy of me,' she said turning to examine the toaster so they couldn't see her expression.

'How did he do that?'

'The usual way – flowers, polite conversation, invitations to events I enjoyed. That sort of thing.'

'You didn't have boyfriends when you were at school, did you?'

'I was at boarding school, it wasn't very practical – and the nuns didn't encourage it.'

'Was that before the permissive society?'

'No – but the permissive society wasn't a popular movement with the Roman Catholic Church.'

'Do you think girls want boys to like the same things as they do?'

Sarah sat down at the table. 'Only if they really mean it,' she answered after a certain amount of thought. 'But it cuts both ways – it's called give and take.'

'We've decided to become vegetarians,' Paul said.

'That's going to solve a lot of problems,' Sarah commented, getting up and walking to the stove where the hamburgers were cooking. As the boys watched, she turned off the electricity, took out the grill-pan and slid the half-cooked meat into the dog's bowl. The Labrador leaped at the succulent feast while the twins looked on in horror.

'There's plenty of salad in the fridge,' Sarah said cheerfully. 'I'm going up to bed. Good-night.'

She was asleep quite soon, but woke up, as she usually did when Colin came into the room. He padded about quietly but she turned to him when he climbed into bed. He smelt of toothpaste and she could tell from the roughness of his beard how long it had been since he had last shaved. They made love with more passion than she had expected, but when Sarah began a conversation afterwards Colin's deep breathing told her that he had quickly fallen into a deep sleep.

Chapter Ten

7.25 a.m. Friday, 17 December

The following morning Sarah was up early, just before the central heating switched itself on; but Colin had already gone. When she left the bedroom the dog emerged from the boys' room and followed her with wagging tail down to the kitchen. She opened the door into the darkened garden but the dog just stood on the threshold and sniffed at the rain-laden air before turning back and collapsing with a sigh next to a radiator.

'I would say you were well and truly domesticated, young man,' she said to him with mock sternness, and as she spoke she suddenly heard echoes of her father in her own voice. The same sentence – spoken long ago, when she was a little girl. That had also been to a dog. She searched her memory . . . of course; they'd had a puppy called Spot, a little black and white terrier. He had stayed on her mother's bed when she was ill. Sarah could see the little creature quite clearly; but her mother's face still would not come to her.

By the time she had made herself a cup of coffee, she heard the papers click into the letterbox. She thought about reading them in bed, and would have done so had Colin been at home; but today she did not want to return to the lonely room. Instead she showered quickly and dressed before taking the papers into the kitchen, which was warmer now. She sat with a second cup of coffee, reading at a leisurely pace.

To her slight surprise, she found her story on Vickie Howard leading the features section. She was puzzled that they had decided to run it after all, but accustomed to the sudden reversal of decisions by newspaper executives she did not bother to speculate for long. No doubt it would all become clear when she got to the office, she told herself, and continued to read the rest of the paper.

Like all journalists, Sarah followed her own routine when she read the morning papers. First she scanned the front pages to see what each had chosen to lead on. Then she read the *Gazette* news section thoroughly, going back to the features and sports section for a more cursory glance. The *Gazette* was a middle-market newspaper with the *Daily Mail* and the *Daily Express* as its closest rivals, so she studied them next, comparing coverage of particular stories that interested her. Next she scanned through the pops then turned to the broadsheets. By the time Emily came down she had absorbed all the information necessary for the beginning of her working day.

'What time did you get in last night?' she asked Emily, who had made herself a cup of tea and was now sitting with the *Guardian* propped up before her.

'Not long after you'd gone to bed,' she answered. 'The boys were cooking bacon sandwiches. They said you gave their supper to the dog.'

'It was meat,' Sarah answered. 'They told me they'd decided to become vegetarians.'

168

'They've decided to become doctors as well,' Emily said. 'But I wouldn't let them take out my appendix just yet. I think the idea was they'd sort of creep up to vegetarianism slowly.'

'How can you creep up slowly?'

Emily shrugged. 'Give up sausages this year, liver next, and so on. Christmas is their big problem. I think they plan to give up turkey in the second half of the twenty-first century.'

Sarah thought for a moment. 'Have they really decided to become doctors?' she asked.

'That's right,' Emily said, still studying the paper.

'I thought they were only interested in sport.'

Emily looked up. 'Martin and Paul are both top of their year in science subjects now,' she said. 'Colin told me he's having real problems keeping up with them. They're way ahead of the stuff he was doing for A levels in his day.'

Sarah felt a sudden lurch of dismay. 'I had no idea,' she said.

'Well, you've been a bit tied up in your work recently,' Emily replied, continuing to read the paper.

Sarah got up and walked to the kitchen window. Events suddenly seemed to be moving very fast. Had she neglected her sons? What could she do to make up the distance between those diverging trains?

'Do you know the girls they're going out with?' she asked Emily.

Emily stood up and washed her mug in the sink. 'They're not "going out" just yet, Mum. They just hang about them trying to push each other over. But I suppose that's some sort of ritual male mating behaviour.'

Sarah felt guilty again. She set about preparing a

169

breakfast for the boys. The scent of bacon soon brought them to the kitchen.

'What's up?' Martin asked. 'We only get a cooked breakfast at weekends.'

'Last day of term,' Sarah answered, taking a maternal pleasure in the sight of their attack upon the food. 'Besides, I thought you might want to have a last slice of bacon. I shan't bother to buy any tomorrow. Emily and I don't eat it.'

'That's all right,' Paul said quickly. 'We talked it over last night. We decided we were going to give up liver and kidneys.'

'That sounds like a useful arrangement,' Emily said. 'As you don't like liver and kidneys.'

'How about giving up Emma Harris and Amanda Phillips?' Emily suggested mildly. Sarah was surprised by the violent reaction.

'Shut your stinking mouth, or I'll stuff a sweaty sock in it,' Martin snarled back.

'*Martin*!' Sarah exclaimed in horror. 'Don't use that sort of language in this house.'

'I didn't swear,' he answered.

'It was coarse and offensive.'

'It was meant to be coarse and offensive,' he argued.

Emily stood up. 'An effective threat as well,' she said, making her Parthian shot. 'He does have a vast supply of sweaty socks.'

'At least I don't sleep with one of Ric Daggert's shirts,' Paul called after her.

Blushing, Emily turned at the door, as angry now as her brother had intended her to be. 'You've been in my room again – I warned you to keep out.' She turned to Sarah. 'Make them keep out, Mum, please.'

170

In the past, Sarah had found their wrangling tedious; but this morning it was strangely comforting – a definite sign that all of their childhood was not over. 'Don't go into her room,' she admonished. 'Girls need their privacy.' She thought for a moment. 'And while I'm on the subject, clear all your junk out of the spare bedroom. It's starting to spread over the house like Virginia creeper.'

'What junk?' Paul asked indignantly.

'Those boxes. Some of them are dangerous.'

'Dangerous?' Martin asked.

'There's some stuff up there that can explode like a bomb.'

The boys exchanged puzzled glances. 'What stuff?' they asked together.

'Something you squirt from a can.'

'Oh, Spray Mount,' Martin said. 'It's only dangerous if you use it near a flame. That's why Pat stopped us using it in the kitchen.'

'Well get rid of it. Life's dangerous enough as it is.'

'We'll do it later,' they promised.

When she got to the office, Stiles was in a bad mood. 'I thought you were on afternoons this week,' he greeted her.

'I switched with Pauline,' she answered. 'I cleared it with George Conway when he was still news editor.'

Stiles was about to say something but changed his mind and just shrugged his displeasure as she went to her desk.

'What's got into him?' Sarah asked Mick Gates who was seated next to her.

'Search me,' he answered. 'He's already bollocked me for not putting in enough bills with my expenses.'

Sarah logged on to her computer terminal and called up her personal file to find out if there were any messages. There was one from George asking her to come and see him as soon as she got in.

She crossed the newsroom to his office and found him with his feet on the desk, whistling while he read a manila file. 'You're in a good mood,' she said. 'Does it have any connection with Stiles's foul temper?'

George swung his feet down and leaned across the desk. 'Look into my eyes,' he said.

Sarah did as instructed. 'Bloodshot – but swimming with the milk of human kindness.'

'They are the deepest blue,' he said blithely. 'I have it on the authority of Sir Robert Hall, no less – the status is official. I am his Blue-Eyed Boy.'

'When did all this happen?'

'Last night. When Simon Marr returned from his protracted discussions with that white trash he was associating with he found Sir Robert with me in Gordon's office. It seems Lady Hall had urged him to do something on rape.'

'Why?'

George held up his hands. 'Some charity she wants to get on that the Princess of Wales is involved with.'

'I would have thought he'd have had enough of good works,' Sarah replied. The paper had been mixed up in a charity scandal earlier in the year.

George continued. 'I was able to call up your story on the terminal before his very eyes. Sir Robert was delighted. He insisted it went into the paper last night.'

'What did Simon Marr say?'

'Simon was impressive. I have seldom seen a more astute piece of bum-crawling in all my years in the Street. He took credit for appointing me as assistant editor in charge of future planning and called in Stiles to tell him I was to handle all big stories in future – with total precedence in the use of staff.'

'That's wonderful news.'

George shook his head ruefully. 'There is a stone in every pair of new shoes,' he said. 'Marr has handed me this piece of nonsense.' He held up the file he had been reading. 'Hitler's last secret weapon. The chairman is keen on it as well: "A rattling good yarn," he called it. Marr wants you to go on working on the rape story and this nonsense at the same time. There's talk of you going to South America to interview Otto the Hun.'

Sarah sat down. 'Oh, no. It's Christmas next week, George. I wouldn't mind so much – but this is one of the gamiest wild-goose chases I've ever been sent on.'

'Relax,' George said. 'I'll stall it.'

'Promise?'

'The word of the Blue-Eyed Boy.'

'I spoke to Joe March about the Vickie Howard case last night,' Sarah said. 'He thinks they've got a good chance of catching the man.'

'Good,' George answered. 'Stick with it – that would be a proper Christmas present for everyone. Including Lady Hall.'

Sarah returned to her desk under the bitter stare of Stiles and saw that there was a blue envelope on top of her computer. There was no stamp on the envelope. Just her name, typed in capital letters.

She opened it, unfolded a heavy sheet of plain white paper, and felt a sudden chill in the overheated office. The paper was curious; thicker than was usual for letters. Then Sarah realised it had been cut from the flyleaf of a book. Written in large spidery capital letters were the words: ROMAN IS COMING FOR YOURS SOON. There was a scrawling arrow pointing to four hairs that were sealed beneath a short strip of transparent tape.

Sarah knew what they were – she took two clean sheets of paper and slid one under the envelope and letter. Placing the other on top she carried it to the news desk.

Stiles deliberately kept her waiting while he issued instructions to a secretary about expenses. It was an old technique of his; petulant but still irritating.'Yes,' he said eventually.

Sarah placed the sheets of paper on his desk and uncovered the letter.

'What's this?' he asked.

'It's from Vickie Howard's rapist. And I think those hairs are from his other victims.'

'They're short,' he said, then he looked closer. 'Unless he plucked them from their muffs.'

'Exactly, as you so elegantly put it,' Sarah said, unable to disguise the contempt she felt for him.

Stiles reached out to pick up the letter and a sharp voice said, 'Don't touch that.' It was George, who had come to the news desk and understood immediately what had happened. 'Fingerprints,' he added in softer tones.

'What shall we do with it?' Stiles asked.

Automatically, George took over. 'Call the police, the incident room run by Colin Greaves. Speak to him if you can; otherwise Sergeant Holland.' He turned to Sarah: 'Let Joe March know what's happened. He'll have to come into the bloody office now.' He called to the picture-desk assistant who sat nearby. 'Get this copied, but don't handle it, and the envelope.' Then to Stiles: 'Find out how this got on Sarah's desk. Then come and tell me in the editor's office.'

Sarah was on the telephone by now. George interrupted her: 'Follow me into Marr's office when you've made the call, and tell March to join us there if he can get here in the next half-hour,' he instructed.

It didn't take long for Sarah to contact Joe March on his mobile telephone. He told her he was in Camden Town and would be back in the office immediately.

Marr was intrigued when he was handed the photocopy of the letter. 'My God, what a great shot this will make,' he said. Up to that point he had seemed quite uninterested in what George was telling him. It was as if he could not connect too well with words, but a visual image brought the reality home to him.

'You're not thinking of using it, are you, Simon?' Gordon Brooks asked anxiously.

'Yes, of course,' Marr answered in surprise. 'It's all right to broadcast when the kids are in bed, don't you think?'

'But people get the *Gazette* in the mornings. Bit strong for a family newspaper, don't you think?' George added.

'Ahh,' Marr said, recollecting the medium in which he now worked.

'Obviously this Roman wants it printed,' George said. 'I'm not sure we should let him have what he wants.'

'Why has he signed it Roman?' Stiles asked. He had

entered the office accompanied by Wally Tate, the head of the building security department.

'It may be a reference to the rape of the Sabine women,' George answered. 'On the other hand it could really be his name.'

Stiles nodded as if he knew all about the history of Rome; then he introduced Wally Tate to Marr. Tate scratched his sparse strands of grey hair when Marr asked him how the letter got to Sarah.

'It just appeared on the reception desk in the morning rush,' he answered. 'The boys on the desk sent it up to the tape room and a messenger put it on Mrs Keane's desk.'

'Have everyone who handled it standing by, Wally,' George said. 'The police will want to fingerprint them for elimination.'

'I'll fix that now,' Tate said and he left them still studying the copy of the letter. A few minutes later Joe March was shown into the room, followed almost immediately by Colin Greaves and Detective-Sergeant Nick Holland. Holland's modern clothes and well-cut hair contrasted oddly with the appearance of March, who now stood beside him. His white shirt and cheap suit were immaculately pressed, but they looked as if they had been bought in the Fifties. He hadn't visited a fashionable hairdresser either; his closely trimmed hair had been attended by a barber of the short-back-and-sides school.

When they had all been shown the letter and told of the arrangements George had made with Wally Tate, Marr turned to Greaves.

'Will you put a police guard on Mrs Keane?' he asked.

Greaves shook his head. 'I don't think that will

be necessary,' he replied drily. 'Sarah's a sensible woman.'

'I would be happier if she had an escort at all times,' Marr said.

'I doubt if this threat will be carried out,' Greaves continued. 'Letters are usually just a way of showing off. I think the man wants publicity. When somebody is actually going to cause harm they usually act out of the blue.'

'But suppose the threat *is* genuine, Superintendent? Mrs Keane is one of the most valuable members of my staff.'

'She's pretty valuable to me as well,' Greaves replied.

March cleared his throat. 'She is connected with Saint Catherine's,' he said.

Greaves nodded. 'But she also wrote the piece in the paper this morning. Roman must know that it was about Vickie Howard, even though her real name wasn't mentioned. It's more likely to be a reaction to the article than the selection of a new victim.'

'But if it isn't?'

The two men studied each other for a moment.

'Then he'll have to come past me to get to her,' Greaves said softly.

'I think I have an opinion in this matter,' Sarah said, ending the silence that followed Greaves's last remark. 'I'm not going to have a bodyguard. My home is very well protected.' She turned to smile grimly at Greaves. 'After all, I've had the locks and other security measures vetted by an expert. As for the rest of the time – well, as Colin says, I'll take sensible precautions.'

*

Sarah walked with Colin from the building. At the front door, he said, 'I'll see you tonight at the school concert.'

'I didn't think you could make it.'

'More work than pleasure,' he answered. 'I'm coming along to warn the audience. I hope it doesn't put too much of a blight on the proceedings.'

'Better sad than dead,' Sarah answered firmly.

'I'm sure you're right,' he said sadly, and raised a hand before departing. Nick Holland waved as well and she watched them as they walked to the car together.

When Sarah returned to Marr's office, March had left, but Fanny Hunter was there and Peter Kirk. The atmosphere was strained. George sat in one of the chairs near Marr's desk, and when Sarah glanced at him he rolled his eyes upwards to inform her that more chaos was afoot.

Marr greeted her with enthusiasm, as if she had not been in his office just a few minutes before. 'I'm impressed by your sensible attitude to that other business,' he started briskly. 'Now let's get on with something that may prove to be a mite more important to all our futures. Fanny's come up with a great angle on the V weapons story,' he said enthusiastically. 'Why don't you tell it again,' he suggested.

Fanny was not happy to have to present her idea to Sarah but Sarah could also detect something unusual in her demeanour. She wants to please Marr, she told herself. It was a new departure for Fanny, who was accustomed to being treated with nervous deference by executives.

'Hitler was an astrology nut, wasn't he?' she began.

'So the history books tell us,' George said.

'So,' Fanny continued, 'let's get our astrologer to give her prediction on the likelihood of this catastrophe taking place.'

'Who is our astrologer?' Sarah asked. The byline on the daily column was just Delphi, with a woodcut of a single staring eye beneath.

'A woman you don't know called Cynthia Padgett,' Fanny snapped.

Marr held up a hand to interject. 'I've read the readers' research and she's one of the most popular features in the paper. It's a great angle to get her in on the story. The idea is that we get Mr Kirk here to interview her, as the science editor. So what do you think?'

Sarah side-stepped the question. 'What does Peter think?' she asked.

They now looked to the shambling figure of Kirk, who stood, hands plunged in his jacket pockets. He paused for quite a long time before speaking. 'When I joined the *Gazette*, some thirty-three years ago, I was given the undertaking that it was a serious news-paper. Indeed, the first editor I worked for gave me his word I would never be involved in anything I con-sider to be rubbish – but sadly, today, that agreement has been breached. I have no other course to take than to tender my resignation.'

'You're going to resign?' Marr asked incredulously.

'No, Mr Marr,' Kirk said stiffly. 'I am not going to resign. I *have* resigned. The matter is in the past tense.'

'Why?' Marr asked.

Peter Kirk smiled. 'Because astrology is pure non-sense,' he said quietly. He held up a hand as Fanny began to bridle. 'I don't think it does any actual harm to the weak-minded people who believe that the movement of the planets affects their daily lives; but I will not take part in any charade that is designed to persuade individuals that the world may be about to come to an end.'

Marr sat at his desk, his brow furrowed with concentration. Then he walked over and stood very close to Kirk. When he spoke his voice was steeped with sincerity. 'Believe me,' he began, 'I understand your reservations, Mr Kirk and I withdraw the request unreservedly. I have far too much regard for your integrity to ask you to do anything that would compromise your standing as a professional journalist.'

'Thank you,' Kirk replied, unsmiling. 'May I go now?'

'Certainly; and thank you for your frankness.'

Kirk left the office and Marr turned to the others. 'I still like the idea. I want you to do it, Fanny.'

'*Me*?' Fanny repeated. 'I'm not sure if it's an idea that's good for my column.'

Marr smiled. 'You're right, I was thinking of it as a separate article. But it can appear on your page – with Sarah's byline of course.'

'Sarah?' Fanny said uneasily. 'What's she got to do with my page?'

Marr turned to George. 'Didn't you say Sarah was your senior staff member on this story?' he asked.

George nodded.

'There you are,' Marr said. 'You'll be sharing your page with another star, Fanny.' As he finished speaking, the door opened after a hesitant knock and

180

Gordon Brooks looked into the room. A crowd of executives waited behind him. 'Are you ready to take conference, Simon?' he asked.

'Wheel them in,' Marr replied, then, 'There's no need for you to stay, Fanny, this story is far more important. Why don't you work out the details now?'

Sarah and Fanny left the room together and Fanny stalked off in the direction of her office without another word.

Sarah went to her desk and waited for George to emerge from the conference. She felt disquieted by the events in Marr's office: it was like taking part in a game where no one had explained the rules. Something was going on that she did not yet understand; but she was determined to find out. Marr seemed to be manipulating the situation to his own satisfaction; she just wondered which side he was on.

When she saw the other executives returning to their desks, she looked for George. He followed some minutes later, gesturing for her to come to his office.

'What's going on?' she asked when they sat together.

George passed her a plastic-covered report. 'Look at page twenty-eight,' he said.

Sarah flipped open the file and saw that it was a market research document. After a moment's study she looked up. 'Fanny's ratings have dropped,' she said.

'Plunged,' George replied. 'She's down to 29 per cent in reader interest.'

'That's still a lot of people.'

'Not enough,' George said. 'Columns like Fanny's have to be up in the high eighties with women and the sixties with men. Fanny has about the same value to the newspaper as the gardening column at the moment.'

'Does she know this?'

George nodded. 'That's why she was trying to please Marr with that astrology pitch. She's got the wind up.'

'So that explains Marr's indifference.'

'Correct. Now look at page forty-two.'

Sarah saw a column of names with figures beside them. 'You're going to have to explain this to me,' she said. 'I fail to see the significance.'

'The significance is very simple,' George answered. 'The percentage figures next to the name give a recognition rating among the readers. Yours comes out very high.'

'But what does it mean?'

'They show your name to the readers on a card and ask them if they recognise it.'

'And?'

'A high rating means a high recognition. The theory is that readers remember what you write.'

Sarah looked at the introduction to the document. 'This research took place at the end of October,' she said.

'That's right.'

'But that's when I was doing the pop-star's wife-swap story,' she explained. 'Everyone was reading that.'

George took back the document with a smile. 'Don't look a gift horse in the mouth,' he replied. 'Marr doesn't know that. He just thinks Fanny's on the skids and your star's in the ascendant. Everybody loves a winner.'

'But Fanny could walk into any other newspaper in Fleet Street. They're always making her offers.'

182

George considered her words. 'If the news gets around that Fanny is box-office poison, they won't be so keen; that's the way of the world.'

'So what's Marr up to?'

George laced his hands behind his head. 'I'd say he was trying to destabilise her.'

'Why?'

'If Fanny is really on the way down, it's a problem. To pay her off would cost a fortune and you know the management won't spend a penny they can avoid at the moment. Marr's trying to get her to resign. Then he won't have to pay up her contract.'

'But they're contemplating buying this trash from Maclean for a quarter of a million pounds – what will the management make of that?'

'And it will cost another quarter of a million to advertise it on television,' George added. 'But if it's a hit series it should put maybe a couple of hundred thousand on the circulation.'

'That won't last long. You know those sort of circulation figures fade away after a few weeks.'

'Yes,' George said. 'But the circulation department can spread the gain over six months and make it look good for the industry figures. The *Gazette* is desperate to keep over one and a half million – otherwise the advertisers will demand a lower page rate and the management can't afford that at the moment. The City isn't too pleased with LOC PLC's performance and our chairman knows Miller will step in if things get any worse. The share price is a bit like the economy of the country. If the financial gnomes don't like it, down it goes, and out goes Sir Robert.'

Sarah put a hand to her forehead. 'I'm just a simple

reporter, George. What on earth am I supposed to do? Just tell me what to get on with, I'd prefer to leave all the high policy decisions to those who enjoy that sort of thing.'

The telephone rang and George answered. 'Right,' he said and hung up.

'Marr wants you again.'

'Oh dear, do I have to?'

He smiled. 'Just get on with it.'

Marr was pacing his office, dictating to his secretary. He paused when she entered. 'I've just had an outraged call from Cynthia Padgett, the astrologer,' he said. 'She didn't hit it off with Fanny.'

'But I thought Fanny didn't want to do the story,' Sarah said, now thoroughly bewildered.

'She must have changed her mind. Anyway it seems she acted in a very high-handed way with Ms Padgett. She was talking of resigning as well. I've told her you'll meet her at her flat in Charles Street and take her to Wilton's restaurant for lunch at one o'clock. We've booked the table and my car is waiting downstairs. For God's sake sort this out, Sarah. I don't want the astrologer to resign as well. She's *really* valuable to our ratings.'

Chapter Eleven

Alf Thomas dropped Sarah outside the house on the corner of Charles Street in Mayfair and told her he would wait in the vicinity. 'Give me a ring on the car phone and I'll pick you up here when you're ready to go to lunch,' he told her. Sarah entered the building and looked around the hallway. At some time in the distant past it had been a private house; but it had long since been divided into flats. She took an open-cage lift that creaked to the gloomy landing on the third floor and rang the doorbell. After a few minutes the door opened and a figure stood silhouetted against the light. 'Cynthia Padgett?' Sarah asked.

There was a pause before a light voice said, 'My God, Sarah Linton. Come in.'

She entered, puzzled by the recognition and still studying the figure whose face was revealed in greater clarity when they stood in the small hallway. Gradually the fine-boned features and long blonde hair were replaced by another image of a plump-faced schoolgirl with large spectacles who had shared her dormitory in her last years at the convent.

'Cynthia Lewis,' Sarah said finally.

'I'm glad it took you so long to realise it was me,'

the woman laughed, leading her into a large room that was decorated in some splendour. Sarah could tell the antique furniture was the real thing; and the rugs and pictures were equally impressive.

'I had no idea you were the *Gazette*'s astrologer,' Sarah said. 'The last I heard you'd married and gone to live somewhere in Africa. Didn't your husband have some grand job with the government out there?'

'That's right,' Cynthia replied. 'Nigeria. Then they sacked my husband and he divorced me.'

'Oh, Cynthia, I am sorry.'

'Don't be,' she replied. 'I didn't know how much I disliked him until we actually lived together.' She gestured for Sarah to sit beside her on a sofa. 'Didn't you marry someone glamorous?' she continued.

'Jack Keane, he was in television – he was killed . . .' Sarah paused for a moment. 'That was a couple of years ago.'

Cynthia reached out sympathetically and took her hand. 'I'm sorry,' she said.

'It's all right now. And . . . well, I've met someone else.'

'Who?'

'A policeman.'

'A policeman?' she repeated. 'Does he drive about in a car or is he still pounding the beat?'

'He's a superintendent at Scotland Yard.'

'How exciting.'

Just then Sarah became aware of a very thin, rather elegant young man, with skin the colour of polished ebony, who was standing before them. So silent had been his arrival, it was as if he had materialised in the room. Cynthia looked up.

186

'Can I get you anything?' he asked gravely. His voice was as English and as cultivated as a well-mown lawn.

'Sarah this is Prince Charles Mananluba, my secretary.'

Sarah wasn't sure whether to stay sitting and shake hands or rise and curtsy.

'Call me Chas,' Prince Mananluba said with a dazzling smile and he took her hand in his own. It was slender and as delicate as a bird's wing.

Cynthia looked at her watch. 'It's past twelve. Shall we all have a real drink?'

Sarah suddenly realised that for Cynthia it wouldn't be the first of the morning. Without waiting for her answer, Chas left the room and returned immediately with a bottle of champagne on a silver tray.

'So how did you become an astrologer?' Sarah asked when the glasses were filled.

'Your story first,' Cynthia said.

Sarah shrugged. 'When Jack was killed, I had to go back to work. I got a job on the *Gazette*. I'd worked there when I was first married.'

'Do you have any children?' Chas asked.

'Twin boys and a girl – how about you, Cynthia?'

Cynthia shook her head. 'No children.'

'So how did you come to work for the paper?' Sarah asked.

'Chas fixed it for me.'

Sarah looked questioningly at him and he waved a deprecating hand. 'It wasn't very hard. LOC PLC owed my family a favour. We were of some use to them in obtaining certain mining rights in my country. I had a word with Sir Robert Hall.'

Sarah turned to Cynthia again. 'But how did you learn to write an astrology column?' Cynthia waved her glass in the direction of Chas again. 'He knew someone. I had to take lessons, you know. I don't just make it all up.'

'Do you believe it?'

'I believe it gets me all this,' Cynthia said smiling. 'My column is syndicated all over America and the Far East.'

'And Europe,' Chas added. 'I haven't told you yet, the Germans and the French chain want it now.'

Cynthia patted Sarah's hand. 'You see – no wonder they advertise me as the star of stars. Now, tell me what all this is about. That dreadful creature Fanny Hunter rang me this morning and began to talk to me as if I were a coolie on her father's estate. She practically demanded I comply with her wishes or she would have me fired. It took me a few minutes to explain to her that the *Gazette* has a contract with me, not the other way round.'

'And very valuable to us you are, Cynthia,' Sarah said quickly. 'That's why the editor told me to come here and smooth things out.'

'So what is it he wants?'

Sarah sat back and took a deep breath. 'There's a man who claims the Germans had a last secret weapon at the end of the war that is going to destroy England quite soon. They want you to look into the stars and see if there's any catastrophe looming that could confirm his story.'

Cynthia sighed. 'Oh, I don't think I shall become involved in that one, darling. If the world ends it won't matter; and people tend to remember if you get

188

those major predictions wrong.' She smiled. 'Still, it did bring us together again. Let's go and have a lovely lunch and then you can go back and tell him that you've talked me into staying with the *Gazette* after long and difficult negotiations.'

They finished the champagne and Sarah rang the office car.

Alf dropped them at the restaurant just off Piccadilly and they were soon at their table, where Chas ordered more champagne. Before they had a chance to drink any he suddenly rose. 'I spy an old school chum,' he said. 'Will you excuse me for a few minutes?'

Sarah and Cynthia gossiped for a time about school-days and then Cynthia paused and said, 'Whatever else happened, Sister Veronica would be proud of your manners.'

'What do you mean?' Sarah replied.

'Chas, of course. You haven't mentioned him. Surely you're dying to ask?'

Sarah could not deny her interest. She waited in silence. But before Cynthia could answer her own question, a waiter came to the table. 'There's a gentleman asking for you Mrs Keane,' he said. And then Sarah saw March standing behind him.

'Hello, ' she said. 'Won't you join us?'

March took a seat and Sarah said, 'Cynthia Padgett, this is Joseph March.'

'Is this your policeman?' Cynthia asked. 'What a delightful surprise, I'm so glad to meet you.'

'No,' Sarah said, 'this is a colleague.'

Cynthia raised her eyebrows as Chas returned to the table. Further introductions were made and March leaned forward and said, 'I thought you'd want to know:

they've got the real name of the man who sent you the letter.'

'That was fast,' Sarah replied.

'He'd left his fingerprints on it, and he's got form. I think you may know him.'

'Who?'

'Anthony Dale.'

Sarah shook her head. 'I've never heard of anyone by that name.'

'Are you sure?' March asked. 'He works in the *Gazette* building. He's one of the commissionaires.'

Immediately the face of the young man in the pub came to her. 'I think I know who you mean,' she said. 'But I didn't know his name. He's been charged with rape before?'

'And stealing cars and assault,' March said.

'Have they arrested him?'

'No, he didn't come to work today and there's no sign of him at his address. It looks as if he's skipped off.'

'Have they got a positive identification from Vickie Howard?'

'She and her boyfriend are away somewhere – out of touch. But it's just a formality, the hairs match those of the other victims.'

Sarah smiled 'I'm glad for Vickie Howard. Maybe she won't have to go through an ordeal in court now.'

March nodded. 'I'm going to the pub where they perform tomorrow night, they're expected back by then. There may be some copy in her reaction.'

'They have a photograph of Dale?'

'They will have. The security department at the *Gazette* keeps one,' March replied.

190

'Well that's a relief.'

'It isn't over yet. They haven't actually caught him. You could still be in danger. Keep your guard up.'

'May I come with you tomorrow night?' Sarah asked.

'If you want to.'

Cynthia and Chas had been listening to them with fascination.

'Won't you explain all this mystery over lunch,' Cynthia coaxed. 'I would be delighted if you'd be our guest.'

March hesitated, as always when he was offered something that might be misconstrued as a bribe. A waiter placed a menu in his hands and he glanced down for a moment before exclaiming: 'How much for fish and chips? – you must be bloody mad to pay these prices.'

When Sarah returned to the *Gazette* after lunch, she found a scene of chaotic disorder. Cables snaked through the corridor approaching Marr's office and as she got closer there were groups of casually dressed, unfamiliar figures lounging around in a bored group while others arranged lights. Marr sat at the centre of it all, casually reclining in his swivel chair, listening to the director, Barrie Loam describe what he was hoping for in the scene he was about to shoot. A make-up girl dabbed at Marr's forehead, unconcerned by the figures who swarmed about them.

'Sarah,' Marr called out. 'How did you get on?'

'The police think that the rapist is one of the *Gazette*'s commissionaires. They're looking for him now.'

'Good, good,' Marr said without any real interest. 'But what about Cynthia Padgett?'

She stepped between the lights and cables and stood before him. 'The good news is: Cynthia will not resign. The bad news is: she won't do any sort of predictions about the Apocalypse.'

'Damn,' Marr said after a moment's reflection. 'That was a good angle.' He spun round to the director. 'How about getting Sarah in this shot, Barrie? Showing me something she's written. Then the others can come in and we can start conference.'

'But I haven't written anything,' Sarah said, starting to back away.

'They won't know that,' Marr said. 'There'll be no dialogue, we can do a voice-over later.'

'Could work,' Loam said, framing Sarah's face with his hands. She looked about her for a way of escape and saw Gordon Brooks signalling frantically from the doorway. Stepping back through the tangled cables she approached him.

'You'll have to stop him doing this,' Brooks hissed.

'Doing what?'

'He's called all the executives in to be filmed holding a phoney conference,' Brooks said in despair. 'If we do that the real newspaper will grind to a halt and the edition will be hours late.'

'Why don't you tell him?' Sarah said.

'I can't talk to the man,' Brooks said despairingly. 'He's started to call me sweetie. Every time I point out something important that must be done, he just says "That'll be all right, sweetie." ' Brooks seized hold of her arm. 'You tell him, Sarah. Tell him if he goes ahead with this the whole production is imperilled.'

Sarah thought for a moment. 'Why don't you get all

the deputies to prepare for the actual conference and then the department heads can take part in the phoney conference without causing any problems.'

Brooks stopped and looked at her as if she had just solved the riddle of the Sphinx. 'Why didn't I think of that?' he said finally. 'This man is turning my brains to garden compost.' He walked away shaking his head and Sarah returned to Marr's side.

'Just stand there and lean forward as if you're pointing something out to Simon in the piece of paper on his desk,' Loam instructed.

'How long will this take?' Sarah asked.

'Not long,' Loam replied. Then he went to the camera. 'How does it look?' he asked.

'Crappy,' replied the cameraman. 'We lit it without her. The shadow's falling on Simon's face now – he looks like the Invisible Man.'

'What?' Marr said, alarmed.

'Take it easy,' Loam said. 'We'll relight the shot.'

'Her hair looks wrong now,' the cameraman said when they had stood for ten minutes.

'Trixie!' Loam shouted. 'Fix her hair.'

An hour and a half later Sarah emerged from the office, having only completed a few minutes of actual filming, to find all of the senior executives standing in a grumbling mob; but she could not see George Conway among them.

As she expected, George was in his little office, reading a book entitled *Lives of the Great Philosophers*.

'You're beginning to like it in here, aren't you?' she said when he looked up.

'Did you know there was a Greek philosopher who lived in a barrel,' he answered cheerfully. 'Who am I to complain? I sit here with my magic machine and all the information in the world comes to me.'

'There's two pieces of information you don't know,' she said.

'Tell me the most interesting first,' he demanded.

'It turns out I was at school with the *Gazette*'s astrologer.'

'Incredible,' he replied with mock astonishment. 'Here I was reading about Jung's theory of synchronicity and you come and tell me that.'

'What's Jung's theory of synchronicity?'

George lifted the book. 'In plain English, some coincidences are so extraordinary they're almost spooky.'

'Are you ready for my second piece of information?' Sarah asked.

He nodded.

'The police are looking for one of our commissionaires – they believe he's the one who raped Vickie Howard.'

For once in their long association, George looked startled by a piece of news. 'You're kidding?' he said quickly.

Sarah shook her head. 'Joe March got it from the police, name of Anthony Dale. His fingerprints were on the letter to me, and the hair matches the victims'.'

George looked thoughtful. 'He seems to have got very sloppy. Who's writing the story?'

'Joe March and me. At least, I will eventually. I'd only just got back when I was kidnapped by Marr to take part in his bloody film.'

George laughed. 'This place is becoming unravelled. Has he told the chairman yet?'

'I don't know.'

George sat with his hands together as if praying. 'Well, all we can do at the moment is a piece saying the police are seeking a Mr Anthony Dale, employed as a commissionaire by the *Gazette*, to help in their inquiries – but we'd better tell Sir Robert all the same.' He reached for the telephone and dialled Marr's number.

'He's not taking any calls at the moment,' the secretary said. 'The cameras are on in his office.'

'This is absolute priority,' George said. 'I'll take responsibility.'

There was a click and Marr came on the line. 'What is it, George,' he said in a terse voice. 'You've just ruined a shot.'

'Sarah tells me that the police are seeking one of our employees for murder and rape,' George replied. 'I think the chairman should know.'

'You tell him,' Marr said without interest and hung up.

Sarah had listened to the conversation and was perplexed by Marr's reaction. 'Do you think he's mad?' she asked. 'That sounds as if he has a career death wish.'

George shook his head. 'No, he just has the most acute case of self-obsession I've ever encountered. Whatever he's doing personally is to him the centre of the universe. Sir Robert suffers from it as well, maybe that's what attracted him to Marr in the first place.'

He picked up the telephone again and called Sir Robert's office. After a few minutes' conversation with a secretary and then a personal assistant, George was told to come up, with Sarah, to the executive suite. They emerged from the lift on the top floor where the atmosphere was very different. Plusher carpets led through a sequence of tinted glass doors past potted plants and black leather sofas to the chairman's domain.

When they entered his office, they had to look up at Sir Robert, who was standing behind a beautiful model of a cluster of glass towers, like Gulliver visiting a Lilliput of the future. Sarah was puzzled but as they drew closer she realised that he was standing on a little set of steps.

It was well known that the chairman was sensitive about his height.

'What's all this about somebody on the staff being murdered, Conway?' he asked.

'You have been given incorrect information, Sir Robert,' George answered crisply. 'The police think someone in our employment is the murderer.'

The chairman looked baffled. 'Who employed a murderer? I want them fired,' he said.

'It's not one of the editorial staff,' George continued. 'The man they're looking for is a commissionaire.'

Sir Robert descended the steps, paced across the office and turned. 'This could be bad for the image of the company,' he said almost to himself. Then he looked towards them. 'Can we keep it out of the paper?'

George pretended to think about the question. 'We *could* keep it out of the *Gazette*,' he said slowly, 'but not the rest of Fleet Street.'

Sir Robert sighed suddenly and sat down in an armchair, where he looked smaller than ever. 'Come and sit down,' he said in almost a friendly voice. Sarah and George did so and Sir Robert rested his chin in a cupped hand. 'Fleet Street isn't the same any more,'

196

he said sadly. 'Once upon a time it was a gentleman's club. Owners could ring each other up and decide what should be printed in the best interests of the nation.' He looked towards the glass towers again. 'It's just dog eat dog now.'

'I think there's a way we can handle the story so that the company is seen in the best possible light, Sir Robert,' George said.

'You do?' he replied. 'What do you suggest?'

George gestured towards Sarah. 'Mrs Keane has worked on the story. Because of the piece she wrote that we ran this morning, the murderer has threatened her life. I think that represents a victory for the *Gazette*. If it hadn't been for your intervention, the story wouldn't have gone into the paper and the murderer wouldn't have been discovered.'

'That's true,' Sir Robert said with sudden spirit. 'In fact you could say we flushed out the murderer by my far-sighted actions.'

'Exactly.'

Sir Robert bounded from his chair and paced about. 'I like this development,' he said with greater confidence. Then he turned to them again. 'Why didn't Mr Marr come and tell me about this, he's the editor? It's his duty to keep me informed. If he's not up to the job he can be replaced, you know.'

'He wanted to,' George said quickly, 'but he's up to his eyes with the V weapon story. Frankly, I've never seen a man so dedicated to his work.'

'That's why I picked him,' Sir Robert said in another mood change. 'This paper needed some energy pumped into it.'

'He certainly has energy,' George agreed.

'I'm glad you took the responsibility of keeping me informed, Conway,' Sir Robert said with even greater friendliness. 'I shall look to you in the future as a man who can keep me up with developments in the editorial department. Mr Marr is under a lot of pressure and he won't always have time. You can prove a loyal colleague by telling me all the little things you think I should know.'

'I shall consider it a pleasure as well as a duty,' George answered with a deferential nod.

Chapter Twelve

While they waited for the lift, George hummed a little tune. Sarah could restrain her curiosity no longer.

'Why did you –' she began, but George interrupted her with an explosive fit of coughing. Once in the lift, he smiled. 'Best not to have private conversations up there,' he said, pressing the button.

Sarah looked at him carefully. 'Are you saying the place is bugged?' she asked. 'Surely things aren't that bad?' Then she noticed they were going up.

'Come on to the roof,' George said. 'Only the pigeons will be interested in us up there.'

They made their way on to the asphalt-covered surface and stood by a parapet that overlooked Gray's Inn Road. It was just getting dark and a blustery wind was blowing dark clouds towards the east.

'Why did you protect Marr?' Sarah asked eventually.

'That was only part of it,' George replied. 'Actually I was enrolling myself in Sir Robert's secret service.'

'Why?'

George looked towards the south. 'Because this lot are destroying the newspaper,' he said. 'It's time we had a new owner.'

'I thought you considered all forms of management a curse.'

George smiled. 'It's a bit like marriage: if you've got to have a wife, you might as well try to get a good one.'

'So what are you up to?'

George looked at her closely. 'If Sir Robert and Simon Marr are allowed to continue in their present manner, they will eventually engineer a cock-up of such monumental proportions, the present management will have to sell the company.'

'So you're going to double-cross them?' Sarah asked. 'Isn't that dangerous?'

'I'm not going to double-cross them,' George said. 'The way to deal with these fools is to carry out every demand they make to the letter. I intend to be the most loyal member of the staff.'

Sarah returned to the chaos of the newsroom. Barrie Loam had moved his camera there to shoot more film and could clearly not understand that people were performing actual functions rather than acting out a charade for nis benefit. Eventually she logged off duty and drove home. Pat was preparing supper wearing her 'best outfit' when she entered the house. She was going with Sarah to the school concert.

'It said on the TV that they know who did them murders,' Pat called out, while Sarah petted the dog in the hallway.

'I know him as well,' Sarah answered when she came into the kitchen.

'You do?'

'He works at the *Gazette*.'

'Blimey,' Pat said. 'They didn't mention that on TV.'

'Read about it in the papers tomorrow,' Sarah answered as she hurried upstairs to change.

When she came down again half an hour later, Pat had her coat on and was standing ready in the hallway. 'The supper's in the oven, I've taken Sam next door, and it's raining cats and dogs again.'

'Oh damn,' said Sarah. 'I've left the car in the road. There's no point in us both getting wet. Wait in the porch and I'll reverse into the drive.' She took an umbrella from the coat stand and went out to face the weather. Rain pounded down on the empty street and made a rushing stream in the gutters. When she reached her car, she fumbled with her keys and dropped them on the pavement. It was pitch dark when she crouched down so it took nearly a minute to find them next to the nearside wheel.

As she was about to straighten up she thought she saw something move in the dark shadows under the high box hedge that separated her garden from the neighbouring house. While she watched, there was the same flickering effect again. Sarah quickly got into the car and drove into the paved area so that her headlights played over the place where she had seen the movement, but there was nothing there.

Pat hurried from the house and got into the passenger seat. 'What a night,' she said as she fussed with her seat-belt. 'It's not fit for man nor beast.'

Man or beast, Sarah reflected as she drove away, what had she seen in the shadows? She dropped Pat at the school gates while she searched the adjoining roads for a parking space. It took some time and the walk back was further than she expected. Eventually she emerged from the network of side streets on to the main road and began to trudge up the hill to the school while cars swished past. There were no other pedestrians in sight. A car slowed down beside her and started to crawl along. She felt a mounting sense of panic and quickened her step, but the car matched her stride. For a moment she felt overwhelmed with fear and the sensation seemed to ebb her strength. Choking anxiety drove the power to reason from her; all she could think of was where she could run to hide.

Then her fear receded. Instead she suddenly felt angry, a cold rage that brought back her ability to think clearly. There were lights in the large houses she passed; she decided to enter the next one with an open driveway, determined to draw attention to her plight even if she had to break a window.

A voice called from the car: 'Sarah, it's me, Joe March.'

Sarah looked towards the car with a flood of relief that matched the pouring rain.

'I didn't mean to alarm you,' he said when she got into the car, 'but I wasn't absolutely sure it was you.'

It was an office car and Alf Thomas was driving. He smiled but didn't speak.

'That's all right,' she answered, still light-headed from the panic. 'Hello Alf. My children will be impressed by a chauffeur-driven car.'

'Parking's bad around here, folks,' Alf said when they arrived at the school and he peered out into the wet darkness.

'I'm not going to be long,' March answered, glancing at his watch. 'Hang about.'

'Just as long as I'm not nicked for kerb-crawling,' Alf said.

'Aren't you staying for the concert?' Sarah asked when they got out.

March shook his head. 'I just wanted to hear Greaves speak. Once he's said his piece, I'll be off.'

The concert was taking place in a new hall located in the extensive grounds at the rear of the original house, where other school buildings had been erected over the years. They walked along a pathway with other groups of adults, guided by signs that led past tennis courts to a large modern building that housed the gymnasium and also the school theatre. In the brightly lit lobby groups of staff greeted parents while sixth-formers acted as ushers for the more illustrious guests who had been allocated seats closest to the stage. Colin Greaves had already arrived. He stood to one side of the entrance hall and nodded to March and Sarah when they all stood together.

Father Robson spotted them and came over; he looked suddenly worried by the group.

'I'll say a few words and then introduce you, Super-intendent. I have a place for you in the front row.' He turned to Sarah and March with a deep frown of embarrassment, 'But I'm afraid all the other seats are taken. You could have had mine, Mrs Keane, but Councillor Hemdale brought a last-minute addition to his party and I've already given it up.'

Sarah smiled at his concern. 'I'm sitting with a friend elsewhere, Father,' she said quickly. 'Mr March and I didn't come together, we met by coincidence, and he's leaving after Colin speaks.'

'I won't need a seat in any case, Father,' Greaves added. 'I won't be able to stay for the music.'

'So I'm promoted to the front row again,' he said cheerfully. Seeing something else that needed his attention he excused himself but made it clear he would collect Greaves before the beginning of the concert. He edged back into the throng.

'How's the search for Anthony Dale going?' Sarah asked Colin.

Greaves spoke so quietly that his lips hardly seemed to move. 'He was due off for a long weekend, so he wasn't at work. We've searched his flat. Nothing interesting. Vickie Howard said he was interested in the theatre; he may have done amateur dramatics, belonged to a theatre club perhaps, something like that, we're checking.' He glanced away for a moment and then looked back at her. 'Do you remember anything special about him?'

Sarah thought before she answered. 'I saw him recently in a pub near the office. The Royal William. Maybe he's a regular in there.'

'Was there anything else, anything that struck you about him?'

'He looked very fit, as if he were in training for some kind of athletic event.'

'Like a runner?'

'No, not a runner; but there was something about his stance. More like a gym instructor: chest out, almost standing on the balls of his feet.'

The ushers began to ask people to take their seats. March moved away to the back of the hall, saying, 'I'll call you tomorrow morning about going to see Vickie Howard.'

204

Sarah thanked him and went to find Pat. She was in the third row, on the aisle, patting the empty seat beside her and offering Sarah a mint.

There was the usual shuffling and scraping of chairs until Father Robson walked down the centre aisle accompanied by Greaves. The audience watched with interest, and a ripple of muttered comment passed through the hall.

They stood before the closed curtain and Father Robson held up his hand for silence. 'Good evening, ladies, gentlemen, and distinguished guests,' he began, with a nod towards the grandees in the front row. 'Welcome to our annual concert and carol service. This, of course, is a joyous event, celebrating as it does one of the highlights in the Christian calendar. The birth of our Lord Jesus Christ. But before we begin, we have a sad duty to perform. As you all may know by now, a series of terrible attacks have been made on women connected with our school.'

There was a murmur throughout the hall, and Father Robson held up a hand. 'I must tell you that the police are hopeful that the man responsible may soon be apprehended; but there is still danger. And until he is in police custody, we must all take special care. Superintendent Greaves of Scotland Yard is here with us tonight, to say a few words, and I am sure you will give him your deepest attention. Thank you.' He turned: 'Chief Inspector . . .'

Sarah thought that Greaves looked almost frail next to the robust figure of Father Robson. Knowing he did not care for public speaking, she wondered how difficult this must be for him. But he was matter-of-fact in his delivery, having long ago taught himself a technique to deal with audiences.

'I'm sorry to bring such a terrible matter to your notice on an occasion that Father Robson described rightly as a joyous event,' he began. 'But I want to talk to you ladies in the audience now.' There was absolute silence while he paused. 'All the attacks that have taken place have happened to women in their own homes, in the place where they should have felt most safe. It was there that they proved to be most vulnerable. All of you must have said to your children: "Be home before dark." This man attacks at twilight, the time when home seems at its most welcoming. Somehow he persuaded women just like you to allow him over their thresholds.' Greaves paused again and looked into the hall. He caught Sarah's gaze for a moment, then went on: 'I have come here to ask you to be more vigilant until we have caught this man. Please do not take your safety for granted. Remember – each attack has taken place just before nightfall.' He stopped again to let his words sink in and the silence continued. A chair scrape seemed to echo around the hall, as Greaves started again. 'Once more, I urge you to be alert. The man we seek may be familiar to you – someone you have trusted in the past. Maybe even someone you thought of as a friend. Please heed my warning – it could save your life.'

He stopped and turned to Father Robson, who stood head bowed at the side of the stage.

'Thank you for letting me speak this evening. I hope you enjoy the rest of the evening, and Happy Christmas to you and your families.' Greaves gave a brief nod to the audience, then left the stage and walked from the hall.

When the door had closed behind him, the curtain drew back and the school orchestra began their first piece. Sarah spotted her own children immediately. Like all the others, they seemed the epitome of innocence in the aftermath of Greaves's grim speech. Gradually the soaring young voices caused her to feel a glow of pleasure; the music seemed to cause the harsh warnings to fade from her mind. There was something deeply touching about the earnest efforts of the young people. Sarah had a good ear for music. If the orchestra was less than professional, the choir excelled. The young voices, pure as silver, rang through the echoing hall, soothing everyone with the familiar carols. Suddenly Sarah felt that Christmas was truly near. Memories of her own childhood flooded back. A time of innocence, when the tribulations of adulthood were unimaginable shadows of the future.

The last carol, 'Silent Night,' moved her to tears. Then something wonderful happened: a memory of her mother came to her so vividly that when she closed her eyes she could see her face with perfect clarity; and finally, a sense of total peace came to Sarah.

She waited for the boys in the entrance hall. It was a cheerful time: she recollected her own days of breaking up from school, when friends had parted from each other for the holidays. Farewells were called out and hugs exchanged. Emily stopped with Ric to tell her they were going for one of their inevitable pizzas. The boys were clustered with another group. Martin broke away and pulled her over to introduce Mr Harris.

'Emma's asked us all to go to a pantomime tomorrow evening. Is that all right?' he said.

Sarah looked towards Mr Harris, a pleasant young man with prematurely grey hair. 'We took a block booking,' he explained. 'The boys will be very welcome.'

'Thank you,' Sarah answered. 'I hope they're not too boisterous for you.'

'They seem strangely quiet around the girls,' Harris replied with a grin. 'I've only got daughters, so a bit of masculine company will make a change. Come and meet my wife,' he added. Sarah joined the group and met Mr and Mrs Phillips as well. The objects of her sons' desires were both mischievous-looking girls with a strikingly similar appearance, pale freckled complexions, snub noses and the sort of curly, red hair that Sarah always associated with the Scots.

'Maybe it's genetic,' Mrs Harris said with a laugh as the children moved away to mingle with another group. 'It's the nearest thing to twins being attracted to twins that I've ever seen.'

'Are the girls related?' Sarah asked.

'Cousins,' Mrs Phillips answered. She nodded to Mrs Harris. 'We're sisters, they both take after our grandfather – at least that's where the red hair comes from.'

They talked for a few more minutes and then separated to make for their cars. The rain had eased so Sarah led them to the place far down the hill, where she had parked. 'We might just as well have walked home,' Paul said when they finally climbed aboard.

Chapter Thirteen

8.05 a.m. Saturday, 18 December

Joe March rang the following morning, earlier than Sarah expected. It was barely light. Greaves, still sleeping beside her, stirred uneasily as she snatched the telephone. March said he would meet her at seven o'clock that evening at the pub in Barnes where Vickie Howard would be performing. When she hung up, Greaves held up his wrist to check the time.

'Hello, stranger,' she said, laying her head in the crook of his arm. 'Sorry to wake you up.'

'Was I asleep?' he said. 'I didn't think it was allowed.'

'Do you want coffee or will you rest for a while?'

'Coffee, I think,' Greaves answered. 'I ought to get up.'

'Have you got much to do?'

He thought for a moment, then spoke with slight surprise. 'Nothing really, the wheels are all in motion. I'm a bit like the First World War general now. The battle's started. I just wait back at the château until it's over.'

'You've got nothing to do?' Sarah asked, rolling closer to him.

'Not until this afternoon. I said I'd watch the boys

play rugby. Do you want me to come shopping with you?'

'Not until later,' Sarah replied. 'Just imagine I'm Mimi, the girl who comforts the general.'

When Sarah eventually left the bedroom, the dog was glad to see her. They made for the kitchen together; but as usual he was reluctant to enter the cold wet garden when she opened the door and ordered him out. Sarah stood at the window while the kettle boiled, and watched him sniffing his way across the lawn, his golden coat showing clearly against the rough winter grass.

Poor fellow, Sarah thought, you've been a bit left out of things lately. She promised him a long walk later in the day.

When she took Greaves's coffee to the bedroom, he had fallen asleep again, hands clasped on his chest. He looks so sad, even now, she thought, like some melancholy knight resting on his tomb; his long patrician features formed by old sorrows. Although he had known all of the advantages wealth could bring, Greaves had endured more than his share of pain in life. His first wife had divorced him after their children had died in a boating accident, blaming him for caring more for his work than his family. Sarah knew that he still thought there was an element of truth in the accusation, and it was a burden he would carry for the rest of his life.

She closed the door softly and returned to the kitchen. When she let the dog back into the house he barked and scrabbled at the door to the hallway. Sarah guessed it was the paper boy, whom he always saw as a challenge to his territory. Because the morning papers were heavier on Saturdays, it was the boy's custom to leave them on the doorstep. After a few sips of coffee, Sarah walked to the front door. When she opened it, the boy was just taking the papers out of his canvas bag. He said good-morning as he handed her the thick bundle, then he reached down and picked up a blue envelope without a stamp that was on the marble floor of the porch and handed it to her.

Sarah recognised the handwriting. 'I'm sorry, I don't know your name,' she said to the boy who now peered at her from beneath the wide rim of a baseball cap.

'Clive Winter.'

'Will you come into the house, Clive?' she said, as she glanced into the roadway. He looked uncertainly at her. 'Please,' she said quickly. 'It's important.'

The boy stepped into the hall.

'Just a minute,' Sarah said and she raced upstairs to where Greaves still slept. It took a few moments for him to gather his wits when Sarah handed him the envelope, then he reached for the telephone on his side of the bed. 'Keep the boy downstairs,' he said as he dialled. 'I'll be there in a moment.'

Sarah returned to the hallway, where Clive Winter was standing in some confusion. 'I need your help, Clive,' she said gently. She could see that the lad was disturbed by her anxiety. 'Will you wait here for a little while?'

'I'll lose my job if I'm late with my other papers,' he said.

'Don't worry,' she replied soothingly. 'I'll ring the newsagent. Everything will be all right.' Sarah went to the extension in the hallway and called the number she obtained from Directory Enquiries. The newsagent sounded agitated when she explained that it was necessary for her to delay Clive Winter.

'It really is important that he stays here, Mr Patel,' she said. 'Don't worry, I'll get my sons to finish his round.'

Clive Winter was looking thoroughly disconcerted by now, but he was reassured when he saw the boys once Sarah had routed them out of bed.

'Hello, Winter,' Martin said, when he came down. 'I didn't know you delivered our papers. How much do you get?'

'A tenner a week,' the boy answered.

'You know each other?' Sarah said.

'We're in the same form,' Martin explained. ' A tenner a week,' he said, impressed. 'How did you get the job?'

'I inherited it from my brother,' Winter answered airily, as if discussing a country estate.

Greaves appeared, unshaven and wearing corduroys and a sweater. Clive Winter explained the rest of his round to the twins, then Greaves invited him into the kitchen where Sarah made him a cup of chocolate.

'Did you see anyone in the street this morning, Clive?' Greaves asked.

The boy nodded. 'The man at Number 11, a jogger and a tramp,' he answered without hesitation.

'What was the man at Number 11 doing?' Greaves asked.

'He leaves for work at this time every morning.'

'Today is Saturday.'

'He owns a shop in Highgate, I think it sells books.'

'What about the jogger? Have you seen him before?'

'Every morning. It's a woman, she always says good-morning.'

'Do you know where she lives?'

'24a Benton Street.'

'Are you sure?'

He nodded vigorously. 'Sometimes I'm early and I see her coming out. She's always on time.'

'What about the tramp?'

The boy shrugged. 'I didn't pay much attention.'

'Was he tall?'

'Taller than me.'

'What sort of clothes did he wear?'

He thought for a moment. 'A long, dirty grey over-coat, old trainers. Some sort of hat.'

'What sort of hat?'

The boy thought again. 'Woolly, I think, like the ones skiers wear. He had a lot of tangled hair and a beard that covered his face.'

'Did he walk fast or slow?'

'Quite fast but it was a funny sort of shuffle.'

'Did you speak to him?'

'No.'

'Were there any cars?'

'I heard one,' the boy said, 'but I didn't see it.'

'How did it sound?'

'In a hurry.'

Greaves smiled. 'Well done, Clive,' he said. 'That's a great help. You can go home now.'

The boy departed and Greaves turned to Sarah. 'I'd better go and check them out,' he said. 'I alerted the local nick, but it's unlikely they'll come up with any-thing. Someone is coming from the Yard to take the letter back to Forensic, but they won't start work on it until Monday. It's pretty much like the other one in any case.'

'May I look at it?' Sarah said.

'I shouldn't bother,' Greaves said. But Sarah insisted.

It was a similar sheet of paper with just a drawing on it this time – a crudely drawn woman with knives sticking from her naked body.

'Wait until I've dressed,' she answered. 'I want to come with you.'

A short time later, Greaves rang the bell of the flat Clive Winter had identified and after a few minutes' wait an attractive and fit-looking young woman came to the door. She was dressed in leggings with a long, thickly knitted open coat over a sweatshirt, no make-up and her straw-blonde hair plaited and piled on her head in a Nordic style. She looked at the both of them with mild interest, surprised at such an early call.

'I don't want to buy anything and I already have a religion that gives me sufficient spiritual fulfilment, thank you,' she said before they could speak. She began to close the door.

'I'm a policeman, Miss –' Greaves said quickly and he produced his warrant card. She opened the door again, puzzled. 'Judy Paine,' she answered.

'This is my associate, Mrs Keane.'

'You're a writer on the *Gazette*,' Judy Paine said immediately.

'That's right, Miss Paine,' Sarah said, surprised. Journalists were rarely recognised by the public.

'You'd better come in,' she said, opening the door wider. They entered a narrow hallway that led into a

214

large bare living room. The only furniture consisted of three plain black leather chairs on a polished wooden floor. Everything else was painted a matt cream, including the fireplace and a large piece of driftwood that was the only decoration on the walls.

'Have you just moved in?' Greaves asked and felt Sarah nudge him in the ribs.

Miss Paine laughed. 'It's taken me over a year to get it in this shape,' she answered. 'Perhaps we'd be more comfortable next door.'

She opened two large shutters to reveal a kitchen that was as warm and inviting as the previous room had been bleak and forbidding. Rugs were scattered on a terracotta tiled floor, there were low, chintz-covered armchairs next to a wood-burning stove, and a Welsh dresser bright with pottery. Bunches of dried flowers in pots stood on the dresser and were hung on the walls. A cat snoozed on the pine table between a vast wooden bowl of fruit and another of vegetables.

'I can see you're more at home here,' she said to Greaves. 'Won't you take a seat?'

Greaves sat at one end of the pine table and looked down at a sheet of paper that was reeled into an old-fashioned typewriter. He read the words: How to make a shark and an octopus out of old toilet rolls. Then he glanced up at Miss Paine, who was now smiling at him with such interest that Sarah felt a sudden stab of concern.

Greaves did not possess the traditional looks that were supposed to bowl a maiden over; he was too English. His understated manners and his long narrow face spoke more of character and reliability than

215

dashing romance, but when women fell for him they tended to melt like sealing wax. And it was usually strong-willed and self-reliant women who suddenly turned soft and pliant under his steady gaze.

'I work for children's television programmes,' she explained.

Greaves nodded. 'I understand you go for a run each morning.'

'And evening,' she replied.

'Twice a day?'

She stood now between Sarah and Greaves, her hands resting behind her on the table, the long woollen coat open so that they could both see her splendid figure displayed to its best advantage. Sarah suddenly felt that her skirt fitted too tightly around her waist and she made a note to lose a little weight after Christmas.

'I'm a marathon runner,' Judy Paine continued. 'I just warm up in the mornings. In the afternoons I go out for more than an hour.'

'Do you always take the same route?'

'In the morning, yes. I vary things in the afternoon.'

'You ran along Cleverly Road this morning. Did you see any other people?'

She thought for a moment. 'Yes, the paper boy, and the man who's always fiddling with his car.'

'Is he always fiddling with his car when you pass?'

She smiled. 'I think he likes to look at my bum every morning.' She thought again. 'And this morning there was a tramp.'

'Did you see a car?'

'Yes, an old Bentley that belongs to Doctor Ventral, he passed me going quite fast.'

216

'You know him well?'

'He's my GP, his surgery is in Burnley Close.'

'Was there anything extraordinary about the tramp?'

She nodded. 'Yes, there was: he didn't walk like a tramp.'

'How do you mean?'

'Tramps aren't usually in a hurry – this one was. It was quite noticeable. There was a sense of purpose. There was something else as well, but I can't describe it – just something not right. I think it may have been the walk but I'm not sure.'

Greaves asked her to tell them what the tramp had been wearing; it sounded much the same as Clive Winter's description.

'What's all this to do with?' she asked finally.

'Nothing for you to be alarmed about, Miss Paine,' Greaves said. 'Just someone who has been bothering Mrs Keane. We think he was in the neighbourhood this morning.'

They got up to leave; and Judy Paine walked with them into the front garden of the house. She looked to Sarah as they were about to depart and said, 'Your children go to St Catherine's, don't they?'

'That's right,' Sarah replied.

'I think I know your daughter. Her name's Emily, isn't it?'

Sarah looked at her, puzzled. Judy Paine was young, but surely not young enough to have attended the school at the same time as Emily.

'I didn't know her when I was at St Catherine's myself,' Judy explained with a laugh, 'but I did some teaching for the little ones a few hours a week when I first left college. Sister Mary asked me to help out.'

Greaves exchanged glances with Sarah. 'I think we'd better come back in for a few more minutes, Miss Paine,' he said. 'There's something I must tell you.'

'Very attractive girl,' Sarah said as they drove towards Hampstead Village.

'Very,' Greaves agreed, glancing severely at a battered Montego that had come close to the offside wing of his beloved Riley.

'I wonder if she'll keep her figure when she has to give up all that exercise?' Sarah mused.

'I should think so,' Greaves answered. 'Look at you, when do you ever take any exercise? But you're as slim as the first day I saw you.'

'You haven't known me all that long,' Sarah replied. 'I was fat before I met you.'

'Then I'm glad I didn't meet you until I did.'

'Do you think you'd still want me if I were fat again?'

Greaves nosed into a parking space and then turned to her. 'I don't know,' he said. 'Blow out your cheeks and let me look.'

She did as he requested and he shook his head. 'Stay slim,' he said without smiling.

'You swine,' said Sarah as she followed him towards Prior's Antiquarian book shop. Mr Prior was younger than she'd expected, although his clothes had a distinctly Edwardian cut. He was of average height and he wore spectacles that she suspected were an attempt to make him look older. When he bade them goodday, Sarah was struck by the lightness of his voice.

'Actually, we're neighbours, Mr Prior,' Greaves said when he had introduced them. 'But we haven't met before.'

218

'I haven't been there long,' Prior said. 'And I've been working very hard on the business. It's a tough racket, antiquarian books.'

Sarah suddenly wanted to giggle. The desire to laugh at inappropriate times was a failing she had endured all her life. The image of antiquarian booksellers fighting like Mafia chieftains for their share of the 'racket' came to her so vividly that she had to turn away for a moment and bite her lip.

Prior could not recollect much about the tramp, but he remembered Judy Paine with absolute clarity. 'I watch her all the time,' he confessed.

'Watch her?' Greaves repeated.

Prior nodded towards a little portable television set on the counter next to the cash register. 'Her programme each afternoon. She's so talented. Paints, sings, does exercises. There's nothing Judy Paine can't do.'

It was obvious Prior was among her greatest fans.

'But you haven't met her?'

He shook his head. 'I keep wanting to say hello . . .' he shrugged, 'but you know how difficult it must be for people in show business. They must get tired of the public bothering them.'

'Maybe we could introduce you,' Sarah suggested.

'Could you really?' Prior said eagerly. 'That would be wonderful.'

'Is there anything about the tramp that struck you as being unusual?' Greaves asked again, as they were about to leave the shop. Prior shook his head. 'Only his walk – that didn't look right.'

'But you can't tell me in what way?'

'Sorry,' he said. 'It just didn't look right, that's all.'

*

There was no one else for them to interview so Sarah suggested that they do their weekend shopping while they were in Highgate. They were earlier than the crowds and had just passed through the checkout counter in Sainsbury's when Greaves turned, loaded with carrier bags, and bumped into George Conway, who was similarly burdened.

'Hello, Colin,' he said gloomily. 'Been turning money into Christmas crap as well, have you?'

Sarah saw that he was accompanied by a slim young woman who wore an ex-army combat jacket, jeans and lace-up lumberjack boots. The sides of her head were shaven, the rest of her hair pulled back in an untidy pony tail. She carried a dark-haired baby that appeared to be bursting with rude health.

'This is Diana, my stepdaughter,' he said. 'And the deprived, underprivileged child in her arms is Aquarius.'

'Come off it, Dad,' the young woman said, and to Greaves and Sarah: 'Forgive me for not shaking hands.'

'They've come home to spend the traditional winter solstice festival at our flat,' George explained. 'We're not having a Christmas tree, I think we'll just dance around a bonfire decked with mistletoe.'

'Christmas is just an extension of the Roman festival of Juvenalus,' Diana said. 'And Prince Albert brought us the Christmas tree.'

'You won't mind eating turkey, will you?' George said. 'I think we got that from the Americans.' Despite his grumpy words, Sarah could tell that he was pleased by the turn of events.

'How long are you home for?' Sarah asked.

220

Diana shrugged, 'We're not sure, we'll have to find the column again.'

'Until it's time to do the washing-up on Boxing Day, I expect,' George said.

'Do people come and go from the column all the time?' Greaves asked.

'Sure,' Diana answered. 'There's no rules. It's all about freedom. We were passing near London so we just dropped out.'

'I was going to call you later,' George said, changing the subject. 'We've got to go into the office tomorrow.'

Sarah sighed. 'What time?'

'Marr wants a meeting at eleven o'clock about the Maclean story. With any luck we should be through before lunch.'

They said good-bye and made for the car. Greaves was in a thoughtful mood on the way back to the house and Sarah was preoccupied with Diana and Aquarius. She had found a new category of concern in which to place Emily, and for a time considered the worries that would arise were her daughter to take to the open road.

That afternoon, Sarah, Colin, the boys and the dog set off for the playing fields next to Highgate Woods, where the twins were to play rugby. The day was ominous with the threat of further rain. Sarah stood on the touchline with the thin straggle of spectators and watched the two teams trot on to the pitch.

The boys appeared self-conscious when she waved to them, nodding briefly and then keeping their heads down until they reached their positions. She noticed that they were a good head taller than the other members of their team, and they looked so much like their father it caught at her throat for a moment. Then she linked arms with Colin. The boys would not look in her direction – then the reason became apparent. Two red-headed girls suddenly appeared next to Sarah, wearing the school colours of her sons' team.

'Hello, Mrs Keane,' they chorused.

'Hello, girls,' Sarah replied. 'This is Mr Greaves.'

They grinned at him and giggled.

'Are you rugby fans, girls?' Colin asked.

'Oh yes,' they answered, watching the game begin. 'We love rugby.' Then Emma asked, 'Why aren't there any goalkeepers?'

'That's football,' Colin answered, slightly surprised. 'There aren't any goalkeepers in rugby.'

The girls looked nonplussed. 'Doesn't that make it easy to score goals?' Amanda asked.

'There aren't any goals in rugby, either,' Colin said patiently. 'The teams score points.'

The dog became interested by the activity on the field and started to pull on the leash, wanting to run on to the pitch. He barked furiously when the boys came close. Despite the participation of her sons, Sarah didn't really enjoy the game, and it was a tedious business restraining the dog. But she stuck it out. Towards the end of the match it began to grow very cold. The wind blew from the north, and the clouded sky began to darken into a deep gloom.

'I think I'll walk the dog for a bit,' Sarah said.

'Don't you want to know how the match ends, Mrs Keane?' Emma asked.

Sarah smiled and shook her head. 'The other side is ahead by thirty points, Emma,' she replied. 'I think I know how it's going to end.'

222

'You mean we're losing?' Amanda said in a disappointed voice. 'And the boys have been so brave.'

Sarah walked away and the dog pulled her in the direction of the woods. When she released him from the lead he headed into the trees.

Chapter Fourteen

At first the pathway was well defined and Sarah walked on without thought while the dog explored the undergrowth to each side of them. Then her mind wandered to the meeting that was to take place the following morning. She was not looking forward to the event with anything but foreboding. There was something about Simon Marr's enthusiasm for the Maclean story that filled her with depression. Everything seemed so unsettled; it was as if the foundations of the newspaper office had been built on shaky ground and it was now slowly sinking into a great quicksand.

She could remember a time when the very idea of the *Gazette* represented stability to her, an unchanging symbol as durable as the buildings and institutions of her childhood; an integral part of England, as reliable and familiar as the Brigade of Guards or the Post Office. Now she could imagine it fading away, like the cinemas that had once stood with such haughty grandeur in all of the local high streets.

To shake off the dreary mood that was taking hold of her she began to concentrate on the tasks she must perform before they could all leave for the cottage.

Briskly she started to tick off her mental list. She had bought the children's presents and stored them in the wardrobe in her old bedroom. There was one that they already knew about and one that would come as a surprise on Christmas morning. Colin's dressing gown was still in the boot of the office car. Perhaps she would be able to collect it tomorrow. She had decided to buy her father a collection of gardening books that she had seen advertised the week before, but now she wondered if they would be exciting enough. It was hard to imagine what he would desire in his wildest dreams – maybe Colin would have some kind of insight. The two men had a comfortable relationship. There was last-minute shopping to be done, the goose and the turkey had been ordered from her butcher and she had arranged to pick them up on Tuesday morning, then do the last food shop so they could drive with laden motor car to Oxfordshire. She wondered how Sam would act on the journey: he wasn't a bad traveller but this was a greater distance than usual. Perhaps there was some pill she could get from the vet. A vintage Riley packed with Christmas fare was no place to nurse a sick dog. She told herself she must buy some blank video tapes, to avoid arguments between the children.

Suddenly Sarah stopped and looked around her. It was really getting rather dark. The clouds that had gathered so ominously throughout the afternoon had now thickened to a density that made the sky the colour of lead, and the woods gloomy as a curtained room. There was complete silence; she could no longer hear the distant shouts of the spectators fringing the rugby pitch or the rustle of the dog in the undergrowth.

225

'Here boy!' she called out, but there was no other sound. The quiet seemed to press about her.

'Here boy,' she called again, but her voice did not seem to carry through the dank air. She heard the snap of a twig: one single distinct crack that could only have been caused by the weight of a human being. She turned in the direction from which she thought the sound had come, peering into the tangle of bare branches and the black trunks of trees.

She felt a curious mixture of fear and anger. How could I have put myself in such a stupid position? she asked. Another crack, closer now. Sarah looked down at the leash in her hand: she would not be able to beat off an assailant with that. Casting around, she kicked at the dead leaves and found a length of dead branch, about the size and weight of a hockey stick. Holding it like a bat she stood with her back to a tree and waited. The footsteps in the rustling leaves were quite clear now. She drew back and there was a pause before the figure came level with her.

There unmistakably was the profile of Anthony Dale. Slowly his head turned towards her and Sarah swung with all her strength and struck him on the side of the temple. He grunted and sank to his knees, and Sarah began to run. Crashing through the undergrowth, she had no idea where she was heading, nor could she tell if Dale was in pursuit. Suddenly, in one heart-stopping moment, the undergrowth parted and the dog emerged, bounding beside her in evident enjoyment. Sarah fell once, heavily; but even though she was partially winded she struggled to her feet and ran on. A sudden jagged flash of lightning lit the woods about her like a star shell, and a simultaneous crash of thunder vibrated through the air. Another flash of lightning forked down, and Sarah saw that she was standing on the edge of the playing field with the storm raging directly overhead.

The game had finished; but some spectators remained huddled in groups along the touchline. The teams had gone to the pavilion to change. Then Greaves saw her; and realising something was wrong, he broke away and came towards her, starting to run when he saw how distressed she was.

'He's in the woods,' she said when he reached her. 'Dale, I just saw him.'

Others had run up now so when Greaves saw that she wasn't badly hurt he left her and ran to the Riley and his mobile telephone.

They returned to the house in subdued silence. The boys had already gone with Emma Harris's parents. Sarah was in a slight state of shock, so Greaves ran a hot bath and made a cup of sweet tea which he laced with whisky. He brought it to her while she lay back in the brimming tub.

'It was almost worth it for all this attention,' she said, when he sat beside her on the bath-stool and held her hand. She smiled up at him. 'Actually, you ought to be angry – even after the warning you gave I wandered off like that. I behaved like a bloody fool.'

'I know,' he answered. 'When you're feeling better I'm going to knock hell out of you.'

'I'm sorry.'

'I forgive you.'

After the bath she fell asleep on the sofa in the living

room where Greaves had lit a fire. She woke up suddenly when the carriage clock on the mantel softly chimed six o'clock. Now she felt refreshed and filled with resolution.

'I'm late,' she said, sitting up. 'I've got a meeting with Joe March.'

Greaves was reading in the armchair opposite. 'Are you sure you want to go?' he asked.

'Certain,' she answered.

He could see that she was determined. 'Then I'm coming with you,' he said with equal firmness.

Sarah did not take long to dress, but it was still nearly 7.30 when she found Joe March in the crowded public house where Vickie Howard was due to perform.

'I'll be around,' Greaves said. 'My presence may cast a pall on your conversation with Miss Howard.'

She found Joe March at the bar. 'I didn't think you were coming,' he said. 'What will you have?'

Sarah asked for a glass of wine.

'They put the play on through here,' March said, indicating a further room, which they entered. 'I've already seen Vickie Howard, she says she'll join us for a drink later.'

Sarah looked about her. The decoration in this part was much older than the rest of the pub. A faded Edwardian barn of a place, it was still lined with ancient foxed mirrors and tobacco-coloured wallpaper embossed with flowers. The ceiling was supported at intervals with cast-iron posts, and rows of bentwood chairs had been arranged on the dusty floorboards. There was already a scattering of spectators who had also carried their drinks in from the saloon bar.

They took the seats that March had reserved with his hat and raincoat. The stage was a makeshift affair, slightly raised at one end of the room and lit by spotlights set high on the walls. There was no curtain and a babble of conversation came from the saloon bar, where a large crowd was drinking oblivious of the production that was about to start a few yards from them. Sarah and March sat in the second row and looked at the meagre props on the raised platform: the corner of a bar, a small table and two straight-backed chairs. Everything was painted black.

The shuffling and murmured conversation died away when the lights dimmed and a young man crudely made up to look much older came and stood behind the bar. He began to clean glasses and suddenly Vickie Howard swept down the centre aisle carrying an empty tray.

'Noisy bastards,' Vickie proclaimed in a disgusted voice. 'I don't know why it's called the saloon bar – pigsty would be a better name.'

It was a clever device. Immediately the babble of conversation behind them had been incorporated into the action of the play.

Sarah enjoyed the production. The play, performed without interval, was a simple enough concept and one that had been explored many times before, but that did nothing to spoil her pleasure. Gerald Trench played a widower who appeared to struggle for dominance over his strong-willed daughter. The father was a monster of selfishness who bullied, pleaded and tricked the only remaining member of his family to stay in the shabby hovel of a public house which had once been the centre of a shipbuilding community,

229

now faded into a fragment of inner-city desolation.

At first the daughter seemed to have sacrificed her own life, but gradually it became clear that she was keeping the father's dream alive, managing to create the illusion of some kind of hope for the future.

Sarah joined in the final applause but Joe March was less enthusiastic. 'Bloody rubbish,' he muttered while Vickie Howard and Gerald Trench were still taking their bow.

'I thought they were very good,' Sarah answered.

'They were all right,' March said. 'The play was tripe.'

After a few minutes, Vickie Howard came out from the back of the stage and spotted Sarah. She accepted a soft drink from March and said Gerald Trench had been delayed for a few minutes but he would have a pint of bitter. March went to the bar, while Sarah and Vickie faced each other at the table. Vickie lit a cigarette and blew a stream of smoke towards the ceiling.

'Is he taking off his make-up?' Sarah asked.

Vickie nodded. 'It only takes him a minute.' Then she looked up and said, 'Here he is now.'

As Gerald Trench walked towards them, Sarah became aware of a curious phenomenon she had experienced before. Once she had covered a story concerning a visiting team of Russian gymnasts. In the display hall she had been astonished by the beauty of their appearance. It was as if she were suddenly among some race from the future, where physical imperfections had been eliminated. Both men and women appeared to be perfectly proportioned. But after the performance, when the athletes were brought to her by the translator, something bizarre took place. As each of them approached, instead of growing larger they seemed to shrink, until she was surrounded by a crowd of people who barely came up to her shoulders.

On the makeshift stage Gerald Trench too appeared to be of heroic proportions – but it was an illusion. Like many short people he attempted to compensate for his lack of height by standing up ramrod straight, especially when he shook hands.

'I thought you were both quite wonderful,' Sarah said when they had all sat down.

'It's all Gerry,' Vickie said quickly. 'I just stand there and do what he's told me. Sometimes I feel like a piece of clay that he's modelled, as if it's not me at all. Mind you, he did go to art school.'

'Pygmalion,' March said softly.

'That's right,' Vickie continued. 'Sometimes I feel exactly like Eliza Doolittle.'

'I wasn't referring to Shaw,' March said. 'I meant the Greek who made a statue he fell in love with.'

'Anyway,' Sarah said. 'I was most impressed by your work. I hope I don't sound patronising, but I wasn't expecting anything nearly as powerful.'

Trench nodded as if he were hearing a speech with which he was in complete agreement. 'Tell me what you didn't like about it,' he said flatly.

There was a slight pause and March said, 'I thought the idea that the capitalists had closed down the shipyard as an act of class warfare a bit naive,' he said, matching Trench's flat tone.

Trench turned to look at him and did not speak for at least a count of ten.

231

'So you support the ruling classes?' Trench said emphasising each word as if he were banging in nails.

March smiled in a lopsided fashion. 'Quite the reverse. The only thing capitalists did for us was put our rent up when I was a kid. That's why I know that if the ruling classes could have made a few bob more by keeping your shipyard open they would have. There's nothing they'd have liked better than a lot of poor sods slaving twelve hours a day – if it meant the profits were still rolling in.'

Sarah decided she was not going to become involved in a political wrangle. 'I don't care about the philosophy of the piece,' she said. 'It was a good vehicle for both your talents.' She turned to Vickie. 'How are you now?'

Sarah noticed that Vickie reached for Trench's hand before answering. 'Fine,' she said, and then after a pause: 'Apart from the odd nightmare.'

'Did they tell you they know who they're looking for?'

Vickie lowered her head and said, 'But they still haven't caught him.'

Sarah decided not to tell of the incident that afternoon. 'I'm sure they will soon', she said. 'And the police will probably have enough evidence to put him away without you being crucified in the dock.'

Trench now turned to Sarah. 'You live with that policeman, don't you?' he said.

'Yes.'

Trench nodded, a smile of understanding on his face. 'The power of the press on one side and the full weight of the law the other. You must sleep pretty sound at night.'

'I don't feel as if I have much power,' she answered. 'I'm just a general news reporter, not an editor. I have no say about whether my work is used or not.'

'Just a hack, eh?'

'If you want to put it that way.'

'But you support the system?'

'I work for the system, yes.'

'And how many women are on the board of your paper?'

'None,' Sarah answered.

'And how many of the senior executives are women?'

'Just Fanny Hunter,' Sarah replied.

'That fascist bitch,' he exclaimed. 'She doesn't deserve to be called a woman.'

At least we agree about something, Sarah thought. But she was already beginning to tire of Gerald Trench; the only thing that kept her at the table was Vickie Howard, who was still gazing at her partner as though he were endowed with godlike wisdom.

The landlord solved the problem. 'Second house!' he called out. 'They're all seated inside.'

Sarah and March said good-night and the actors left them. Sarah looked around the crowded bar and finally saw Greaves seated at the counter nursing a pint of bitter. He appeared to be in conversation with an elderly man and woman. March slipped away saying he was due at his sister's house, and Sarah joined Greaves.

'What happened to March?' Greaves asked later when they were walking to the car.

'He had to go to see his family,' Sarah explained.

233

Greaves looked at his watch. 'Do you fancy a meal? It's a bit late to go home and cook.'

'I thought you'd never ask.'

Greaves drove them to an almost deserted Chinese restaurant in Richmond where the young girl who served them looked confused when he spoke to her in a language she clearly could not understand.

'Just a minute, I'll get my grandfather,' she answered. A few moments later a puzzled man emerged from the back of the restaurant. He beamed when he saw Greaves and they began a rapid conversation in Cantonese.

'What did you order?' Sarah asked, when the man returned with a bottle of clear liquid and poured them both drinks.

'An Emperor's feast,' Greaves answered, raising the glass in salute to the owner.

When they got home they found the boys in the living room looking through the old gramophone records.

'What was the pantomime like?' Sarah asked.

'Smashing,' they replied together.

'There was a terrific song in it,' Martin said. 'Mr Harris said it was a big hit when he was a little boy. We're trying to find it.'

'Be careful with those,' Sarah said.'They break easily. What was it called?'

' "They Tried To Tell Us We're Too Young," ' Paul said. 'Do you know who sang it?'

'It's just called "Too Young" and there's two versions,' Sarah replied. 'One by Jimmy Young and, I think, Nat King Cole, let me look.'

She soon found the version she was seeking, and

after the boys had played it for the third time, Sarah and Greaves decided to go to bed.

'Do you know that song?' Sarah asked as they were reading in bed.

'Yes,' he replied, looking up. 'We had it at my parents' house in Hong Kong. My sister played it incessantly one summer when I was home from school.'

'Why?'

'She'd just fallen in love for the first time with a young naval officer. I seem to remember they met at a dance. Eventually he sailed off in his battleship and she inflicted Jimmy Young on us for the rest of the holiday.'

'Do you remember your first love?' Sarah said, laying aside her book and nestling closer to him.

'Very well.'

'Who was she?'

'Anthea Owen. Her father had a confectionery and tobacconist's shop in Holland Park Avenue and she used to help in the shop. When I lived with my aunt I went in there every day just to look at her.'

'Do you ever wonder what became of her?'

Greaves shook his head.

'No?' Sarah asked in surprise. 'Why not?'

'I know what happened to her,' Greaves replied. 'She married the son of the local greengrocer.'

'I was in love with Brian Regan,' Sarah said sleepily. 'He was the butcher's boy in our village. He used to ride past on his bicycle and pull faces at me. I thought he was wonderful.'

'It's a miracle we both didn't go into trade,' Greaves said, closing his book and turning to her.

Chapter Fifteen

10.30 a.m. Sunday, 19 December

Sarah set out for the office the following day with reluctance. It wasn't that she resented working on a
Sunday – she had grown used to that many years before – it was the nature of the business in which she
was now involved. Although news reporting was essentially the harvesting of hard facts and the arranging
of them in a coherent order, much of how one went
about it was based on intuition. She had talked about
it with Greaves and discovered that it was similar to
police work.

   Sarah could feel there was something deeply wrong
with the Maclean story. Too many people wanted it to
be true because it suited their own ambitions and
Sarah knew that the best confidence tricks always began
with a story the victims wanted to believe. Like someone in mourning seeking a medium to put them in
touch with their loved one, the victim suspends belief
because they want so much for the story to be true.
That was why she was puzzled that Maclean wanted
her to be involved. He was aware of her scepticism.
Perhaps he had told himself that if he could persuade
her the story was sound then others would be infected
by her conviction.

The traffic to the office was almost as heavy as it was during weekdays. Whatever happened to the day of rest, she asked herself, good old English Sundays when people stayed at home dozing over the papers after their roast beef.

She met Harry Porter in the vanway, puffing on one of his eternal cheroots, and a sudden thought occurred to her. 'Do me a favour, will you, Harry?' she asked as they rode up in the lift.

'Ask and it's yours, darling,' he replied. 'As long as it doesn't involve Christmas shopping, or leaving the office while football is on.'

'But football is on TV all afternoon, Harry,' she said.

'Why do you think I like working Sundays?' he replied. 'There's never any stories to go out on and the wife spends all afternoon watching old films on television. Coming in here is like having an extra day off.'

'Don't you miss Sunday lunch?'

'Nah,' he replied. 'I like dinners when they come out of the oven with all the gravy hard around the edge of the plate. Now, what do you want?'

They got out of the lift and stood in the corridor. Sarah looked to see no one was watching and then said, 'There's a man coming to a meeting in the editor's office at eleven o'clock. I want you to snatch a picture of him.'

'Why?'

'Just say it's a favour.'

'Doesn't Marr want it taken?' he asked with a sudden gleam in his eye.

'Not really,' Sarah said. 'He doesn't want to upset the man.'

'Tell me what he looks like,' Harry said cheerfully.

During the fifteen minutes left before the meeting started Sarah gossiped with Pauline Kaznovitch. She became aware that Jackie, Fanny Hunter's secretary was hovering close to them, waiting to speak.

'Hello, Jackie,' Pauline said. 'What are you doing in on a Sunday?'

Jackie looked over her shoulder before she spoke. 'Miss Hunter's got a big job on. She says I can't have my half-day for Christmas shopping unless I come in today to make up for it.'

'How can I help you?' Sarah said.

'It's a message from Miss Hunter,' she replied. 'She says you're to tell Mr Marr that she can't come to the meeting today, and that you're to take a full shorthand note so that she can know exactly what went on.'

'Do you know where Fanny is at the moment?' Sarah asked.

The girl looked miserable. 'She says I'm not to give anyone the number.'

'Just tell me where she is,' Sarah said. 'Then you won't have broken a confidence.'

Jackie looked around again. 'She's at a special meeting at . . .' Jackie couldn't bring herself to speak the name, but she leaned forward and wrote it on a piece of paper. Sarah looked down and smiled. 'Don't worry,' she said. 'I won't let her know how I got the number.'

When Jackie departed, Pauline looked at the sheet of paper. 'What's she doing there?' she said, intrigued by the name.

'I've a feeling she's shopping for a new job,' Sarah

238

said reaching for the telephone. The switchboard operator of the rival newspaper was very helpful. 'I don't think the editor is in today,' he said. 'He doesn't usually come in on Sundays unless there's a big story. Are you sure you don't want me to try the deputy?'

'Just try the editor's office?' Sarah said. 'I don't mind hanging on.'

A secretary answered.

' I have an urgent message for Miss Hunter,' Sarah trilled in the impersonal tones of a message service operative.

'Please hold,' the secretary said. A moment later Fanny came on the line.

'What is it, Jackie?' she said sharply.

'Wrong again, Fanny,' Sarah said sweetly. 'I just wanted you to know that I won't be delivering any messages or taking a shorthand note of the meeting.'

There was a long pause when Sarah thought that Fanny's hatred was actually passing along the telephone line. 'I shall deal with you later,' she said finally. Sarah heard the receiver slam down: it was a pleasing sound. She walked towards the editor's office in quite a lighthearted mood and met Harry Porter coming towards her.

'Got your man,' he said.

'Did he see you?' Sarah asked.

Harry looked at her with an expression of mock outrage. 'Do me a favour,' he answered. ' I was snatching pictures before Leonardo painted *The Last Supper*.'

'I'll see you later,' she said.

'Not while football's on,' he called after her.

When Sarah entered the editor's outer office she found George Conway and Charles Trottwood waiting. The duty secretary smiled apologetically. 'He won't be a moment, Mrs Keane,' she said. 'He's got Mr Maclean and some other gentlemen in there with him at the moment.'

'All well?' Sarah said to George, who smiled and shrugged without answering.

'Bit of a cock-up, I believe,' Trottwood said, with a certain amount of relish.

The door opened eventually and Marr gestured for them to enter. He was obviously in a seething rage but trying to keep it under control.

'Take a seat,' he snapped as if he were ordering a team of performing dogs. 'We've got a change of plans. The chairman wants the series to start in the paper this coming week.' He flopped down in his chair and gazed at the ceiling. 'This of course ruins our plans to coincide the series with a television slot.' He indicated Loam, who was sitting to his right with a petulant expression on his face. 'What we're going to do is film the whole business of getting the story and publishing it in the paper and then aim for it to go out when the book is published.'

'Who's writing the book?' George asked.

Marr waved dismissively. 'That can come later. What I want to know now is, can Sarah be ready with the launch piece tomorrow?'

Sarah sat forward. 'What launch piece?'

Marr spoke irritably. 'The launch piece of the series, of course.'

George coughed. 'This story is in no shape to go into the paper yet, Simon.'

'Why not? I've told the chairman we've buttoned it all up.'

240

'All you've done is negotiate the contracts. No writing has been done at all.'

'Well that won't take long, will it,' Marr answered. 'Sarah's used to writing stories every day. She hasn't got to go anywhere, or chase any information, it's all here,' he said stabbing a finger towards Maclean, who sat in a chair against the wall smoking a cigarette. He looked towards Sarah and she thought there seemed to be a certain triumph in his expression.

'We have to check the facts, Simon,' George said gently.

'How are you going to check the facts?' Marr asked with a burst of irritation. 'Ask Adolf Hitler? Surely we either believe Mr Maclean or we don't?'

'Has anyone talked to the government?' Trottwood asked mildly.

'Yes,' Marr said shortly. 'I had a word with the Ministry of the Environment myself. The chief press officer, in fact.'

'What was his reaction?'

'Usual bloody bureaucratic red tape. He told me it was a matter for the Ministry of Defence.'

'Let me get this straight,' George said. 'You want Sarah to write a story saying there could be time bombs in the country's water supply and we're going to publish it this week?'

'That's right,' Marr answered. 'And we're filming the preparation of the story, *cinéma vérité* stuff, hand-held cameras.' He stood up. 'Now, can we all get on with it?'

'Do you think this is the best story to publish just before Christmas, Simon?' George asked.

'It's a rattling good yarn,' Marr said. 'People will

talk about this. What do you think the reaction from the public will be?'

'I think the sales of Perrier water will soar,' George said. 'And possibly people will begin to hoard bottled beer.'

Marr ignored his comment and turned to Sarah. 'Can you begin this afternoon, Sarah?'

'I suppose so,' she answered in a resigned voice.

'Hold on,' Loam interjected. 'I can't have a crew ready until tomorrow.'

'In the morning then?' Marr said.

'I want the interview to take place at the hotel,' Maclean said, speaking for the first time.

'Ten o'clock suit you?' Sarah asked.

'Fine,' he answered.

Loam nodded.

'That's fixed then,' Marr said with relief. From his tone it sounded as if the whole business had been completed. They stood up and as they were leaving, Marr said, 'Sarah, will you hang on for a moment.'

When the others had filed out, Marr asked her to be seated again. 'Sarah,' he began, 'now that's all out of the way, let's discuss the book. I want you to write it.'

Sarah took a deep breath. 'I'm not sure if that would be the best thing for me to do,' she answered. 'I'm a reporter, not an author. With something as . . . important as this, don't you think it would be better to hire someone more experienced? After all, my name wouldn't mean much to the book-buying public.'

Marr looked surprised. 'Oh, I was thinking of it going out under my name.'

'You want me to ghost it for you?'

'You would have a credit in the foreword.' He leaned

242

towards her and put a hand on her knee. 'You could refer to all the work you've done in your column.'

'Column?'

Marr nodded. 'I'm going to fire Fanny Hunter and I want you to take over the page – when you've done the V-3 story, of course.'

Sarah could feel the ice splintering. She thought for a few moments and then looked up. 'Let's see if this collaboration will work, shall we?' she replied. 'Suppose I do the first story and you can add a few touches yourself. Then it could go out under your name.'

'Yes, that could work,' Marr answered thoughtfully. 'Then I could appear in the television advertisements.' He looked up, his features suddenly transformed into an expression of sly cheerfulness. Walking Sarah to the door, he rested his hand on her shoulder. 'Keep up the good work,' he said.

Sarah was still puzzling over the good work she was supposed to have done as she walked to George's office. Since Marr's appointment she had produced practically nothing for the paper.

'What was all that about?' she asked. George nodded for her to close the door, and then said in a low voice, 'Marr paid half the money into Maclean's Swiss bank account yesterday.'

Sarah sat down. 'He must be mad.'

'Yes, that's a conclusion the chairman is rapidly coming to.'

'Didn't Marr clear it with him?'

'He didn't know Marr had the power to draw that amount. Editors didn't before Marr – but when he joined, Sir Robert put him on the board of Gazette Newspapers as well, and in doing so he automatically conferred the same financial discretion other directors enjoy. When Sir Robert found out what he'd done he demanded that the story go into the paper right away. He expects the circulation increase to justify the expenditure to the rest of the board.'

'But the circulations of all newspapers go down after Christmas, everyone knows that.'

George smiled.'Sir Robert says that is a circulation department myth.'

Sarah sighed. 'Well I've managed to persuade Marr to put his own byline on the story.' She related her last conversation with the editor and George nodded his agreement when she came to the end. 'What are you doing now?' he asked.

'Going home,' she replied firmly.

She went to her desk to collect her possessions and was about to leave when she saw Prince Charles Mananluba, his arms full of large brown envelopes, standing close by, talking with one of the features department subs.

'Hello, Sarah,' he called out. He placed the bundle of envelopes on her desk and shook her hand.

'Hello, Chas,' she replied. 'What are you doing here?'

'I brought in Cynthia's copy for the next month,' he answered. 'A boring task, but one I undertake with a happy heart.'

'What's all this?' she said, tapping the pile of envelopes.

'Syndication,' he replied. 'I make copies of her articles and then send them to the other papers that take her column.'

'How do things look for the month ahead?' she asked.

244

'Turbulent,' he replied. 'But prosperous for those born under Taurus. That's Cynthia's sign, I need hardly add.'

Sarah picked up her bag and coat.

'Do you have time for a drink?' he asked her.

'I don't,' Sarah answered. 'I have to be home for lunch, but I can drop you off if you like.'

'That would be delightful. If you could take me to the Savoy, I shall be eternally in your debt.'

When Sarah got home she found Emily and Greaves cooking the lunch. The boys were in the living room playing the record she had heard so many times the night before.

'I'm beginning to regret I found that for them, ' Sarah said with some feeling when she joined Emily and Greaves in the kitchen. She sat down at the table with a glass of wine and watched Greaves carefully separating the yolks from eggs. They had invited Nick Holland and his girlfriend Lucy to lunch.

'What are you doing?' Sarah asked. 'Can I help?'

'No advice please,' he replied. 'But unstinting admiration would be appreciated.' Emily showed him a bowl of vegetables she had peeled. 'Excellent,' he said. 'Now just cut them lengthways once.'

'What are those?' asked Sarah.

'Parsnips,' Emily replied.

'The boys don't like parsnips,' she said. 'There's no point in cooking that many.'

'Yes they do,' Emily replied. 'Mrs Harris gave them baked parsnips last night, after the pantomime. They say they've never had anything so delicious.'

Feeling superfluous, Sarah went back to the living

room, but was driven out by the record. She decided to take a turn in the garden with the dog and had just pulled on wellington boots when she remembered Harry Porter's photograph of Maclean. She rang the office and got a casual in the photographers' room.

'You've missed him by seconds. Harry's just gone out with Joe March,' he said. 'Some story about a girl being beaten up. The news desk monitored the story on the police band.'

As Sarah put down the telephone she could hear Greaves's private line starting to ring. She stood in the doorway while he took the call. When he hung up his face was grave. 'Vickie Howard has been attacked again. Dale came back to her flat.'

'How is she?' Sarah asked.

'Apparently just shaken up. No real damage, just superficial bruising. This time her boyfriend was there. He fought Dale with a kitchen knife. Judging from the amount of blood the constable on the spot reported he must have half killed him.'

Chapter Sixteen

Greaves drove the Riley to Vickie Howard's flat, where he found a policewoman sitting with her. Gerald Trench was on the sofa looking pale, his right hand heavily bandaged.

'The bastard got in again,' he said to Greaves. 'Where were your people?'

'Just tell me what happened,' Greaves said, refusing to respond to Trench's anger.

'He just pushed in again,' Vickie interrupted, her voice trembling. 'He had me by the throat, he was punching me.

Greaves could see more bruising on the left side of her face. 'Where were you?' he asked Trench.

'In the kitchen. I grabbed one of the knives and stabbed him in the back.'

'How many times?'

'I don't know. Twice in the back, I think, it didn't go in very deep. He turned round and I stabbed him some more times. Then he let go of Vickie and ran off.'

'What happened to your hand?'

Trench looked down at the bandage. 'I cut myself when I was stabbing him,' he smiled bitterly. 'That's something that never happens in the movies.'

A uniformed constable came into the room and waited until Greaves looked up at him. 'A Mr Nathanson on the next landing down saw a man running from the flats, sir,' he said in a low voice. 'And there's a reporter and a photographer from the *Gazette* outside.'

'What are their names?'

'March and Porter.'

'Tell the people downstairs I'll be there in a minute.' Greaves went to the door and nodded to March. 'Hello, Harry,' he said.

'Is it true Vickie Howard has been attacked by the same man again?' March asked.

'Quite true,' Greaves said.

'May we talk to her?'

Trench had come to the doorway behind Greaves. 'Let them in,' he said.

'That's up to Miss Howard,' Greaves said mildly.

'Vickie,' Trench called out, 'come and ask Mr March into the flat.'

Vickie came to the door and asked them to enter. Leaving her with March and Harry Porter, Greaves descended to the Nathansons' flat. In complete contrast to the rooms above it was brightly lit, and sparkling with the attention Mrs Nathanson, a blue-rinsed matron, had lavished upon every surface. Mr Nathanson was dressed as if his wife had included him as an accessory to the living room. His fawn trousers and neat woollen cardigan, with its patches of suede, matched the velvet-covered sofa that he now perched upon like a grey-haired bird. Bright inquisitive eyes watched Greaves suspiciously when he took the chair opposite.

248

'Would you like a cup of coffee, Superintendent?' Mrs Nathanson asked.

'Thank you,' he replied. 'I would indeed.' He looked back at Mr Nathanson. 'I understand you saw someone running from the block of flats earlier, sir,' Greaves began.

'That's right,' he replied. 'I was just coming back from taking the dog for a walk when he came out of the entrance. It gave me a bit of a turn.'

'Why?'

'Well he was a big lad, and I thought he was drunk. Then I saw the blood on him.'

'He's got to take things easy,' Mrs Nathanson, said, returning with the coffee on a silver tray. 'He's got high blood pressure. This sort of thing shouldn't happen to him, he's not as young as he was.'

'It shouldn't happen to anyone,' Mr Nathanson said irritably. Then he turned to Greaves. 'I ask you, what kind of expression is that: "He's not as young as he was"? Who's as young as they were?'

'You know what I mean,' his wife said, handing Greaves a delicate cup and saucer.

'Go on,' Greaves said.

'When I saw he was hurt I said to him, what's the matter, can I help?' Mr Nathanson continued.

'He did first aid in the RAF,' Mrs Nathanson said quickly. 'He was a medical orderly. He saved our David's life when he nearly choked to death.'

'I slapped him on the back, that was all,' Nathanson said with a shrug. 'Anyway, the lad downstairs pushes past me and smears blood on my raincoat sleeve.'

'Did you see where he went?' Greaves asked.

'I followed him to the next turning,' Nathanson said. 'He got into a light-blue Ford Escort.'

'I don't suppose you remember the number?' Greaves asked without much hope.

Mr Nathanson reeled it off immediately.

'Are you sure?'

'He was an accountant for forty-three years,' Mrs Nathanson said proudly. 'He never forgets a number.'

'Thank you Mr Nathanson,' Greaves said. 'I wish all witnesses were so precise.' He turned to the policeman who stood in the doorway: 'Get that off right away.'

Greaves returned to the gloom of Vickie Howard's flat a few minutes later and found Nick Holland standing with Joe March.

'They let us have everything,' March said, then paused. 'It's not going to look very good – girl attacked twice by same man.'

Greaves shrugged. 'You know we can't guard everyone. The odds against this happening were pretty long.'

'A million to one, I'd say,' March replied. 'But the public won't see it that way. They'll say it's police incompetence.'

Greaves smiled wearily. 'Aren't you glad you're not a copper any more.'

'At times like this,' said March.

Harry Porter joined them, winding on the film in his camera. 'All done,' he said.

'OK,' said March. 'Let's be off.'

Greaves turned to Holland when they had gone. 'I wasn't going to bother to bring you out on this one, I could have told you about it when we met later,' he said.

As they were leaving the dimly lit hallway, Holland reached down and picked up a small leather wallet that was wedged behind the open door. He flipped it open: it was Anthony Dale's security pass. There was also a folded sheet of paper. It was another crudely drawn figure, this time a skeleton sprawled across the page, with the words: ROMAN VIRTUE written below.

In the kitchen where the light was better they examined the wallet again. There was something else slipped behind the security pass: a ticket for Camden Public Libraries and a slip of paper with the characters: 4X361 12–3 21 written neatly with a fibre-tipped pen. They puzzled over it for a moment. Greaves put it away when Trench came into the room. 'We're going to leave a policeman on duty here, Mr Trench,' he said.

'Don't bother,' Trench answered. 'He won't be back now.'

'As you wish,' Greaves answered as politely as he could. He said good-bye to Vickie Howard and left the flat. On the drive back to Hampstead, Greaves talked the situation through with Nick Holland. 'He's badly wounded, judging from the amount of blood in the flat, so he'll need medical attention. If he doesn't go to a hospital, someone is going to have to look after him. Let's go through his records again and check who his closest relatives are.'

'I did that,' Holland said. 'He doesn't have any family left. His mother and father lived on an estate in south London, but they both died years ago. No grandparents, aunts or uncles. There was a brother but he went off just after the parents died.'

'Where to?'

'The neighbours weren't sure. They said he was the local bright boy. Always working at his books – too stuck up to play with the other kids on the estate. Anthony was the extrovert: good at games, used to look after his brother if there were any fights, although he was the younger one.'

'Maybe he went away to study,' Greaves said. 'Let's check his school records.'

'It'll have to be tomorrow,' Holland answered.

'Read out those numbers again.'

'4X361 12–3 21.'

'Four times three hundred and sixty-one is – '

'One thousand four hundred and forty-four,' Holland answered after a few moments' calculation.

'What the hell does it mean?' Greaves asked.

At the house, Sarah was waiting. 'How is Vickie?' she asked.

'Not too bad, considering,' Greaves answered.

'Lucy is coming here,' Sarah said to Holland. 'I asked her to supper, we didn't expect you'd be back so soon.'

They stood in the kitchen and Greaves took out the two pieces of paper once again. While they were studying them, Martin came in to get some orange juice. 'That's good,' he said glancing down at the sketch of the skeleton.

'Do you think so?' Greaves asked.

'It's a bit rough,' Martin went on, 'but the bones are correct.' He leaned over. 'All the parts are there – even the right number of ribs. And look how well he's drawn the pelvis. He'd get an A for anatomy in our group.'

'Curiouser and curiouser,' Greaves muttered and put the piece of paper away. Lucy arrived a little while later and they played Scrabble in two teams after supper. But everyone was too preoccupied to enjoy the game.

8.30 a.m. Monday, 20 December

The next morning, Sarah's father was due to take Emily and the boys to the Oxford cottage ahead of Sarah and Colin. Greaves had already left the house and Sarah was studying March's story on the second attack amid the chaos the boys made preparing for their departure. Emily had done her packing the night before and was sitting next to her in the kitchen drinking coffee and reading the *Guardian*. 'By the way,' she said, not looking up, 'I've sorted those old toys you wanted for Father Robson's Christmas appeal. I put them in the boot of the car.'

'Oh, well done,' Sarah replied. 'Will he still be at the school?'

'Until Boxing Day. He said you can drop them off any time.'

'I'll try to do it today.'

Sarah's father arrived just after nine o'clock looking brisk and alert. 'You must have been up for hours, Dad,' Sarah said when she made him a fresh pot of tea.

'Plenty of time for lying about when I'm in my grave,' he replied, glancing down at the story she had been reading. 'This looks a bit of a mess.'

'Poor Colin,' she said. 'He's worked so hard. It sounds as if the police have done nothing at all.'

'The result isn't always equal to the effort expended, you know.'

Sarah smiled. 'You always used to say that when we worked in the garden.'

253

'Did I? My father used to say it to me. Funny how things get passed on.'

'Tell the children,' she said as she handed over the keys to the cottage.

'Will you post these for us, Mum?' the boys asked as she kissed them goodbye.

'What are they?'

'Christmas cards.'

'Just one each? I can't guess who they're for. Be good. Do what Grandpa tells you.'

They waved as she left for the office. Thank God I didn't have to write the Vickie Howard story, she told herself in the car. It would be bad enough for Colin without reading my name on it. Sarah went straight to the Staffordshire Hotel and found Maclean in his suite, but no sign of Loam. 'Have you spoken to Doctor Frichter recently?' she asked while they waited.

'Last night. He rang me, actually,' Maclean answered. 'He's not in the best of health, you know. I hope we can get out to South America before his heart fails altogether.'

There was a silence and then came the muffled sound of a violent altercation just outside the suite.

'I'd better go and check that,' Sarah said eventually.

In the corridor she found Loam shouting at a harassed-looking man in a dark suit, and two technicians loaded with equipment watching with detached boredom. Loam turned to Sarah. 'Tell this arsehole we're filming inside the room!' he ordered.

Sarah gestured for them to go into the suite, then turned to the hotel assistant. 'My name is Mrs Keane, I know these gentlemen,' she said. 'I'm sorry for the misunderstanding.'

254

'Forgive me, Mrs Keane,' he said. 'My name is Ian Kempton, I'm an assistant manager. We have strict orders not to let anyone near this suite without permission. They just barged into the hotel. I thought they might be a television crew trying to get a story.'

'You were quite right, Mr Kempton, thank you for being so vigilant. I shall make sure the manager knows how helpful you've been.'

Placated, Kempton departed and Sarah entered the suite.

'Get us some coffee, will you?' Loam said not bothering to look at her. Sarah walked over and tapped him on the shoulder. 'Yeah?' he said in surprise.

'Come into the bedroom for a moment, please,' she said. He looked over at his technicians and raised his eyebrows before following her.

Sarah closed the door behind him and folded her arms. 'I want you to listen very carefully, Mr Loam, because there's no danger of me repeating myself. I am neither your servant, nor your minder. I am a reporter on the *Gazette*. If you continue to behave in your present manner I shall walk away from this job; and as I am the only person connected with this nonsense who has any hold on reality that might seriously jeopardise your fee. So mind your manners when you're around me. Do I make myself clear?'

Loam looked at her and made a sucking sound with his teeth. 'Sure,' he said finally.

They returned to the main room of the suite and Loam carried out the rest of his business in a more orderly fashion. Sarah went over the story of how Maclean met Frichter again and by twelve o'clock she had enough material to begin to write. Excusing herself, she made her way to the office and found George Conway. 'I'm starting to write now,' she said.

'Marr has booked you on a flight to Brazil tomorrow morning,' George replied. 'It's going to be a close-run thing.'

'Not for me, George,' she answered. 'Because I'm not going.'

'I know,' he said. 'I'm working on it. Something will turn up.'

At her desk Sarah started to write the story. It took a long time, as each paragraph sounded hollow and unconvincing, but she pressed on. At last it was finished and she made the commands to pass it into Conway's file. Then she printed it out as hard copy for Marr. Conway strolled up when she had finished. 'Have you read it?' she asked.

He nodded.

'Poppycock, isn't it?'

'The Chinese invented the art of flying kites, but I would say Mr Maclean has surpassed them.'

'Well, at least my name isn't going on it,' she said philosophically.

'I'll come in with you,' George said.

When they entered Marr's office they found him in a state of uncontrolled frenzy. Papers from his desk were scattered around the room and a chair was overturned. His usually sleek hair was in disarray and he had even unbuttoned his shirt collar.

'The story has leaked!' he shouted. 'Some bastard has talked – I want to find out who the traitor is, if it means firing the whole bloody staff!'

'What's happened?' George asked.

'Some bloody newspaper has rung up Maclean at

the hotel and made him another offer, that's what's happened.' He raked a hand through his hair so that it stood up as though he had received a powerful electric shock. 'Who the fucking hell can it be? I want to know – I won't rest until I find out.'

'I know,' George said mildly. 'So does Sarah; but she's too decent to shop anyone.'

'Who is the bastard?' Marr demanded, his voice cracking.

'Fanny Hunter, of course,' George said. 'You really shouldn't have put the wind up her, Simon. Hell hath no fury, remember . . .'

'What shall we do?' Marr said.

George smiled. 'There's a flight to South America tonight, I've checked. If you send her to interview Frichter and announce it on the front page, she can hardly sabotage the story. It would look like failure; and we all know Fanny couldn't take that.'

'Brilliant,' Marr said. 'You do it, George. If she won't go, threaten her with exposing her treachery. That would blow her reputation for being a straight shooter.' He looked happier and reached out for the copy Sarah held. After he had read it through quickly he looked up with a smile. 'This is good stuff,' he enthused. 'A bit rough, but I'll polish it up. Just leave it with me.'

'Delighted,' said Sarah, with some feeling.

5.30 p.m. Monday, 20 December

Greaves sat in his office looking down at the sheet of paper with strange numbers on it. He was waiting for Holland, who had spent the day checking on Dale's brother. It was raining again, and Holland was soaked when he finally arrived.

'I found someone who remembered the family,' he said. 'Dale's brother, Stephen was a bright boy, local comprehensive, then Manchester University, reading chemistry. He got a good second and started teaching six years ago. I tracked one of his college mates. It seems he married an Ellen Glass, whom he met at Manchester. They had a child. The friend thinks Stephen was teaching at a school in Hammersmith until they lost touch. I haven't made any more calls yet.'

'Good work,' Greaves said, looking at the wall clock. It was 5.40 p.m., ten minutes after office work ceased in most parts of Britain. It would now be almost impossible to find an office that could give them information.

'We'll have to leave it until the morning,' he said. 'Let's hope someone spots that damned car.' He rang Sarah. 'How was your day?' she asked.

'I've known better.'

'Was there much comment about Joe March's piece?'

'Ribald as well as cutting.'

'To hell with them,' she said with feeling. 'If they say anything else, tell them you're going to walk out.'

'You're not going to believe this,' he said. 'But that's just what I'm about to do. I'm finished for the day.'

'You're not going to believe this either,' she answered, 'but so am I. And there are no children at home. Where do you fancy going?'

'First to a box at the theatre, then supper at Romano's. After that, champagne out of a chorus girl's slipper and finally, a ride home on a milkman's horse.'

'I can manage the slipper and the champagne. What else will you settle for?'

'How about a Big Mac and an early night?'

'Double portion of French fries and onion rings?'

'You're on.'

10.40 a.m. Tuesday, 21 December

The next day, Nick Holland got lucky. After three calls he'd obtained the name and address of the school where Stephen Dale was last employed as a teacher. It took a little time to track down the headmaster, a dry-sounding man called Palmer.

'You were lucky to get me,' he said when he answered Holland's call. 'I was just about to leave for the holidays.'

He listened to Holland for a time and then said, 'Yes, I recollect Stephen Dale very well, he taught here until three years ago.'

'Did he leave a forwarding address?'

'I'm afraid not, Sergeant. Mr Dale had no address after he left here. He took to the road.'

'A tramp?'

'He might just as well have been, but no – he and his family became what I believe is known as New Age travellers.'

'You don't happen to know the type of vehicle he used?'

'I remember it well: it was a converted school bus. The sixth form worked upon it as a special project for over a year. Then, to our astonishment, Mr Dale departed from the school in it. I suppose that demonstrated a certain amount of panache even if it was

259

slightly dishonest. We had no idea he was the owner of the bus; everyone thought it had been donated to the school.'

'You don't happen to know the number plate?'

'I'm afraid not. The whole business was an occurrence I would rather forget. Schoolchildren are impressionable, you know. It wasn't the best example to set our sixth form.'

Holland thanked him for his help and hung up.

'Try the West Country police forces,' Greaves said. 'Someone may have something on the vehicle. I wonder if anyone knows anything about New Age travellers.'

'There's Beamish, the new man in traffic,' Holland suggested. 'He was with Wiltshire until recently. They have a lot of travellers passing through.'

'See if he can spare us some time,' Greaves said.

An hour later, Beamish was released from his duties in the traffic department. He was an open-faced young man. God, Greaves thought when he sat before him. Policemen are even beginning to look young to me.

'Tell me about New Age travellers,' Greaves said.

'What kind of thing do you want to know, sir?'

'Let's start with what kind of people they are.'

'All sorts, sir.'

Greaves sighed. The young man was going to be hard work. 'Don't worry,' Greaves said gently. 'You're not giving evidence or sitting an examination. It's gossip I'm after. Imagine we're just chatting in a pub.'

'I don't go in pubs, sir, I'm a Methodist,' Beamish said, a little shocked by the suggestion. Greaves could see Holland trying not to smile. He had to control his own features as well.

'Then imagine you're having a cup of tea with an uncle,' Greaves said.

Beamish looked happier. 'Well, they're a mixed lot really. Some are nice – quite gentle sort of people. They look after their kids, no doubt about that. But there's some nasty types as well. The ones I couldn't stand were the Crusties.'

'Crusties?' Greaves replied.

'The ones that don't believe in washing. Stink they do. Turns your stomach.'

'Tell me more about the others.'

Beamish thought for a moment. 'A lot of them pretend they're free spirits and all that; but really they're just work-shy, and some of them are bent.' He paused. 'Bit like the rest of the general public, I suppose.'

'How about the groups, do they stay with the same column all the time?'

'Mostly; but there are always some at the fringes who join up for a few months and then move on. Some people are naturally restless, even when they're moving about all the time.'

'So somebody new joining a column wouldn't cause a stir?'

'No one would pay much attention,' said Beamish.

Greaves thanked him, and sent him back to traffic.

'Good place to hide out,' Holland said.

Greaves sat forward. 'Get on to the computer and see what columns are where. At least we'll get some kind of idea on how wide the search could be.'

An hour later, they stood before a map dotted with coloured pins. 'I had no idea there were so many of them,' Holland said.

Greaves nodded. 'Not all of them are New Age,' he said. 'Some are old-fashioned travellers, some gypsies.'

'Christ this is going to be a long job, unless we get lucky,' Holland said softly.

Greaves sat back in his chair and studied the map. 'Why are they called New Age travellers?' he asked, almost to himself.

'Something to do with the age of Aquarius, isn't it?'

'Aquarius,' Greaves repeated. Then he reached for the telephone.

Chapter Seventeen

10.45 a.m. Tuesday, 21 December

When Sarah got to the office she found Tony Prior and Pauline Kaznovitch hanging paper chains across the reporters' desks. It was party day at the *Gazette* and the atmosphere anticipated the festivities.

'All set for the Features thrash tonight?' Prior called out.

'I'm not sure I'll make it,' Sarah replied.

'Come on,' Prior urged. 'Guaranteed fun for young and old.'

'Does it say anything about the middle-aged?' Sarah said, passing them by. In the ladies' lavatory she found a group of secretaries showing each other the dresses they would change into later in the evening. Two of the news-desk assistants were wearing Santa Claus hats. Mick Gates was acting as whip for the reporters' lunch, which was due to take place in an upstairs room at the Godfather's restaurant.

'Twelve forty-five on the dot, Sarah,' he called out when she returned to her desk. 'No hanging about in the office, sucking up to the bosses.'

'I promise I'll be drunk by one o'clock, Mick,' she answered.

There were two unfamiliar faces among the reporters,

both young women. They were casuals, called in for the day in the certain anticipation that most of the staff would be unfit for testing stories by the afternoon. To add to the joys to come, that evening the Features department party was to take place in a private room in the Lion.

Sarah had dressed for both events, deciding that a dark blue suit was smart enough to show she had made an effort. In truth she was not looking forward to either with much pleasure. The reporters' lunch tended to develop into the sort of masculine celebration where trousers were dropped, beer thrown, and arm-wrestling took place; and after a time the Features party would degenerate into a noisy drunken disco. She did not disapprove of the behaviour of her younger colleagues, it was just that experience had taught her cheap red wine was not necessarily a key to true happiness.

There was a great deal of noise around the reporters' desks, like thunder on a summer day: fair warning of the storm to come. Sarah saw George standing in his shirt-sleeves at the doorway of his office. There was something on his shoulder but she could not quite make out what it was. As she drew closer she saw that it was the model of a robin redbreast attached by Sellotape.

'That's a nice touch,' Sarah said.

'Metaphorically it's a bluebird,' George answered.

'Why?'

George began to sing softly: 'Zip a dee doo dah, zip a dee ay, my, oh my, it's a wonderful day . . . ' He stopped and smiled. 'That's from *The Song of the South*, a very underrated movie.'

264

'I've taken the children to see it, George.'

'Then you'll remember Brer Rabbit begging not to be thrown into the briar patch?'

'I do.'

'Welcome to the briar patch,' George said, handing her a cable. It was from Fanny Hunter, addressed to Simon Marr. It read: Otto Frichter died on 5 November. Cremated 7 November. I resign. Fanny Hunter.'

Sarah reached for George's telephone and called the Staffordshire Hotel. When she hung up, she turned to George. 'Andrew Maclean vacated his room last night. No forwarding address. They're sending the bill to Mr Marr, as arranged.'

'Something tells me it's going to be an interesting day,' George said.

Outside his office Sarah bumped into Harry Porter. 'Morning, my old darling,' he said. 'Are you going to buy me one before the lunch?'

'You can count on it,' she replied, then remembered something. 'Harry, what happened to that picture of the man you took for me, the chap going into Marr's office?'

'I left it on your desk,' he answered. 'I put it in an envelope.'

Sarah shook her head. 'I didn't find it.'

'Well it was definitely there, I did it myself.'

Puzzled, Sarah returned to her desk. Her telephone rang; it was Cynthia Padgett. 'Darling,' she said. 'Can we meet later for a Christmas drink?'

'I'd love to, Cynthia,' Sarah answered. 'But it's rather a full day here.'

'I just wanted to tell you a little secret,' Cynthia continued. 'I think Chas has been rather a naughty boy.'

'How?'

'It's the most extraordinary thing,' Cynthia continued. 'Do you remember seeing him in your office on Sunday?'

'Yes.'

'He had a lot of envelopes – copies of my column – and when he got home there turned out to be an extra one. God knows how it came into his possession, but it contained a photograph of someone he recognised.'

'Go on,' Sarah said.

'It was a chap Chas knew in West Africa. His real name is Ian Fisher, but he sometimes calls himself John Kneller and on very rare occasions Andrew Maclean.'

'What did he do with the picture?'

'Well, when he saw the story in your paper this morning, I'm afraid he sold it to a friend on the *Evening Standard*.'

'Why did he do that, Cynthia?'

'Well it was that frightful woman Hunter's fault,' she explained. 'Chas tried to renegotiate my contract last week and she was extremely rude – princes are very sensitive, you know. Chas felt Fanny Hunter had forfeited his loyalty.'

Sarah looked across the newsroom and saw George signalling with some urgency. 'I must go, Cynthia,' she said. 'I'll call you later.'

George ushered her into the room and shut the door. 'Marr wants us to go into his office – he sounded disturbed.'

'I don't blame him,' Sarah said, and told him about her conversation with Cynthia.

George whistled and then slowly plucked the robin

from his shoulder. 'I think matters are reaching what my old science teacher called a critical mass. Let's see how Marr is standing up under fire.'

They were about to leave when the telephone rang. 'Hello, Colin,' George said. 'Do you want to speak to Sarah?' He was about to hand the receiver to her, but stopped. 'Yes,' he said. 'That's right, they're at home.' He gave his address and then hung up. 'He says he'll call you later,' George said, puzzled. 'He's gone to talk to my stepdaughter.'

Greaves and Nick Holland parked in the forecourt of a block of mansion flats in Highgate. George's front door was answered by his second wife, Tina, a buxom and well-preserved brunette. She was slightly apprehensive when they asked to see Diana, but she visibly relaxed when her daughter recognised Greaves and greeted him in a friendly fashion.

'I thought she might be in trouble,' Tina said wearily. 'Gypsies are always in trouble with the police.'

'Mum, how many times have I got to tell you, I'm not a gypsy,' Diana said. 'Why don't you go and make us a cup of tea?'

They entered a living room which was scattered with plastic toys. 'Sorry about all this,' Diana said. 'Dad keeps buying them for Aquarius. God knows what he'll produce on Christmas morning. A model printing press, I expect.'

When they were seated, Greaves asked her about travellers. She responded warily at first, until Greaves explained about the connection with the murders, then she became co-operative. 'You'll be lucky to find them at random,' she said. 'And the local Old Bill won't be much help. We don't get on with the law very well, you know.'

'Can you suggest anything?'

'Not really.'

'Tell me,' Greaves asked, making one last stab in the dark, 'does this mean anything to you?' He produced the slip of paper containing the indecipherable numbers they had found in Dale's wallet. Diana glanced at it and said, 'Well, there you are, I don't know why you're bothering with me.'

'You understand what it means?' Greaves asked.

'Course I do,' Diana said, looking down at the paper again. '4 crosses 361, they're roads, the A4 and the A361. Twelve dash three means someone will be waiting between twelve o'clock and three o'clock on the twenty-first,' she glanced up. 'That's today.'

Greaves looked at his watch – he and Holland had some fast motoring to do.

When she and George entered Marr's office, Sarah was struck by the difference in the atmosphere from the newsroom. Outside all was cheerful anticipation, smiling faces and good-humoured banter. Here, she encountered the weighty gloom of a funeral parlour. Charles Trottwood stood before the desk with the sepulchral demeanour of the undertaker and Simon Marr was slumped in a lifeless fashion in his swivel chair, like a corpse ready to be laid out. Only his eyes moved to them when they stood in the doorway. The silence was so complete, Sarah could hear the distant thud of traffic in the Gray's Inn Road through the double-glazed windows.

'I've been betrayed,' Marr said softly.

'By whom, Simon?' George asked.

Slowly Marr sat up straighter but his shoulders still sagged. 'Everyone,' he replied. 'Tell them about the call from those bloodsuckers,' he instructed Trottwood.

Charles spoke with grave concern, but Sarah could hear the pleasure in his voice. 'A reporter from the *Evening Standard* has rung to ask if Mr Marr knew that Andrew Maclean is the notorious confidence trickster, Paddy Reilly, also known as Ian Fisher. He's calling back in a few minutes.'

'What do I tell them?' Marr asked hoarsely. His voice seemed to have collapsed with his spirit. 'Why didn't you warn me he was Paddy Reilly?'

'Because we didn't know what Paddy Reilly looked like until now,' George answered. 'That's the art of being a confidence trickster, Simon. Keeping your identity a secret.'

'But he's done this sort of thing before. You should have been prepared.'

George sat down on the sofa and indicated that Sarah should do so as well. 'Paddy Reilly has tricked three national newspapers in the past – those are the ones we know about. I don't think he got quite so much money on previous occasions.'

'He's made me a laughing-stock,' Marr said. 'How could you let this happen?' He looked up at Sarah, his face bleak. 'I hold you responsible for this. I must say it could seriously damage your career.'

Sarah stiffened and leaned forward, but George held her gently by the arm and said, 'I think the thing to concentrate on now, Simon, is protecting the reputation of the *Gazette*.'

'What about my reputation?' Marr replied. 'Who gives a sod about a newspaper? It's just a dead thing, only fit for lighting fires and wrapping rubbish. I'm a living person, with a public who cares about me – can't any of you see how upset and wounded all the little people will feel if I'm made a scapegoat for this heap of crap?'

'Some of us feel differently about the *Gazette*, Simon,' George said in a mild voice. 'We think the newspaper comes first, and it's people that come and go.'

'Fuck this business,' Marr answered with deep feeling. 'I want to get back to television where they know how to treat a star.' He looked up again. 'So tell me what I'm going to do for Christ's sake.'

'Tell it straight,' George said. 'Say we made a mistake, all newspapers get things wrong from time to time. We own up and say we're sorry. You can remind them gently that Paddy Reilly has taken other papers to the cleaners before. That won't do any harm.'

'I'll still look a fool,' Marr said bitterly. 'I thought dog didn't eat dog in Fleet Street, that's what they always used to say.'

'That was in the days when there weren't so many dogs about,' George said. 'It's a tougher world now.'

'Who's going to tell the chairman?' Marr said. 'I tried to find Brooks but he's off sick and not answering his telephone.'

'I think the chairman may already know,' George replied. 'He has ways of getting unpleasant news early.'

There was a buzz on Marr's communication box and he switched on the speaker. 'Mr Barrie Loam is here with his television crew, sir,' the secretary said.

270

'Oh, God,' Marr replied. 'Tell them to wait down-stairs.'

'They're actually in my office,' she said.

'Tell them I'll be out in a moment.' Marr leaned forward and buried his head in his hands. George and Sarah took the opportunity to leave.

'Take the morning conference in Brooks's office,' Marr said, looking up as they were departing. 'I shall be unavailable.'

Sarah sat at her desk for the rest of the morning, while all around her the other reporters indulged in horseplay. At twelve o'clock, a sudden exodus took place when they all departed for the Lion to have drinks before lunch. Sarah did not go with them. She made an excuse, saying she would catch up, then went to the library to get out the cuttings on Paddy Reilly. When she returned to the newsroom it was fairly quiet. There was just Joe March seated at one of the vacant desks reading a file of some sort.

'Not going to the reporters' lunch?' she asked.

'It's not compulsory is it?'

'Not if you're over twenty-one.'

'I think I'll pass.'

Sarah collected her possessions and made for the exit. As she was passing the messengers' department one of them called out: 'Here, Sarah, take a look at this.' He showed her a pile of the first edition of the *Evening Standard* he was about to distribute. Sarah paused and looked down. In a panel on the top of the front page was a reproduction of that morning's story in the *Gazette* plus a picture of Simon Marr next to Andrew Maclean. The headline read: GAZETTE HOAXED: The Skeleton in Simon Marr's Closet.

271

Sarah passed on slowly, shaking her head.

Greaves was driving west along the M4 motorway with Holland beside him. It had started to rain when they passed Reading and the car now hissed along the wet surface of the road as if they were aquaplaning towards their destination. Holland had been on the telephone since their journey had begun. He replaced the receiver and said: 'Wiltshire Constabulary say they located Dale's Ford Escort in a lay-by near Silbury Hill. There's a lot of blood inside.'

Greaves's eyes were on the huge lorry ahead he was about to overtake. When they had passed through the curtain of spray the juggernaut threw behind it he said: 'How long have we got?'

'One forty-five,' Holland replied. 'Not far now. We take the next turning off the motorway.'

The secondary roads bore a fair burden of traffic, but Greaves used all his skills and authority to force their pace. Occasionally motorists would look with anger as he overtook through the pounding downpour. When they reached the junction of the two arterial roads, a police car was waiting for them. The driver stood in the rain at Greaves's open window and leaned down. 'The vehicle you described is heading towards Chippenham, sir,' he said in a country accent. 'There's a car tailing them but not interfering, as you instructed. I guess they're on their way to rejoin a column that's heading towards Bristol.'

'Thank you,' Greaves answered. 'How long do you think it will take for me to catch up with them?'

'Half an hour at the most, sir, if you stick on our tail.'

The constable returned to his car and they set off.

Holland sensed that Greaves was more relaxed now. 'God, I hate motorways,' he said after a time. Then they saw the police car ahead signalling them to slow down.

Sarah got to the restaurant cursing the rain that had soaked into her best shoes. When she entered, she could hear the sound of 'Silent Night' being bellowed by the assembly above. She recollected the contrasting sweetness of her sons' choir, before trudging up the staircase to the room where the reporters' lunch was being held.

The time they had spent in the Lion had not been wasted; already there were signs of the anarchy to come. George had removed his jacket, and once more Sellotaped the robin to his shoulder. Three reporters were trying to knock it off with bread rolls taken from the baskets on the table while he stood on a chair at the far end of the room. Pauline handed her a glass of red wine and said, 'Some day we'll look back on this and laugh.'

Stiles was standing close by. He turned to Sarah. 'Was there anything on the wires about trouble at the office when you left?' he asked.

Sarah told him about the *Standard* page one and he looked back to Bernard Train, one of the reporters on the City page. 'Did you hear that?' he asked.

'That could be it, old boy,' Train replied with the fruity delivery of the very drunk. 'The LOC shares were doing a tango when I left to come here.'

'What a cock-up,' Stiles said bitterly. He gestured around the room. 'You know what that means, it's good-bye to all this. I think I'd better get back, I may

273

be needed.' He put down his drink and left the room.

'What does he mean by that?' Pauline asked.

Harry Porter, who had joined them, shrugged. 'I can only imagine the little prick's referring to his own position,' he said cheerfully. 'The reporters' lunch has been this good since 1946; and I should know, I haven't missed one.'

Harassed-looking waiters had managed to place the first course of antipasto before the vacant seats. Then Luigi appeared and announced that luncheon was served. Sarah took a seat close to the staircase at the end of the long table, as far away as she could manage from the more raucous members of the party.

The noise intensified as the party continued, bouncing from the white rough-cast walls and tiled floor in a general cacophony of sound that made conversation below the shouting level impossible. Rows erupted, toasts were made, undying friendships pledged and old feuds renewed. It was, as Harry Porter had pointed out, exactly the same as the lunches Sarah had attended in her youth. Even the people seemed the same, although only a few faces remained from the time she had been a new girl on the *Gazette*.

As Stiles had returned to the office, it fell to George to make the customary speech by the news editor. He did it with his usual brand of barbed good humour. Red faces roared with laughter at each insult he heaped upon those selected for special recognition. When the final toast was made, Sinclair announced he would perform the highland fling on the table. Others struck their throats in imitation of bagpipes as he made a few faltering hops before falling among the litter of plates.

Pauline was urged to demonstrate a Russian dance, which she managed quite creditably. Then Dave Thomas, inflamed with his own brand of nationalism, said he would show them an Irish jig. With a cheer from the others, he was hoisted up and after a deep bow, began to crash his way along the table top, his heels drumming a staccato beat. One heel came in contact with a half-consumed plate of Spaghetti Bolognaise, which described a graceful arch through the air, before coming to rest on Sarah's lap. She was philosophical about it, knowing that such things were almost inevitable. 'Next year I'm going to wear a boiler suit,' she said to Pauline.

'No one will notice when it dries out, Sarah,' Bernard Train said, raising his head from the table, where he had rested it like the Dormouse at the Mad Hatter's tea party.

'But I shall know, Bernard,' she answered with a rueful smile, and decided to withdraw from the rest of the proceedings.

Chapter Eighteen

Stephen Dale's school bus was surprisingly comfortable inside, Greaves thought, when he and Holland entered, more like the interior of an expensive motor cruiser than a gypsy caravan. There was a fitted galley, a portable lavatory, well planned bunks and wall heaters that brought a cosy fug after the sharp air outside. Stephen Dale sat on a folding chair, opposite his wife and a small child, who watched the two intruders with wide, unafraid eyes.

Anthony Dale was lying on a bunk, unconscious and deathly pale.

'How is he?' Greaves asked.

'He's lost a lot of blood but he'll be all right,' Ellen Dale answered.

'Are you sure?' Holland asked.

'I used to be a nurse, I've seen people worse than this.'

'Have you given him anything?' Greaves asked.

She shook her head.

'Do you know why we want him, Mr Dale?' Greaves asked.

The man nodded and put out a hand gently to touch

his brother's forehead. 'It wasn't him, you know,' he said almost to himself.

'He has previous form, Mr Dale,' Holland said, keeping his voice normal, aware there was a child present.

Stephen Dale shook his head. 'That woman was lying, everyone on the estate knew her, she was putting it about all over the place. Tony's not too . . . sharp, you know. I mean, he didn't do so well at school. But girls were always chasing him. Deborah Hallan was married to a nutter, he was working on oil rigs and she was knocking off anyone who would buy her a bag of chips. She took Tony up to her flat. Then when everyone found out, she said it was rape so her husband wouldn't give her a hiding. Tony didn't stand a chance. He's not the one who's been killing these women.'

'There's a lot of evidence to the contrary,' Greaves said.

'Who says?'

'The girl he met in the library.'

Stephen Dale laughed. 'She's the one who's accused him?'

Greaves nodded. 'And there's the letters he sent.'

'Letters?' Stephen said sharply.

'That's right.'

Stephen Dale looked at his wife and then back at Greaves. 'That's not possible, Superintendent. My brother only took books from the library to look at the pictures. You see, he can't read – so if the rapist has been sending letters it can't be Anthony.'

'How did he get a job at the *Gazette* if he can't read and write?' Holland asked.

Stephen Dale looked back at his brother. 'I filled in the form for him. There's no paperwork in the job. Just a few telephone numbers to memorise.'

Greaves felt a lurch in his stomach. Suddenly he knew that Stephen Dale was telling the truth – and he thought of Sarah.

These shoes are ruined, Sarah told herself as she walked back to the office through the continuing storm. When she got to the newsroom, she saw that Joe March was still studying the same file. He didn't look up but Stiles, who was standing at the news desk, waved her over.

'The editor wants you to write a piece explaining how you were duped by Paddy Reilly,' he said shortly. 'They're going to set up the TV camera and shoot you while you write. Simon thinks they can turn it into a funny piece, give it some humour, change the whole base of the story and show how all of Fleet Street has been conned by Reilly.'

'I don't think so,' Sarah replied.

'What do you mean? Are you refusing to carry out an instruction?'

'If you want to put it that way, feel free,' Sarah said, her spirits lightening by her decision.

'That's a sacking offence,' Stiles said. 'You wouldn't have a leg to stand on.'

'Well, in that case I won't have much to do in future,' Sarah answered. 'So I'll be able to spend all my time preparing for an industrial court. If this isn't a clear case of wrongful dismissal, my name is Margaret Thatcher.' She turned and walked back to her desk, head held high, she was boiling with rage.

The telephone rang. She was about to storm from the office, but mothers never ignore a ringing telephone.

'Hello,' she snapped into the receiver.

'Have I called at a bad time?' a timorous voice asked.

'Who is this?'

'Vickie Howard. I'm sorry to bother you.'

Sarah felt her anger drain away. 'It's all right, Vickie,' she answered. 'What can I do for you?'

'I just needed to talk to somebody,' she said. 'I feel terrible, and Gerry is away . . . I just don't know what to do.'

'Where are you?'

'In Hampstead, I went for a walk on the Heath and got wet . . .'

She sounded like a lost child.

'Look,' Sarah said, 'I've got to go home for a time, why don't you meet me there?' She gave her the address. 'We can have a cup of tea and a good natter, then I'll drive you to your flat.'

'Are you sure?' Vickie said. 'I don't want to be any trouble . . . it's just I feel . . . so terrible.'

'Tell me about it when we meet, I'll be there quite soon. I've just got to make a short stop on the way.'

'I hate to be a nuisance.'

'That's perfectly all right,' Sarah said soothingly. 'Look, my next-door neighbour, Jenny Pinner, has a set of keys to the house. I'll give her a ring and tell her to give them to you, so you can let yourself in.'

'You won't be long? I'll be waiting for you.'

'I'll be home before dark,' Sarah answered.

While Greaves headed back to London, Nick Holland tried to make contact with Sarah on the car telephone. It was a frustrating business. When he tried the news desk, a sulky Alan Stiles snapped that she was at the reporters' lunch. When he called the restaurant, a slurred voice told him that Sarah was not there, and he could hear discordant singing on the other end. Pauline Kaznovitch took the receiver and told him that Sarah had left the restaurant some time before because of the accident.

'What's happened?' Greaves asked. He had only been able to hear snatched fragments of Holland's conversation.

'Somebody spilled a plate of food over her and she left, but they're expecting her back for the Features party later this evening.'

'She would have gone home to change,' Greaves said with certainty.

'Ring the house.'

Holland did so but there was no reply.

'Call my number there,' Greaves instructed. There was still no answer.

Holland could feel Greaves coaxing even more speed from the car. 'Try again in five minutes,' he said grimly.

Sarah found a parking space close to the school gates and hurried through the rain to the shelter of the main doorway. She was carrying two large plastic bags that she had taken from the boot of her car. She rang the bell to Father Robson's rooms and waited for some time before the door opened.

'Mrs Keane,' he said in surprise. 'What a busy day I'm having with you people from the *Gazette*.'

He could see by her puzzled expression that his

words meant nothing to her. 'Mr March was here, until a few minutes ago, you've just missed him,' he explained.

Sarah smiled. 'My visit has nothing to do with the newspaper,' she answered. 'I brought some clothes and toys for your Christmas appeal. Nothing very grand, I'm afraid, but quite serviceable.'

'How kind,' the priest said. 'Please come in. Leave them here in the hall, Sister Margaret will sort them later.'

'What did Joe want?' Sarah asked when she had left the bags.

'He was returning some papers Mrs Hathaway loaned him; they're the original school files for the victims of these terrible crimes.'

'Original files?' Sarah asked.

Father Robson nodded. 'The ones Mrs Hathaway keeps. I put everything on the computer, but she prefers to keep a full set of paperwork as well.'

Sarah followed Father Robson into his study where he tapped a pile of brown manila folders on the edge of his desk. 'These are the files loaned to Mr March.'

Sarah could see that he had been working on his word processor. The screen still glowed. 'Are you just putting these on the computer now, Father?' she asked.

'Oh, no, I did those weeks ago,' he replied. 'But, as I said, Mrs Hathaway hasn't quite mastered the system yet, so she keeps a hard copy of everything.' He paused. 'Curious jargon, isn't it? Hard copy – it suggests something much more formidable than pieces of paper.'

Sarah looked around the tiny room. She could see no filing cabinets.

'Come with me while I put these away,' he said, picking up the folders. 'There's something I want to ask you.'

Sarah walked with him through the deserted building to the first floor where he unlocked a large, rather splendid room which was half filled with piles of chairs and desks. Against one wall was a bank of old-fashioned wooden filing cabinets.

'This was the ballroom of the original house,' Father Robson explained. 'It was the lecture hall and gymnasium until we built the new wing in the grounds. These days, it's not used much.'

Sarah watched while he placed the folders on top of the cabinets and began to open various drawers.

'By the way,' he began in a distracted voice, 'how do you feel about Colin being received into the Church?'

'I'm sorry,' Sarah replied, astonished. 'Are you *sure* it's my Colin?'

Father Robson was making a tutting sound as he tried to make sense of the filing system. 'This really is most baffling,' he said to himself. Then he looked up. 'Oh yes, quite sure. He's been taking instruction from me. A rather stimulating experience, he has a rigorous intellect; but I expect you already know that.'

Just then, Mrs Hathaway entered the room.

'Ah, Helen. Thank goodness you're here. I'm afraid I still can't make head or tail of your system. I was trying to replace the files you got out for Mr March.'

'It's quite simple,' Mrs Hathaway replied. She took the bundle from him, opened a drawer and placed them all in the same slot.

'Aren't they filed alphabetically?' Father Robson asked in surprise when he saw what she'd done. 'They are on the computer.'

She shook her head. 'There's not enough of them. This is the file for occasional workers.'

'May I look?' Sarah asked with sudden interest.

Mrs Hathaway opened the cabinet and handed her the files again. Sarah began to flip through them. 'Who knew they were all kept in the same file?' she asked.

'I really can't say,' Mrs Hathaway answered.

'Did the police look at these?'

Mrs Hathaway looked at her in confusion. 'I certainly didn't show them. Did you Father?'

'No,' he replied. 'The police checked my computer discs for all the information they wanted.'

'Would any outside people still use this room?' Sarah asked.

Father Robson shook his head. 'It's not used for very much these days. I can't say for certain who's been here.'

'Miss Carter would know,' Mrs Hathaway said. 'But she's gone to her sister's for the holidays. She left this morning, I know, so she should be there by early evening. Is this information important?'

'It might be,' Sarah answered. 'Could you give me her number, Mrs Hathaway?'

'Certainly,' she replied. 'If you'll come back to the office.'

They returned to Father Robson's room and Mrs

Hathaway wrote out the number. Sarah thanked her and then glanced at her watch. 'Goodness,' she said. 'I must hurry, someone is waiting for me at home.'

'Yes, Mr March,' Father Robson said. 'He said he was going to find you after he'd studied these files.'

They walked with her to the door and wished her a Happy Christmas. She was getting into her car when Mrs Hathaway turned to Father Robson and said, 'Father, do you recollect those actors who came to the school?'

'Actors?' he replied, waving to Sarah.

'Oh, no, you wouldn't,' Mrs Hathaway said. 'You were away in Normandy at the time.'

'What about them?'

'They used the old lecture hall.'

'They used the room?' Father Robson asked. 'Are you sure?'

'Oh yes,' Mrs Hathaway replied. 'I remember it well. The gymnast team were practising in the new hall.'

Father Robson tried to catch Sarah's attention, but she had turned to watch for oncoming traffic before she pulled away.

The rain had thinned to a light, misty drizzle when Sarah turned into her street; the last moments of twilight cast deep shadows into the neighbouring gardens and lights already shone in some windows. She had expected some sign that Vickie Howard would be waiting, but the house was as still as the grave when she entered the hallway. It was cold, and there was no dog to greet her; then she remembered she had turned off the central heating that morning.

There was no sign of Vickie in the living room or kitchen and when she tried the light switch nothing happened.

'Fused,' she muttered, then smiled when she realised the dog was not there to hear her. 'Talking to a dog is all right, Sarah, but talking to yourself is a sign of old age.'

She felt chilled and strangely lonely. The house was usually alive with children and warmth, but now its coldness seemed almost hostile. Suddenly she wanted to hear the sound of another human being. She switched on the radio in the kitchen and a newsreader began to speak in detached tones about the balance of trade between EC countries. She was about to change channels when the woman came to the end of the item and said: 'In a surprise move on the London Stock Exchange this afternoon, a sudden flurry of frenzied trading saw control of London and Overseas Communications PLC pass from Sir Robert Hall into the hands of Charles Miller, chairman of the Miller Corporation, a City conglomerate that has until now had no dealings with the media industry. There has been considerable speculation about the future of LOC PLC, which is the parent company of Gazette Newspapers Ltd, due to the unorthodox style of Sir Robert Hall, who recently surprised the newspaper industry by appointing Simon Marr, the television personality, to the editorship of the *Gazette*. A recent story concerning secret weapons from the Second World War which still threatened Britain was denied by the government, who accused the *Gazette* of irresponsibility and scaremongering. The story turned out to be a hoax perpetrated by Mr Paddy Reilly, a well-known confidence trickster who specialises in hoaxing national newspapers . . .'

Sarah hurried to the telephone in the next room to call George, but when she picked it up, the line was dead. She climbed the stairs to their bedroom to try Colin's private line, but that was also out of order. It was growing even darker now and she decided she had better do something about the fused lights.

Returning to the hallway, she opened the door to the cupboard under the staircase and saw something whitish reflecting in the gloom. Leaning forward, her eyes became accustomed to the half-light and in a terrible moment of recognition she saw that it was Vickie Howard. The only part of her that caught the fading light was her contorted features. Her mouth hung open and her eyes were rolled up so that only the whites showed. A length of rope was wound around her throat.

Sarah stood frozen with horror, unable to speak or move, her vocal cords constricted with fear. Then there came a sound behind her, as soft as falling rain. She turned and felt her skin crawl with horror as she stood facing a fearsome apparition. A man, holding a long hunting knife pointing at her stomach, was panting like an animal before her. His head was encased in a livid-coloured rubber mask and his torso was naked but for chains crossing his hairless body. Some kind of strap around his waist and under his

286

crotch held a grotesque leather phallus erect before him. Sarah could smell him now – a musky feral odour.

Sarah forced herself to concentrate on the knife. The blade was matt black, with only the edge gleaming with razor-like sharpness. Fighting her panic she told herself that it was only a man before her, nothing supernatural. And he wasn't too big. Although his naked body was muscled and taut she was at least as tall as he was. She fought to remember the lessons Greaves had taught her about self-protection and was about to move against him when she felt herself grasped from behind in powerful arms. Sarah struggled to turn and see her new assailant. A familiar voice spoke in her ear.

'Just playing dead, Sarah,' Vickie Howard said in a whisper. 'Time to go upstairs now.' She pushed her forward and said, 'In a moment my little friend is going to hold his knife against your windpipe. If you move he will slice through it and you will die here in the hallway with your blood pumping out of you like a fountain. Nod gently if you understand. '

Sarah nodded.

'Put your hands together behind your back,' Vickie instructed. Sarah did so and could feel a cord being wound around her wrists.

Like a prisoner being taken for execution, she was led upstairs to the bedroom she had shared with her first husband. Once inside, she found another nightmare. Before the bed, Joe March sat in one of the chairs from the dining room, his hands and feet bound with tape, his mouth sealed with the same material.

Another chair stood at the foot of the bed, as if for the comfort of a spectator.

Sarah was pushed down on the bed and while the hooded man held the knife to her throat, Vickie Howard tied her feet to the base of the bed. She could see Joe March's eyes, wide with horror.

'Undo her hands so she can take off that jacket herself,' Vickie Howard said, now sitting in the vacant chair. She sat back and lit a cigarette. The man held the knife against her throat so that Sarah could feel the edge of the blade touching her skin. He pulled her to one side and began to pluck at the cord ineffectually.

'You aren't pleading, Sarah,' Vickie Howard said in a chiding voice. 'The others begged for their lives.'

'They'll catch you now, Vickie,' Sarah answered.

'Are you going to be defiant?' Vickie said. 'Oh, good. The others were just terrified. Some of them lost control completely – opened their bowels, wet themselves with fear. Breaking you down is going to be much more entertaining.'

Keep her talking, Sarah told herself grimly. While she talks I live.

'You've made too many mistakes,' Sarah said quickly. 'They know why you're doing this now.'

Vickie inhaled deeply. 'They understand the Theatre of Fear?' she replied. 'I doubt it.'

'The Theatre of Fear?' Sarah said. 'What does that mean?'

Vickie drew deeply on the cigarette and then lit another on the stub before grinding it out on the carpet. 'You've seen me performing,' she said in a conversational voice. 'I worked hard to become an actress – for years. I told them I wanted to go on the stage. They told me I was dreaming, that I ought to find a proper career. I told them I wanted something else. I gave my soul for the job. Who cares? Even when I work in some slum of a public house, audiences sit like cattle, they can't feel the emotion I put into my work. Well, now you can. You can feel the torment I feel when I'm raped by an audience. And as you choke to death, you can know how it feels to be regarded with total indifference by another human being as if you're a piece of meat, a flayed animal ready for the butcher's block. People eat animals. They eat actors too – now you can share the sensation.'

Sarah could feel the cord on her wrists coming loose. She didn't have much time.

'Why did you choose those women?' she asked. 'What had they done to you?'

Vickie sighed. 'The women were nothing, silly, it was the school. When I was at Saint Catherine's they never wanted me to be an actress. They even tried to stop me going to drama school.'

'You did all this as revenge on Saint Catherine's?'

'That's right.'

Vickie could see that Sarah's hands were now free, but the knife was still at her throat. 'Now take off your jacket and blouse,' Vickie ordered. 'Gerry will cut off your underwear, he likes doing that, the poor dear can't get an erection. Do you like the one I provided for him?'

'Doesn't he speak for himself?' Sarah said.

'He can't speak or think for himself, unless I've told

him what to say,' Vickie continued. 'He's just a ventriloquist's dummy, really. The poor darling, he never had any fun until I found him.'

With the knife still touching her, Sarah began to remove her jacket.

'Faster, Sarah, this isn't a striptease,' Vickie ordered, eyes narrow now from the smoke of the cigarette she kept between her lips. Sarah began to feel a terrible despair. Don't give in, she told herself. Find something to fight with – anything.

There was a noise from below: the sound of the front door opening and a voice calling out, 'Hello! Anybody at home? It's only me.'

Pat Lomax! The interruption was the opportunity Sarah had prayed for. At the sound of the voice, Trench had taken the knife from her throat for a moment and turned his masked face to Vickie for guidance. It was enough. Sarah seized the rubber-clad hand that held the knife and clamped her teeth into the still raw wound beneath the bandage. Trench gave an animal howl. The hunting knife flew from his grasp and clattered to the ground in front of Joe March.

Vickie Howard moved fast. Uncoiling from the chair in a snake-like motion, she reached for the blade. Sarah could see that she would hold it in a moment. Twisting away from Trench, she reached down into the box that the twins had left by the bedside. Her hand found the can of Spray Mount and she squirted the liquid into Trench's eyes.

Grunting, he swayed away, scrabbling at the eye slits of his mask.

Sarah now swung round to face Vickie Howard, who had retrieved the knife and was moving towards her, the cigarette still hanging from her mouth. She squirted the can again: the cold liquid caused Vickie Howard's head to snap back as it was enveloped in a cloud of petroleum vapour and liquid rubber solution. There was a second while Vickie's momentum carried her forward, and then the glowing end of the cigarette in her mouth ignited the mixture and her head was engulfed in a blazing fireball. Screaming, she stumbled away, dropping the knife and beating at her burning hair and face. Sarah seized the knife and slashed through the bonds at her ankles. She turned to Trench, but he was still on his knees clawing at his eyes.

Sarah saw the roll of tape that had been used to bind Joe March. She pulled Trench to his feet, and he cowered away from her.

'My eyes, my eyes,' he whined. 'Please don't hurt me.'

She secured him with the tape. As she turned away the door was pushed open and Pat stood on the threshold of the room, carrying the blackthorn stick from the hall stand. Vickie Howard had beaten out her burning hair and now lay whimpering at the foot of the bed, holding her face in her hands, her body curled into a quivering ball.

Slowly Sarah walked over to Joe March and cut through the tape sealing his mouth and binding him to the chair.

'Thanks,' he muttered after a few moments. 'I'm glad the play had a happy ending.'

Sarah slumped down on the bed, bone-weary. 'I think I'll skip the Features party this year,' she answered.

Epilogue

'She was a better actress than I imagined,' Sarah said, when Pat handed her a cup of tea.

'Clever, too,' March added.

'Insane and clever,' mused Greaves who had by now reached the house. 'I suppose that's the worst combination you can have in a criminal.'

'How about throwing in ambitious and manipulative as well?' Holland added, passing the sugar to March. They were sitting by the fire which Pat had made up in the living room, like soldiers resting after a battle. Trench had babbled out everything to March once he had been separated from Vickie Howard. Now the police cars and ambulance had departed with the pair of them.

'If they'd stabbed Anthony Dale to death instead of just wounding him would they have got away with it?' Pat Lomax asked. She was anxious to fix every detail in her mind so that she could relate the whole story to her sisters.

'It depends what details had come out in court,' Greaves said. 'If the prosecution hadn't brought in the letters, Stephen Dale wouldn't have pointed out that his brother can't read. If that had been the case, they might well have got away with it.'

'So how did Anthony Dale get involved?' Pat asked.

'They really did meet in the library,' Greaves said. 'Only it wasn't a chance meeting. Vickie had planned it. She'd chosen Dale after watching him operating in the Royal William. He was the one. She'd heard from pub gossip that he'd been charged with rape before so she knew his fingerprints would be on record. When he came to her flat she got him to handle some books. It was easy to write the letters on the flyleaves afterwards, so she could fix somebody else for the murders.'

'Why, did she think you were getting close?'

'I like to imagine so, but I don't think that really is the case.'

'Then what?'

Greaves shrugged. 'I think she knew she'd be caught in the end – wanted to be, actually. Involving Dale was just an extension of the performance, drawing someone else into the drama. Subtext, I believe dramatists call it.'

'Are you saying it was all just a play? All those terrible murders . . . those poor women – a kind of game?'

'No, for Vickie acting was real life, not a game. Pain, death, fear were a play. There were no real emotions – just technique.'

Pat continued. 'So what really happened with Anthony Dale?'

Greaves nodded to Joe March, who took up the narrative. 'Vickie picked him up. But he thought he was making all the running. She got him to come to her flat – he thought he was on to a sure thing. After she'd seduced him, he went on his way. She bruised her own cheek, then she cried wolf and called for the police.'

'Why did Dale go on the run?'

'One of the other commissionaires read Sarah's story in the *Gazette* to him. He recognised himself in the story and panicked. Remember, he'd been accused of rape before. He wanted to prove his innocence, but didn't know how. His brother had done all his thinking in the past. He left his flat and started living in his car. He was going to approach Sarah a couple of times, once in St James's Street, when she'd left the Staffordshire Hotel and later outside her house, the night of the concert. He wanted to tell her his version of events, but when he did come face to face with her in Highgate Woods, he was clouted with a lump of wood for his efforts.

'So finally he went back to Vickie's flat to plead with her. She was with Trench and they saw a way of bringing the drama to an end. If they killed Dale, it would have seemed like a neat ending; but he was stronger than they thought. He managed to get away and make for the rendezvous he'd already arranged with his brother.'

'Why did she choose those women to attack?'

March continued: 'She found a list of names and addresses in the filing cabinet when she was rehearsing in the ballroom at Saint Catherine's. Remember, she was in a rage of rejection at the time. She thought she was returning to the school in triumph and then she was told that they weren't even going to perform in the proper theatre. She'd been relegated to the old hall. Even the gymnast team took precedence. It must have been enough to tip her over the edge. The names became a fixation.' March paused and looked at Sarah. 'When I returned the files to Father Robson, I wanted to ask you if you'd known any of them personally. I rang the office and Pauline told me you'd gone home. As I was in Hampstead I thought I'd pop round here. Vickie Howard let me in.'

'Who was the tramp in the street?' Pat asked.

'Vickie Howard, she delivered the letter herself. They took Dale's wallet when they were attacking him. They planted it for us to find, but they overlooked the coded message from his brother.'

Holland looked at Pat. 'Why did you come to the house?'

Sarah looked at her as well. 'Yes, I wasn't expecting you today.'

Pat smiled. 'No, I thought you'd all be out. I brought round your presents; I was going to put them under the tree as a surprise.'

Greaves looked towards Sarah and said, 'Thank God for Christmas.'

Sarah folded the dishcloth with a sigh of satisfaction and glanced around the tidied kitchen. The remains of the turkey rested beneath a shroud of tin foil, ready to provide the sandwiches the twins would ask for later in the afternoon. She poured the last half glass of red wine that remained in the third bottle of claret they had drunk and sipped appreciatively. Her father had chosen well; there *was* the scent of flowers and fruit in the heady aroma; just as the wine snobs said.

From the window she watched a sudden breeze ruffle the surface of the lake. The rain had stopped and two majestic swans glided gently towards the willow-clad island where they nested. Mated for life, she remembered; one of nature's marriages. Two magpies strutted near the sun dial pecking aggressively among the winter grass in the last hour of daylight.

She turned away and walked through the house towards the sitting room where the scent of burning apple logs filled the warm air. Before the fireplace, her father knelt with the boys, pointing to the two paper skeletons spread beside them as he spoke the Latin names for the bones he indicated. The twins repeated the incantation like medieval monks taking part in some ancient, holy litany.

Emily was upstairs in one of the bedrooms, on the telephone, talking to Ric somewhere in Suffolk. Greaves sat on the sofa, legs stretched towards the burning logs, resplendent in his new dressing gown, which he had insisted on wearing after lunch. There was a glass of malt whisky at his side while he dipped into the copy of *Pilgrim's Progress* Emily had given him.

As she entered the room, the dog looked up hopefully from where he lay at Greaves's feet and then lay back with a reproachful sigh.

'Oh, all right, then,' she said. 'I'll take you for a walk before it gets dark.' The dog lumbered to his feet and circled her legs in anticipation.

Greaves closed the book and stood up. 'I'll come as well,' he said. 'There's no need,' Sarah answered. 'You look so comfortable.'

'You can't have everything,' he smiled.

They found coats in the hallway and Greaves selected a walking stick from the umbrella stand.

The air was fresh and slightly chilled when they set

off. Sarah had intended to walk beside the lake; but instead, Greaves guided them along the bridlepath that led towards Enstone church. Sarah linked arms and rested her head on his shoulder while the dog ran ahead to burrow in the hedgerow.

'Happy?' Greaves asked after a time.

'As a magpie,' Sarah replied after a moment's hesitation.

'I thought it was sandboys that were happy.'

'I don't know any sandboys so I've no way of judging,' she answered. 'I see magpies all the time.'

'This way,' he said suddenly, leading her into a water meadow beside the pathway.

'We should have worn wellingtons,' Sarah said. 'The grass is soaking.'

'There's a Taign Su tree in this field,' he replied. 'I wanted you to see it.'

'What's a Taign Su tree?'

Greaves led her closer to the hedgerow. 'It comes from China, someone must have brought it to this country. Sometimes it bears winter fruit; look, here.' He stopped before a certain tree, its branches bare, but sparkling still from the rain.

'Are you sure?' Sarah said doubtfully after a brief study. 'It's more like a hawthorn to me.'

'Look closely,' he answered. 'The branch to the left of your face.'

Sarah did as he suggested and then saw other gleams in the failing light. A stone red as wine clustered with tiny shafts of emerald fire. She took the ring from the tree, it was old and exquisitely fashioned. Then she looked at Greaves again – he did not smile.

'If you find fruit on the Taign Su tree you have to

298

grant a wish to the first person you meet,' he said softly.

'What do you want?'

'I want you to marry me,' he answered.

Sarah reached out for him. 'Who says you can't have everything?' she said, her heart now filled with happiness.